# the
# DIRt
# eaters

—

## DENNIS FOON

ANNICK PRESS

TORONTO + NEW YORK + VANCOUVER

We acknowledge the support of the Canada Council for the Arts, the Ontario
Arts Council, and the Government of Canada through the Book Publishing
Industry Development Program (BPIDP) for our publishing activities.

Edited by Barbara Pulling
Copy edited by Pam Robertson
Cover art by Susan Madsen
Cover design by Irvin Cheung/iCheung Design
Interior design by Tanya Lloyd Kyi

The text was typeset in Centaur.

Cataloging in Publication
Foon, Dennis
    The dirt eaters / written by Dennis Foon.

(The Longlight legacy trilogy)
ISBN 1-55037-807-4 (bound).—ISBN 1-55037-806-6 (pbk.)
    I. Title. II. Series: Foon, Dennis. Longlight legacy trilogy.
PS8561.062D57 2003          C813'.54          C2003-900790-I
PZ7          ·

Printed in Canada.

| Published in the U.S.A. by | Distributed in Canada by: | Distributed in the U.S.A. by: |
|---|---|---|
| Annick Press (U.S.) Ltd. | Firefly Books Ltd. | Firefly Books (U.S.) Inc. |
| | 3680 Victoria Park Avenue | P.O. Box 1338 |
| | Willowdale, ON | Ellicott Station |
| | M2H 3K1 | Buffalo, NY 14205 |

Visit our website at: www.annickpress.com

*This book is dedicated to*
*Shirley Louise Wiss.*

# contents

# Longlight

in the shrouded valley, the people
of Longlight evaded destruction.
for seventy-five years they quietly
thrived, isolated from the world,
nurturing a small flame of hope.
it took less than one hour for them
to be annihilated.
                    —the book of Longlight

A snow cricket leaps between two smoldering buildings onto a collapsed stone wall. It sits for a moment, antennae probing, then jumps to a footprint in the snow. It vaults again and again, from footprint to footprint, moving past snow-covered boulders, until it stops at a thick patch of blue bramble and settles beneath the thorns, on a mound of snow speckled red.

The white cricket sings one sweet, resonant note. The mound shudders and, within it, a pair of eyes snaps open. The eyes belong to Roan.

Roan listens, afraid to move. In the distance, the sullen cawing of crows. Stiff, cold, he considers sitting up. But then—crash! He stops breathing, terrified of being seen.

*His father's anguished face.*

*—Quick, quick, Roan, move, move, move!*

*Hands pulling him up, throwing clothes on him. His sister, Stowe, clutching her straw doll, shaking. His mother, kissing him, hugging him, then pushing Roan and Stowe through the open window.*

*—Go! Hide in the blue brush! Run! Run!*

There's another crash, this one landing at Roan's feet. It's only melting snow falling from the bramble. Hearing no human sounds, he rises. Slowly. Staying invisible inside the mass of thorns. Roan's head pounds. He feels his temple. There's a crust on his hair. He scratches off a piece and groans as he examines it. Scab-matted blood.

Smoke rises from the other side of the hill. The village they called Longlight is silent. No voices, no screams. Desperate to see, terrified of what he'll find, Roan breathes deeply to slow his pounding heart. Then, painstakingly untangling himself from the bramble, he crawls over the snow-spotted hill. His eyes catch something. He moves quietly through the brown whip-grass, staying low. A bit of purple cloth—Stowe's doll, wrapped in its vivid shawl, the one she dyed herself. It's been ground by a horse's hoof into the half-frozen mud. Hands trembling, he lifts the precious object.

*Shouts. Explosions. Crazed, skull-masked invaders on horseback, waving torches, slashing, burning. A eerie, rumbling sound pulsates from the village, like hundreds of voices humming in unison.*

*Scrambling, sliding on the icy whip-grass, Roan and Stowe race, closer every step to the blue bramble, to safety. A piercing scream. Stowe's finger-nails rip Roan's palm as a hideous red skull leans down, lifts her. The masked rider kicks off Roan's bleeding hand. Stowe is reaching, reaching for Roan, but high in the air above her the rider's bone club swoops down.*

Shivering, head throbbing, Roan gently places the ruined doll in his pocket. He inches close enough to see the smashed walls of Longlight. Beyond them, smoke rises from the shells of crumbled wood and clay houses. No sign of riders. No human sounds at all. Trembling, he edges closer, then rushes toward the broken gate and dives for cover. He is lifting his head for another look when a black shape whirls past him. He ducks, terror-struck, waiting for the death blow. It doesn't come. He waits, then peeks again. The ground past the gate is a mass of foraging crows, shattered pots, burned woven baskets.

How did they find us?

An acrid smell flares in Roan's nostrils. From the Community House. Burning plastic: the solar energy panels. Years spent scavenging the parts to make one unit. Gone.

House after house, all smoldering, all empty. Drag marks scar the gravel walkways. Past the Worship Place, across the Forum, to the Fire Hole. Roan hesitates, dreading his next few steps. Every year his father spoke where Roan stood now.

*We stand for the Remembering. Fire Holes like this one opened when the Madness began. Earth, sickened by the Abominations inflicted on its surface, spewed its insides in an attempt to purify what was fouled in the world. Many died. When the scorched lands cooled, the First Ones arrived. Many holes had been filled, but this one was left untouched, its fiery waters unquenched. The First Ones constructed their village around it, the shrine at our center. So we would not forget what we were. Once a year, during the Remembering, this stone gate is opened and a day is spent fasting and praying to remind us of why we set ourselves apart. This is the most sacred place in Longlight.*

The most sacred place in Longlight. It didn't matter what we remembered. They still came to find us.

There's a foul smell. Pieces of scattered clothing in the wind. A woman's blouse, a man's torn shirt. A worn leather shoe, covered in patches. Roan, collapsing, clutches it, this shoe his father constantly mended. His father must be here. He must be close. Roan's eyes dart around the stones. Crows hover over the Fire Hole. Roan scrambles past the stone wall that surrounds the sacred site.

First he sees a mass of brown hair caught on the edge. A bit of flesh connects it to a white skull. Bobbing on the steaming surface, bones. Human bones. Rolling one over the other, hundreds of human bones. Roan's legs go weak. His vision blurs. Everyone he knew, everyone he loved. Roan staggers away from the pit, throat thick, eyes burning.

His legs buckle. He kneels, his face in the hard clay, trying to say the words his father taught him, the prayer of passing, the utterance of safe journey. His lips move but he can't speak, there are too many, he can't find air to make sound. There are too many, so many souls.

He cannot lift his face from the dirt, and the smoke hangs over him.

A sound draws Roan out, bringing him back to the world. He lifts his head and breathes. There, on his shoulder, a white cricket.

Time to go home.

Dazed, still gripping his father's shoe, Roan makes his way past the broken walls, down the gravel path, past the ruined houses of his friends and relatives. He knew every single dwelling, had eaten or played or visited inside them all. Now they were empty husks.

Unlike the others, his own house still stands, its walls intact. But the front door, so carefully crafted by his mother, has been smashed into jagged splinters. He'd taken so much pride in her artistry. It's difficult not to let grief overtake him as he cautiously steps through the defiled threshold. His grandmother's table and chairs, his great-uncle's fire-glazed bowls, all shattered. His father's bookcases upended, books strewn everywhere.

Roan slips into his bedroom. His bed's been thrown over, his belongings shredded, ripped, ruined. He reaches down and grips the bed frame. It's solid. His mother made it strong. He rights the bed, tugs the woolen mattress back onto it, picks up the crumpled blankets. He lowers himself onto the only bed he's ever slept on, pulls his knees to his chest, and stares at the wall.

His people had planted gardens to heal the earth, nurtured and loved one another, shared all that they had. There was nothing to take, but the raiders had come anyway, and now everything was lost. Everything. Everything.

A SPECKLED BROWN RAT WITH A LONG PINK TAIL SITS ACROSS FROM ROAN. THEY ARE ON A PLAIN OF DRY YELLOW CLAY, THE SUN BELOW THE RED HORIZON. THE RAT RAISES ITS HEAD.

"IT'S TIME. GO. NOW."

Roan jolts up, startled awake by the strange vision. It was unlike any dream he'd ever had. Still, his mother taught him to always pay them heed. This dream said to go. He can still feel its urgency. He has to move, now.

He pulls up a floorboard. His stash box is still there. Inside are his great-grandfather's five silver coins, each more than two hundred years old. And in its sheath is the gleaning knife his father gave him last month for his fifteenth birthday. Roan straps it around his shin with a leather thong. With his pant leg slipped over it, the knife is invisible.

Moving purposefully, he spots his mother's rucksack and shoves in a blanket roll. He rushes to gather supplies—fills his water bag, finds some scraps of dry food, carefully places his father's shoe and his sister's doll in the rucksack's side pocket—until he's stopped by a peculiar sound.

It's faint, but quickly growing louder. Roan rushes to the window. On the gravel path, three hundred yards away, a man is riding something Roan's seen only in pictures: a motorbike. The driver, flowing black cloak and long braided hair whipping behind him, is heading straight for Roan's house. Roan dives under a bookcase that's collapsed against the wall. As he hides himself, he feels something in his pocket. The white cricket. Just then the driver walks in the door. Roan holds his breath and silently pulls the knife from its sheath.

"What a waste," the man mutters, and Roan hears him shuffling through the books heaped on the floor. The stranger's hands reach under the bookcase, feeling around. Roan clutches his knife as the fingers grasp a torn-in-half volume and pull it out.

"My name is Saint. What is yours?"

Roan freezes.

"Terrible thing that happened here. Are you alright, boy?"

Roan lurches out of his hiding place and bolts for the door.

"Hey, hey, you don't need to—" Saint calls out, reaching for Roan. He's the biggest man Roan's ever seen. Roan wildly swings his blade before charging out the door. Not to the bramble, no time to conceal himself there. Instead, Roan runs the way he always ran with his friends, straight to the eastern wall. He's headed for the Hollow Forest.

The forest goes on for miles, the tall trees still standing despite the fact the only green they sport is moss and lichen. According to his grandfather, the trees were drained of life when a chemical plant far upriver was bombed. Planting new growth, specially chosen to aid and detoxify the earth, was one of Roan's favorite chores. He devoted many long hours to it. But nothing seemed able to resurrect the Hollow Forest.

The engine! Not much time. Roan's fingers dig into the trunk of Big Empty, a massive, hundred-foot tree more than three centuries old. Like the other trees in this forest, it is completely hollow. Roan pulls at a perfectly matched piece of bark and squeezes through the entry hole he and his friends carved a few summers before, then carefully plugs it behind him.

Roan reaches for the first carved handhold and then works his way up, aiming for the top, where the light streams in. Beside each handhold is the mark of one of his friends: Max, Esta, Lem, Rolf, Aiden. He remembers how the six of them would clamber up together, a knot of warmth and laughter. No more. At the very top he sees his sister's spot, her name carved in big letters. Stowe. That was her place, always. He reaches across, sliding his finger through the S. Where is she now? His hand burns where hers was torn from his grip.

Soaked with sweat, his pockets heavy with rocks, Roan pokes his head cautiously from the broken treetop. With the sun pouring down on him, he sits on the rope seat they all strung together so long ago. He strains his eyes, searching. Has the stranger given up the chase? Roan decides to stay as long as it's light, not start traveling until the cover of night. But travel where? He's never been outside this valley. He has no idea what's out there. All he knows is he can't stay here. Home is dead. Then he sees him.

A hundred feet below, Saint drives slowly through the trees, eyes on the ground. Roan knows the stranger will spot the broken lichen, the grass crushed by his feet. He was running too fast to cover his tracks.

As Saint rides straight to Big Empty, Roan lowers his head and presses his back against the tree wall, heart thumping. Will the man find the entrance? A rush of air from below answers his question.

"I have no wish to hurt you," the man calls up, his head masked in shadows far below. "I saw the smoke. Was that your home?"

"Yes."

"I can feed you, clothe you. After what you've been through, I'm sure you can use a friend."

"I'm fine. Leave me alone."

"I can't do that," says Saint. "You'll die out here alone."

But when Roan looks down, he sees that Saint is gone.

The tree sways. But there's no wind. Roan feels it move again. It creaks, its whole length trembling. He anxiously grips his handhold with the realization: Saint is pushing on the tree. Can a man push a tree of this size over? Not a live, healthy one, but a long-dead tree with rotting roots is fair game for two or three very strong men. This is one man. But no ordinary man. Saint is twice the size of Roan's father.

The old roots snap and the tree buckles. Big Empty starts to fall. Roan falls too, his hands flailing uselessly, his body bouncing against the sides of the hollow.

# the company of friends

the friend gave him the word. and
the prophet took the word and
spoke it. and those who heard him,
followed. and so the brotherhood
of the friend began.
——orin's history of the friend

A MOUNTAIN LION SITS ON A FIELD OF SHORT GREEN GRASS, A SPARKLING RIVER BEHIND, THE SUN BRIGHT, WARM. THE SPECKLED BROWN RAT SITS BY THE BIG CAT, THEIR EYES INTENT ON EACH OTHER.

AN ANCIENT WOMAN, TWO SMALL HORNS ON HER HEAD, LEGS AND TAIL OF A GOAT, APPEARS BESIDE THEM. "YOU BELIEVE HE'S WAKING?"

THE RAT TWITCHES. "HE IS AWAKE."

THE LION CLEANS HER PAW, THEN GLANCES AT THE GOAT-WOMAN. "IT'S TOO SOON. HE'S NOT READY."

"IT CANNOT BE HELPED."

THE GOAT-WOMAN SIGHS. "CAN WE MOVE HIM?"

"HE IS SAFEST WHERE HE IS."

THE LION LOOKS AT THE RAT. "HOW WILL WE SHIELD HIM?"

"IF WE EVEN CAN," ADDS THE GOAT-WOMAN.

THE RAT RISES. "THERE IS NO CHOICE."

Roan wakes to the pungent smell of incense. He's alive. He was sure the tree fall would kill him. That rat again. What was this dream trying to say? But the memory of it drifts when he feels a wriggle in his shirt pocket. The snow cricket. Roan's sore all over, but nothing seems to be broken or swollen. His eyes blearily take in his surroundings, a room with walls of black fabric. Some kind of tent.

As he pulls himself up for a better look around, a gaunt young man steps through the woolen threshold. "So you're finally awake." He gawks at Roan with stark inquisitiveness, as if he's in the presence of some strange, foreign creature.

"What are you staring at?"

"Sorry," the boy says. "I didn't mean anything by it. I'm here to see if you're hungry."

Roan looks at him, confused. "Where am I?"

"With friends."

"How long?"

"Almost two days since he brought you, I think. You were pretty banged up," the boy replies. He is small, with green eyes, and looks a little older than Roan. "They call me Feeder, on account of I do most of the feeding around here." Feeder hands Roan a bowl filled with a dark gruel. "Mostly potato and tripe."

"What's tripe?" Roan asks.

"Sheep gut. Just spit out the chewy bits, everybody does."

Roan stares at the stew, aghast. In Longlight, sheep's milk and wool were taken, but the animals were never eaten.

"Saint will see you once you're done eating," says Feeder.

Saint. The tree-breaker. He was the one who'd brought him here. Aching, heart-sick, Roan sniffs the gruel. It has a pleasant enough smell, and the terrible rumbling in his stomach is a fierce reminder of how long it's been since he's had any food. He dips in the spoon, closes his eyes, and tastes. He has to work to swallow, and it's an effort to hold the food down, but the second bite is easier, and by the third he is eating without pause. Wiping his mouth, he stands shakily, takes a deep breath, and pushes through the knit doorway.

The room he steps into is much larger, with a tall pole holding up the canopy's peak. His eyes need a moment to adjust to the candlelight, but then he sees Saint across the room, sitting with his bare back to Roan. Saint has the strongest-looking torso Roan's ever seen, all muscle and tendon. Yet he sits delicately cross-legged on a woven carpet, facing an altar, deep in meditation. As he waits, Roan studies the dimly lit statue that dominates this place of worship. A man half-straddles a bull, pulling its head back by the nostrils and plunging a dagger into its neck. A raven sits on the bull's tail, and a serpent, a scorpion, and a dog are grouped at the bull's feet. In the silence and the flickering light, Roan puzzles over the meaning of the scene.

Saint bends over the incense smoke, brushing it toward his face with his hands. Roan sees that each of the big man's arms is laddered with a column of thin white scars, climbing from his wrist to his elbow. Turning abruptly, Saint locks his deep-set eyes with Roan's. Roan returns the gaze, wondering what Saint hopes to glean from him. Finally, Saint breaks the impasse, puts on his shirt, and speaks as if nothing at all has occurred.

"I'm sorry I had to bring you here this way, but you left me no alternative. You would not have survived out there on your own."

"That should have been my choice."

"I couldn't let that happen," says Saint. "Our faith does not allow it."

"Is that statue part of your faith?" asks Roan, nodding at the altar.

"It's the center of it. The Friend kills the bull, destroying evil and creating life. Like him, we fight evil and nurture life."

"So you couldn't let me die."

"Exactly."

"And when I'm ready, you'll let me leave?"

"Spend some time with us," says Saint, a gentle smile on his face. "Accept our hospitality and let yourself heal. There's much for you to learn here from me and my followers."

Saint doesn't appear to want to hurt him, but Roan's still not willing to trust him. He has too many questions. What was Saint doing in Shrouded Valley? How did he know where to find Roan? And why does he want Roan to stay in this place? Roan suspects that Saint's connected to what happened to Longlight, and he wants to find out how.

"Alright," says Roan, "I'll stay a while."

"Then you have to tell me your name."

"Roan."

"You lived in that house?"

"That's right," replies Roan. "Did you get everything you wanted from there?"

"I saved some books. Whose were they?"

"My father's."

"He could read?"

"Of course."

"He taught you to read?"

"He, and my mother."

Saint's brow furrows. His voice acquires an almost reverential tone. "Your mother was a reader too?"

Puzzled, Roan nods.

"Did everyone in Longlight know how to read?"

"Yes."

"Amazing," Saint mutters.

"Why do you say that?"

"You've never been outside your village, or that valley, have you?"

Roan, cautious, makes no reply.

"If you had, you'd be aware that few people know how to read," says Saint. "People are suspicious of learning."

Roan is bewildered, though he hides his real concern. No one in Longlight ever spoke much about the Outside, and it had never occurred to him to ask why. What else was hidden from him?

"Why are they suspicious?" he asks.

Saint sighs. "They blame the Abominations on books."

"And you don't?"

"I blame men." Saint moves close to Roan and bends down to face him. "You have a gift that became even rarer when your people were lost. Share it with me. Teach me to read, Roan of Longlight."

I have something he wants, Roan thinks. Should I give it to him? If Saint has some darker purpose, teaching him to read could be disastrous. But then Roan remembers what his father often said: *Reading is like breathing. Words are like air.*

"I've never taught before," Roan says cautiously.

"I'm patient. It may take us a long time, but I'm sure you'll manage. Help me with this. Of course, we would have to agree on some form of compensation."

Roan chooses his words carefully. "You're already providing me with food and shelter," he says.

"I've done nothing more than help someone in need." Saint breathes slowly, contemplating Roan's face. "Perhaps there are others in need. You may not have been the only one from your village to survive."

Roan can't stop the quake that surges through his body.

Saint's eyebrow lifts. "You agree. It might be possible."

Despite himself, Roan whispers, "It might be."

A smile spreads across Saint's face.

"Teach me to read, and if any are alive, we'll find them."

If any are alive. The words make Roan shudder. Suddenly he's overwhelmed with rage, an emotion he's unable to hide.

"My offer makes you angry?"

"Your offer seems . . . fair," Roan chokes out.

"Could it be the thought of what was done to your people?"

Roan nods, not trusting himself to speak.

"You want vengeance."

Roan imagines finding the killers of Longlight, the skull-masked invaders; pictures himself clubbing them, then throwing them screaming into the Fire Hole. He tries to stop the hideous thoughts, but he can't. They're too strong. Roan looks up at the giant and the word lurches out. "Yes." The snow cricket stirs in his pocket, scratching hard against his heart.

"I can help with that too," says Saint. "I will teach you the Way of the Friend. You will find He is always there when we are in need."

For a moment boy and man regard each other in silence.

"So, Roan of Longlight, do we have an agreement?"

"We do."

Saint smiles and pats Roan on the shoulder.

The camp is on a rise overlooking a wide valley. A stream leads off to a nearby mountain. In a paddock, powerful horses stand grazing. Everywhere Roan looks there are tents and looming tent-like structures. All of them are covered with grass and branches, no doubt making their presence invisible from a distance. Under a low canopy protected by a rock wall, seven men bundled in black fur with cowls over their heads sit silently tapping grains of colored sand into the center of a giant flat stone.

"It's a form of meditation," explains Saint. "It takes four seasons to complete the image. When finished, it's swept away and they begin again."

"What will the image be?"

"A tribute to Him we serve."

Roan's attention is drawn by a clanging sound.

"Come. There are other activities you may find intriguing."

Saint takes Roan to a flat area at the edge of another rise, where men in loose tunics practice intricate sword movements, led by a brawny man with a shaven head. Slashing, leaping, they move with grace and precision. Despite his misgivings, Roan watches with fascination.

"Did they practice like this in Longlight?" Saint asks.

"We had no swords," says Roan. "They were forbidden."

"How did you protect yourselves?"

"We didn't."

"But I saw evidence of a great battle."

"There was no battle."

"Surely when attacked, your people defended themselves."

"We do not fight," repeats Roan, his eyes locked on the flashing blades.

Saint makes a small gesture to the man leading the exercises. With a word to his brothers, the bald man joins them, bowing to Saint.

"Friends to all," he says.

"The Friend is true," Saint replies, also bowing, though not as deeply. "Roan of Longlight, meet Brother Wolf, our movement master. Roan has joined us today, Brother. His journey here has been a hard one."

"Everything is only as difficult as the mind perceives it to be," Brother Wolf says, his eyes meeting Roan's.

"The massacre of my village was more than a perception," retorts Roan.

"The greater the pain, the greater your will must be to master it," Wolf tells Roan, "unless you wish to be a slave to it."

"I'm not a slave."

"Then you will find our training useful," says Wolf, and returns to the acolytes.

A numbness sweeps over Roan. The commitment he's made to this strange place suffocates him. There is no going back, no hope of rescue. Longlight is gone. And now he is here.

Touring the camp with Saint, Roan sees that though no walls surround it, a formidable gully of jagged rocks protects the perimeter. High in the trees, wooden platforms are manned by cowled Brothers whose eyes never stop scanning the valley below. Saint draws Roan away from the camp's defenses, introducing him to the Brothers' other activities.

Some Brothers are horse trainers, some are metal craftsmen, some are hunters. Seventy-five Brothers in all, Saint tells him.

At a tent that stands between two alder trees, a gray-bearded man greets them.

"Brother Saint! I have a salve I think may help that sore wrist of yours."

"Thank you, Brother Asp."

Brother Asp's eyes pore over Roan's face, penetrating beneath the surface. But the examination doesn't threaten Roan; quite the opposite. The Brother has a kind, open face that puts Roan at ease.

"Roan of Longlight. I'm sorry I didn't meet you earlier, but I've been tied up with some medical emergencies."

Roan wonders why Brother Asp seems so different, so much softer than the others. Almost like someone from Longlight. Perhaps it's because he's a healer.

Dinner gathers everyone in the main tent around five long tables. Feeder delivers steaming pots of stew and potatoes, ignored by the Brothers as if he's invisible. Roan's about to dig in when he notices that no one is touching the food. All stand in silence behind their seats.

Saint enters and comes to the empty space beside Roan. He lowers his head and speaks. "Born from stone, the First Friend reaches from the sky, giving us all that we have."

The seventy-five men speak in one voice: "Born from man, we reach for the sky."

"His heavenly blade freed us from evil," intones Saint.

"With His love we will free the world."

"We are Brothers. We are Friends."

"We are Friends."

Saint looks around at the assembled Brothers. "Before we eat, I would like you to meet our newest novitiate: Roan of Longlight."

There's an awkward moment before someone shouts "Welcome, Brother!" from a far table. The men applaud loudly and stamp their feet with no sign of stopping. A wild-eyed man with long yellow hair winks at Roan.

"They'll keep going until you return the courtesy."

Roan, catching on, claps his hands. The Friends cease applauding and break into a huge cheer. Everyone around Roan grins and shakes his hand. Then Saint sits and begins to eat and all the Brothers follow his lead.

Saint nods to the yellow-haired man. "This is Brother Raven, Roan. One of my most valued companions."

"You are unique, Roan of Longlight," says Raven, a crooked smile on his face. "Most novitiates don't arrive strapped on the back of Saint's motorcycle."

"He didn't leave me much choice."

Brother Raven emits a high-pitched cackle. "Choice! That's good!" Raven leans into Roan. Roan notices that the brother's breath has an unfamiliar scent, thick and tart. "If you have any problems, talk to me. I'm the helper and the fixer. That's me."

"Good to meet you," Roan replies courteously, but he can

sense the knife behind the man's smile. The Brother is insincere, it's obvious, he doesn't even bother to hide it. Roan eats his stew in silence, mulling over his situation. The Brothers talk quietly amongst themselves, and though he can tell he's the focus of their conversation, no one interrupts his ruminations.

When supper comes to a close, Saint speaks to finish the meal, raising his right hand. "Friends to all."

"The Friend is true," the brethren reply, raising their right hands in response. Then the clearing of tables begins.

As Roan adds his dirty plate to the pile, Feeder takes it. "You'll get used to this place soon enough," he whispers. "It's an honor to have you here."

Before Roan can ask him what he means, Feeder scurries away, and Brother Raven is quick to fill the gap. "Roan, let me show you to your quarters."

Raven escorts him out of the crowded dining tent. The pathway is lined with lit torches, and as they walk, Raven points out the Assembly, a small sloped amphitheater, with tiered benches looking down on a round, flat area. Before Roan can inquire as to its purpose, Raven indicates the "all-important" multiple outhouse structure and the communal washing area, where wooden basins are used for bathing. Roan stares at the very public space.

"Confused?" asks Raven.

"You wash together?"

"And we all crap together, too," chuckles Raven. "So uncivilized, don't you think?"

"Just different."

Raven lifts an eyebrow. "Different? How do you mean, different?"

Roan peers at this strange Brother, feeling he's somehow being tested. "It's all new to me," he carefully replies. "Unlike anything I've ever seen."

Raven chuckles. "A very politic response!"

"It's the truth."

"Of course, of course! Don't worry, I come from the middle of nowhere too. A little hamlet near the Rain Plateau. We barely had a visitor in all the time I lived there. I was younger than you are when I left."

"Where did you go?"

Raven gives Roan a probing look. Then, with a glint in his eye, he says, "To training school."

"What kind of training?"

"To tell the truth, I never completed it. I heard a fascinating tale: that a mortal man had become a Prophet. Gone to a mountaintop and descended with a message from a new God. I was curious, so I volunteered to leave and join the Prophet. I was one of the first to meet Saint. I'll have been with him and the Friend eleven years next spring."

Stopping in front of one of a long row of smaller tents, Raven opens its knit doorway. "This is yours," Raven says. "Get a good night's sleep, because tomorrow you start the schedule Saint's devised for you. You won't be needing those clothes anymore. You'll find the proper attire in your tent. After we raise the sun, you'll spend your mornings with Brother Wolf and your afternoons with Brother Stinger. Oh, and Brother Asp has requested what remains of your free time." Raven gives Roan a confidential look. "You might find the routine a little onerous. If you do, talk to me. I'll speak to Saint for you. Fix things. Remember, any problems at all, my tent's next to yours. Barge in anytime."

"Thank you," Roan says, ducking into his doorway, glad to get away from the cloying man. Inside his tent, by the light of a few candles, he sees the floor's covered with rugs. A thick black tunic lies folded at the foot of his bed, which is a simple wool mat. Roan crawls under the warm blankets, but he still feels cold. He reaches for his pack and pulls his father's shoe out of the pocket, fingering a patch as he lies back down.

The faces of the Brothers whirl before him. In one day, he's met seventy-five strangers, yet it was only a few days ago that he'd encountered the first stranger of his life. The first who had ever come to Longlight. Early that morning, an envoy riding a white horse had arrived unannounced at their gates. Everyone was stunned, but there seemed no reason to turn a single man away. Even more peculiar was the stranger's clothing: a gown completely covered in feathers. On his head was a helmet in the shape of a beak.

In the Shrouded Valley, birds other than chickens and crows were scarce, and no one had ever seen feathers like these before: bright yellow flecked with dazzling vermilion; irides-cent shades of mauve and silver; feathers a foot long, ivory with red speckles. The children of Longlight followed the Bird Man as he walked through the village, trying to touch his amazing gown. He welcomed their touch, letting out a high, cackling laugh. The children laughed too. But the adults were not amused. Roan could see the fear in their eyes, and for the first time in his life, he felt uneasy.

The councillors of the village escorted the Bird Man into the community's meeting room. Before the doors were pulled shut, Roan saw their worried glances, their trembling hands. Roan's father, his face set in a grim mask, was one of the ten who heard the envoy speak. The meeting went on and on as the children hovered outside the doors, brimming with curiosity. The twins Max and Esta, born a year after Stowe, tried to peek in but were quickly shooed away. Most of the children were excited, certain the envoy was here to sell feathers. But Roan's best friend, Aiden, was his usual cynical self. "What good are feathers?" he sniped. "It's not as if you can eat them." Stowe protested. "They're beautiful. I'd trade my two favorite drinking bowls for one of the shiny red ones."

Roan recognized some of the stranger's plumes from books. As they waited, Stowe begged him to name the long-extinct birds. Peacock. Eagle. Swan. Cardinal. She loved the sound of the words and made Roan repeat them over and over, made him write them down as she chanted them. To her it was an event like no other. This fabulous stranger was a feast for the eyes, a springtime in midwinter.

After a few hours, the meeting room doors swung open. The Bird Man left abruptly. His smile had vanished. Ignoring the children who begged for another touch of his plumes, he climbed onto his horse and was gone. Roan lingered behind, watching as the councillors emerged somberly from the building, his father in the lead.

Later that night, he was awakened by his parents' agitated discussion.

"Couldn't we pay him?" his mother asked.

"The only price he would accept," Roan's father said, "we would not pay." What he said next was obscured by the sound of a bowl, thrown, shattering on the floor.

"We have to leave," Roan's mother said. "We have to leave now!"

"No. It's the Prophecy."

"That's only a myth!"

"It's our reason for being here. It's the fulfillment of our existence."

"You'd sacrifice our lives—our children—for what could be nothing more than a fairy tale?"

"Look at me. Your instincts cry out against this. But you know the truth. We always knew this time would come."

Roan heard something in their voices he'd never heard before: terror. He wasn't cold, but he found himself shivering. His mother's voice, wracked with sobs, tore through him.

"Why today? Why now?"

"There can only be one reason," his father replied.

Suddenly, a rumbling sound. Something like thunder, but thunder had never made the floor tremble at Roan's feet. And then, silence. It was as if everyone in the village had caught their breath in the same moment.

"All will not be lost," said his father. Then his mother's voice, strong and focused: "Wake them. Go, go, go! Get them out of here!"

In his new tent, in the camp of the Brothers, Roan's stomach churns. Where is he? What is this place? Who are these people? What do they want from him? He slips his father's shoe back into his pack and steps outside for a glimpse of the moon. It's waning, and he can see craters on the shadowed side.

"Nightmares?" Roan cringes at Brother Raven's honeyed voice. "It's fortunate that I was coming by."

Roan doesn't take the bait, but Brother Raven is undeterred.

"Don't you like your quarters?"

"They're fine."

"Then why out so soon?"

"For some air."

"Be careful of the night air."

"Why?"

"You never know what might bite you." Raven laughs. "You're a very lucky boy, and you don't even seem to realize it."

"What do you mean?"

"You're here in our camp, instead of out there. You could

be roasting on a spit, or being swallowed by Blood Drinkers, or having your head severed and stuck up on a stake. But instead you're under the protection of a man touched by God. Lucky boy."

Roan, not letting on how unsettled he is by Raven's words, smiles politely, nods good-night, and returns to the relative peace of his quarters.

He lies on his bed and closes his eyes.

*A piercing scream. Stowe's fingernails rip his palm. The raider in the hideous red skull lifts her. Stowe is reaching, reaching for Roan.*

Roan's eyes fly open as he tries to shake the terrible memory. Heart pounding, aching to run, he forces himself to be still. The snow cricket scrambles out of his pocket and onto his chest. In a sliver of light, Roan gazes at its delicate antennae, its eyes unwavering black dots. A comforting sight. The cricket is content, Roan thinks. The cricket stays. So will I. Roan's eyes, heavy, finally close.

# the novitiate

the city issued the edict. bulldoze
the schools, bomb the libraries,
burn every book. dissent will not
be tolerated. everyone agreed and
it was done.

—the war chronicles

In the dim light of near-dawn, a tolling bell awakens Roan. His breath clouds in the frigid air. He slips into his new black tunic and pants, woven wool, thick but supple. To all outside eyes, he is one of the Brothers, the Friends. Feeder appears in the doorway with a covered bowl. "I brought you a snack to tide you over till breakfast. Eat it fast, we're due to make the sun rise."

Roan quickly swallows the porridge. Feeder seems content watching his every gesture, so Roan says nothing. As soon as he is ready, they step out of the tent and follow the other Brothers.

In a voice filled with trepidation and awe, Feeder whispers, "Is there really such a place as Longlight?"

The question puzzles Roan. "Why wouldn't there be?"

"Everyone's heard about it, but nobody's ever seen it. I didn't know if it was real."

"Well, it is." A pain flashes through his chest as Roan corrects himself. "It was." Before Feeder can ask him anything else, Roan speaks again. "How did you come to this place?"

Feeder gives him a nervous look. "Same as everyone."

Same as me? Roan wonders.

As they approach a rise at the perimeter of the camp, Saint joins them. "Thank you for escorting Roan here, Brother Feeder."

"You're wel...welcome, Brother Saint," Feeder stammers, apparently tongue-tied in the presence of the great man.

Turning to Roan, Saint nods. "Follow me."

Roan doesn't miss the look of disappointment on Feeder's face as he leaves him behind to follow Saint in the half-light. They climb in silence to the highest clearing in the camp. In this gray predawn, Roan gasps at the sight of seventy-five men standing in rows, looking down at the dark valley below. Its vast expanse is seemingly commanded by the sound of their breath, exhaling and inhaling in slow unison.

Saint cries out, fist to the sky. "For us He raises the sun! For us He brings the dawn."

While all watch in silence, Brother Wolf hands Saint a crossbow. Saint fits an arrow, its tip wrapped in cloth, into the bow. Wolf lights the cloth, and Saint sends the flaming arrow into the sky. Reaching its pinnacle, the bolt of fire arches downward, disappearing from view.

For a moment, nothing. No one speaks, no one seems to breathe. Then, at the edge of the horizon, a blaze of light appears. The sun. The Brothers cheer, a roar so loud Roan's ears hurt. Saint raises his hand. The assembled men fall silent.

"Thank you, Friend."

And all repeat: "Thank you, Friend."

The Brothers bow deeply to the sun, a gesture Roan joins. The silence almost seems to echo a reply, but the spell is broken as the procession heads back down to camp for breakfast.

Roan is finishing his second bowl of porridge, blissfully free of meat, when Brother Raven appears. "Good, you're ready. Time for your morning class."

Along the way, Raven stops at a well, where he pumps some water into a drinking cup. "Go ahead, taste it! Best water in three hundred miles!"

Roan drinks. "It's good," he says politely. But it has a metallic taste, not like the water in Longlight. That water was fresh and sweet.

"Completely untreated," brags Raven. "Fed by the mountain snows. This little area is unique, untainted. You can even drink the water from that stream. But in the villages, it's bad. Utterly toxic. Everyone needs water, though, don't they?"

"Didn't you say it was time for class?"

"Yes, yes, of course," says Raven. "Mustn't dawdle."

He escorts Roan to a clearing where Brother Wolf is leading twenty men through an elaborate series of kicks and arm thrusts. "I'll be on my way. The rigor of the noble warrior has a deleterious effect on my appetite." Raven grins, and with a pat on his stomach, he goes.

Brother Wolf looks up to see Roan. "You're late," he snaps. "Never be late again."

Roan nods, biting back his desire to blame Raven.

"Do your best to imitate what we're doing. I'll fill in the gaps for you later."

Wolf pivots, swoops, and jabs. With each movement, he makes a huge exhalation, a booming noise. His students copy both movement and sound. Beneath the cacophony, from his tunic's pocket, Roan hears the cricket sing.

Roan focuses on Brother Wolf's movements. Although he knows it's impossible, the exercises seem familiar to him. He throws himself with fierce precision into every extension and kick, losing all sense of time and place, until the master dismisses the group. At that moment the cricket stops singing, and Roan stops moving too. He's surprised to see how high the sun is in the sky; the entire morning's passed in a blink. Brother Wolf calls him over.

"Where did you learn these movements?"

"I've never seen them before," Roan replies. "I just followed, as you asked."

Wolf eyes him curiously, then retrieves a sword that's shaped like two crossed crescents from the weapons rack. "Have you ever encountered one of these? It's called a hook-sword."

Roan stares, fascinated. He's never come across anything like it.

Wolf takes Roan's hand. "The hook-sword is held like this," he says. Then he lifts out a battle-axe. "Defend yourself."

He brings the axe down on Roan, who instinctively blocks it with his sword. Wolf shifts his weight back and swings the axe at Roan's head. Roan dives, avoiding the blow, then is up again, ready to ward off the next strike.

Wolf holds up his weapon and shouts, "Attack!"

Roan just stands there.

"Attack! Now! Go!"

Roan looks at him, confused. He can understand warding off a blow. But to attack? That kind of thing was forbidden in Longlight, even in play.

Brother Wolf puts down his weapon and gazes at Roan for a long time. Roan seems to detect a trace of concern in his eyes, but Wolf's hard exterior is an effective mask. "Good balance, excellent reflexes, internal calm. You've had no training, ever?"

"None," Roan mutters. Then he remembers the new and waning moon celebrations in Longlight. They'd practice the postures and movements practically every day. "Well, we did work on a series of stances. Rising Tide ... Dragon Eats Its Tail ... they were like dances."

"So you're a dancer." Wolf laughs, then turns serious. "With some work, you might turn into something. This discipline requires power, speed, and technique. You have potential for speed, an obvious aptitude for technique, but you have to work on strength, stamina, and skill. Not to mention a determined offense, which was obviously not a priority in your dance class."

Roan senses that Wolf is a good, serious teacher, and the Brother exhibits no trace of Raven's deceit. Training with him would be wholly against the precepts of Longlight, would fill his parents with horror. How can it be that the movements had seemed right, made Roan's body exalt? But now, his survival depends on partaking in these practices.

Brother Wolf smiles, taking back the sword, and for the first time since his arrival in the camp, Roan smiles back.

Roan leaves the clearing and heads for the well. In the distance, he observes Brother Wolf talking to Saint. After a few minutes, Wolf bows to Saint, who goes back into his tent. Roan can't help wondering if the meeting was about him.

Pulling up the pail, Roan drinks deeply. The hook-sword felt so comfortable in his hands. The fighting, the thing Longlight most abhorred, seemed like second nature to him. It makes him sick and exhilarated at the same time. Roan douses himself with the remaining water, trying to wash away the tension.

Collapsing against a tree, he closes his eyes. The snow cricket wriggles out of his pocket, settles on his chest, and sings.

STANDING ACROSS FROM ROAN, BRIGHT IN THE MOONLIGHT, IS THE ANCIENT CREATURE.

"WHO ARE YOU?" HE ASKS.

HE REACHES FOR HER, BUT WITH A SWIFT JERK OF HER HAND, SHE KNOCKS HIM DOWN. HE LEAPS UP. SHE GRABS HIS ARM AND THROWS HIM BACK ON THE GROUND, HER CLOVEN HOOF PLANTED ON HIS CHEST. ROAN STRUGGLES, BUT HER HOOF IS FIRM.

"LET ME GO!"

"MAKE ME," SHE WHISPERS.

A bell sounds and Roan wakes into the glare of the afternoon sun, feeling agitated. He can't remember ever having had dreams as vivid and strange as these back in Longlight. But having uncanny dreams after your life's been torn in pieces might not be so unusual.

Roan feels his grief welling up, and he's grateful to see Feeder wave to him, a perfect distraction. Containing his emotions, Roan joins Feeder outside the cook tent. The enticing smell of food causes Roan's stomach to growl.

"This is my favorite part... Watch!" calls Feeder. With one pull, he yanks off a rabbit's entire skin, revealing the pink musculature.

Roan tries not to vomit. In Longlight, they consumed eggs from chickens and milk from goats, but to take the animals' flesh was unthinkable. But now that he's eating meat, he'd be a hypocrite to avoid the sight of an animal being butchered or skinned. And when the time comes for him to leave the camp, knowing how to prepare meat will be a useful survival skill. So he forces himself to watch, stomach churning. Feeder grins.

"I can do it blindfolded with one hand. Wanna see?"

"No, that's alright."

"You're not gonna believe this."

"No, I do, I do."

Feeder flicks his knife on a rabbit's neck, then turns his back to it, reaches behind himself, yanks, and holds the dripping skin proudly in the air. "Not bad, eh?"

"Impressive," murmurs Roan.

"Come on," says Feeder, "let's get you some lunch."

"Not hungry."

"You will be." Feeder drags him into the empty cook tent, sits him down at the table, and pours him a glass of goat's milk. "I bet you never saw a rabbit being skinned before."

"How'd you know?"

"Your face is green."

Roan laughs and sips the milk. "How did you end up being a cook here?"

Feeder doesn't look at him, just sharpens a knife. "That's what I'm best suited for."

"So you picked what you do?"

Feeder lets out a low laugh. "Nobody picks their job. That's up to the Five. Brothers Saint, Raven, Stinger, Wolf, and Asp. As for me, it wasn't much of a decision. This is all I'm good for."

"I don't understand."

"This is what I do best," Feeder says, with finality.

Roan, realizing the subject is delicate, changes direction. "I understand what each of the five do, except for Brother Raven. Does he have a function?"

"Yes. A very important one."

"What?"

Feeder gives Roan a guarded look. "Business affairs."

Roan nods, not quite sure what to make of that. "Have you noticed the smell on his breath?" he asks Feeder.

Feeder bites his lip.

"Do you know what it is?" Roan persists.

"Scorpion hooch."

"It's a drink?"

"Scorpion tails marinated in corn liquor."

"Wouldn't that kill you?"

"It contains just enough poison to numb the brain and make you a little crazy."

"But Brother Raven likes it."

Feeder motions Roan closer and whispers, "I've heard Brother Asp nagging him not to drink so much. The scorpion hooch is hard to come by, and Asp's usually the only one who's got a supply. He keeps it for medicinal purposes. Brother Raven can't mooch more than a couple of sips a night. I've heard Brother Stinger say to him, 'If you got your hands on a whole bottle, I'd hate to see what would happen.'"

Roan hesitates, fearing to breach protocol.

"What is it?" asks the cook.

"I'm probably imagining it."

"What?"

"Brother Raven seems to be following me around."

Feeder laughs with what seems to Roan a twinge of bitterness. "When you finish the milk, leave the glass there." He walks out of the tent, leaving a bewildered Roan behind.

Roan throws back the drink and turns, startled to find a dark man with a short, black beard standing before him. "I am Brother Stinger," the man says, and he motions for Roan to follow.

The seven devotees sit bent over the circle on the huge flat stone. The inner part of the circle now contains the charcoal outline of an intricate drawing that's partially complete, though it's still impossible to make out the subject of the artwork. Brother Stinger looks at Roan. "Your color will be sienna."

He hands Roan some furs and some fingerless gloves. After Roan has put them on, Stinger gives him a small, tube-like funnel and a pot filled with red-brown sand.

"What's the purpose of this?" asks Roan.

"Its purpose is to allow the Brothers to practice patience, perseverance, and concentration. Where the design has small diamonds, you place your color. These are the last words I will speak to you."

The rest of the afternoon is spent in silence, each Friend gently tapping his funnel to drop a few grains of sand at a time into their appointed place. Roan tries to stay with the task, but his mind drifts.

*Stowe is reaching, reaching for Roan. He grasps for her, so close, but before he can touch her fingers, the rider's bone club swoops down.*

Roan wrenches himself back to the present, but too late. His sand has poured out too rapidly, spilling past his designated areas. Brother Stinger notices but says nothing.

His mistake is painstakingly difficult to correct, and Roan is relieved when, just before sunset, the camp's bell rings. His every joint is stiff and sore, as if he's been sitting there a week, yet he's accomplished almost nothing. The sand painters rise, bow deeply. Then each of them picks up an unlit torch and heads toward the rise on the western side of the encampment. Roan follows and at the top finds the entire Brotherhood assembled. Every eye is focused on the sun hovering above the horizon. Brother Asp stands in front of the group, also holding an unlit torch.

"The light dies to live again."

The Brothers reply. "His light lives forever."

The sun melts out of sight, spreading red embers across the sky. The instant it sets, Brother Asp lights his torch. "We live by the light of the Friend."

As each Brother ignites his torch from Brother Asp's, Roan curses his ill fortune. Brother Raven has neatly dovetailed in front of him. "There you are! I've caught you just in time. Brother Saint has invited you to sup with him in his lodgings."

"Thank you, Brother. I know the way," says Roan.

But Raven smiles chummily and strolls along with him. "What an impressive first day you've had. In my humble opinion, you're the most intriguing novitiate to come our way in years."

"You honor me, Brother Raven."

"Little Brother, the honor is all mine. To be in the presence of one so favored by the Prophet. So tell me, Roan. Which appealed to you more today, fighting or sand painting?"

"I'm not sure. I suppose they both have their purposes."

"Yes, they do. And what's your purpose?"

"I'm not sure what you mean."

"Surely everyone has a purpose. How else would one give meaning to this wretched existence?"

"Maybe I'm too young to know," Roan replies. "What's your purpose, Brother Raven?"

"Why, to serve the Friend, of course."

"Perhaps when I learn more about the Friend," says Roan, warily choosing his words, "my purpose will be the same."

"I'm sure it will. I wonder, my good fellow, why Saint's arranged to eat with you."

"I couldn't begin to guess at his reasons."

"Yes, yes, Saint always has reasons. And now you've gone and dashed my hopes of having some light shed on them."

"I wish I could be of more service."

"Hmm. Me too." Brother Raven's face opens in a bountiful smile. "It's so very advantageous to have friends."

Roan is thankful when they arrive at Saint's tent.

"Be careful how brightly you burn, Little Brother," warns Raven.

Despite his nervousness, Roan's glad to finally cross Saint's dim, narrow threshold. He passes several empty rooms, following a glimmer of light that takes him into a large tent attached to the main structure. He's surprised to see a fire burning in the center of the area, the smoke rising through a hole near the tent's peak. Saint sits on a carpet decorated with images of serpents. Books are scattered everywhere, and Saint is picking through them.

"Good, you're here. Roan, tell me what these are about."

Roan kneels on the rug and lifts a volume. "This is called *Alice in Wonderland.*"

"Ridiculous. What else?"

Roan picks up another. "This is the Holy Bible."

Saint takes it from him. Feels it with his hands. Sniffs at it. "So this is what the old God smells like."

"Would you like to learn to read a passage?"

"Heresy and lies," Saint snarls, throwing the book into the fire. Roan leaps and pulls it out, smothering the flames in his clothing. In Longlight, books were treasured. The thought of burning one infuriates Roan.

"Our Friend is the first God and the last God. There's no room here for pagan lies. Throw it back in the fire," Saint commands.

Roan hesitates, controlling his fury. "This text is thousands of years old. It records two of the great religious movements. The struggles and the wars of their prophets."

Saint is silent, mulling over the boy's words. Then he

speaks. "You have a strong mind, and I will not argue with your logic. Put the book in that box."

Roan, satisfied, places the Bible in a large chest, adding it to a pile of books inside. Beside them, he notices some lockets of hair, tied with ribbon, and a few children's toys. A play-ring, a rattle, a wooden top.

"Are there children here?"

Saint takes a moment to reply. "Not here." Then, "Find me a book," he orders.

Roan picks up book after book, reading Saint the title and giving a brief description of the contents. Sappho's love poetry, *Frankenstein, Hamlet,* a Volkswagen Beetle repair manual, *Crime and Punishment,* Plato's *Republic,* a biography of Michael Jackson, *The Biology of Orcas,* the *Kama Sutra.* Dozens of books. But Saint keeps muttering the same thing: "Useless!"

"What kind of book are you looking for?" Roan asks querulously, immediately regretting it as Saint bellows, "Something I can use!"

Roan sifts through the dusty volumes until he discovers a history of the combustion engine and describes it to Saint. "That's more like it," says Saint, who leafs through the book and then puts it in the chest. "You're on the right track. Keep going."

Roan finds another well-worn book. "Here's one on soil decontamination." He opens the cover, and his chest goes tight. "This is from my father's library," he says, his eyes smarting. He remembers his father holding this book, hunched over it, taking notes. *I'm touching what you touched, Father.*

Saint's voice breaks in. "Was the soil contaminated in Longlight?"

Roan breathes, trying to let his sadness go. "Yes. When the First Ones arrived, this book showed them what plants would introduce bacteria to detoxify the earth."

"We'll put that book on our list, then," says Saint. He points at a gold-embossed volume. "What's that?"

"It's called *The History of the Qin Dynasty in China,*" replies Roan, scanning some pages of the thick text. "In 221 B.C. one man conquered all the other warlords and created an empire."

"Where was China?" asks Saint.

"It was a very old, huge country on the other side of the great ocean. This man, he called himself King Zheng, was the first to unify the country."

"We'll read this," pronounces Saint.

Roan turns back to the title page and shows Saint the first word on it: "The." Saint stares at it.

"Do you recognize the letters?" asks Roan.

"Of course I recognize the letters," snaps Saint.

"The T and the H make a sound together: 'th,'" Roan explains.

Saint squints at the letters. Then, after a few moments, he turns to Roan. "How did he conquer the other warlords?"

Roan scans the table of contents. "That's not until chapter 3. We'll get there eventually. Read the first word."

Saint shrugs. "Let's start with chapter 3."

"We should read the first two, they'll provide—"

"Chapter 3. Now."

"Chapter 3 won't be any easier."

"Doesn't matter. *You're* going to read."

One look at Saint's intimidating face convinces Roan that, whatever Saint's motivations, he'd better start reading fast. And so he begins the tale of King Zheng. He reads, both fascinated and repulsed, about how the king used spies to ferret out his rivals, how he employed terror to demoralize his enemies and brilliant battle strategies to decimate them.

"A brilliant man, inspired," Saint sighs.

"I suppose."

Saint eyes Roan. "You don't agree?"

"I find it difficult. All the brutality and murder."

"Yes," says Saint, "you were no doubt shielded from these things in Longlight. But there are many men like King Zheng in the world, and the more we know, the better prepared we will be for them. That's enough for now. We will continue with this book tomorrow."

"You don't want me to teach you how—"

"Time is short, Roan of Longlight. It will be more productive if you read to me. Now, let's have our supper."

Roan follows Saint to a smaller, canopied room where a table is set with roasted rabbit and potatoes. Indicating that Roan should sit, Saint cuts up the meat and places a charred leg on each of their plates.

"Thank you," mumbles Roan. Following Saint's lead, he

picks up the leg in his hands, bites into it, and chokes the meat down.

"You did very well in the practice session today," says Saint.

Roan, watching Saint ravage the meat, breathes deeply. "Brother Wolf is an excellent teacher. He made the moves easy to follow."

Saint studies Roan's face. "With no experience, you kept up with some of my most skilled disciples."

"I hope I didn't offend anyone."

Saint laughs. "Of course not. You have a gift."

"I'm not aware of any gift."

"Your people must have known of your talents. Why didn't they do more to protect you?"

Roan, bewildered, struggles to make sense of Saint's words. "I don't understand."

"The Friend teaches us that life is precious and must be defended. There is no sin in that. You excel in the art of combat. You accomplish with ease where others struggle. This is no accident. It's a gift. It has always been in you and should have been nurtured. By denying it, you make yourself weak."

At the sound of horses and men dismounting outside the tent, Saint wipes his fingers on a cloth, rises, and puts his hand on Roan's shoulder. "I look forward to our reading tomorrow."

In the frigid night air, Roan nearly collides with a large stallion. Steam jets from the animal's huge nostrils, and a crossbow is strapped to its saddle. Roan stares at the formidable weapon and a group of four hulking Brothers, their cloaks mud-crusted, swords hanging from their belts, who have their road-weary eyes set on him. Roan nods to them as Saint, an imposing shadow against the light of the entryway, motions them inside.

Roan lingers a while, gently patting the horse's muzzle. He shivers in the cold. For the first time in his life, he is questioning what he has always taken for granted. Would the people of Longlight have survived if they'd known how to defend themselves? Why were they so opposed to fighting? Why did their values seem so wise then and so foolish now? And what was his gift? Had his father known about it? Would he disapprove of Roan using it now, despite all that had happened?

Roan knows he mustn't trust Saint and his silver tongue. But why not gain whatever skills he can while he remains here? Saint had said that Roan wouldn't survive outside the camp without Saint's protection, and he can't help but feel the truth of that. There is so much he doesn't know.

Roan is suddenly aware of Brother Raven's presence. Raven doesn't approach him, though, so Roan pretends he hasn't noticed. Walking alone, he winds his way to his tent. He will practice some of the exercises he learned this morning. Surely there's no harm in that.

# the prophet's destiny

it is said our world once shimmered
with messages carried on beams of
light, connecting thousands of cities.
in the wars the light was snuffed out
and only one city survived. our city.
the city.

—orin's history of the friend

THE FIRST SIGNS OF SPRING are the dandelions that rise
defiant despite the unyielding ground. The land around
the Friends' camp is barely thawed, but the weeds are bigger
than any Roan's ever seen, and every part of them is gathered
and eaten. The snow cricket, like Roan, is particularly fond of
the tender new leaves, while the Brothers are most interested
in the flowers, which are fermented and made into wine.

There's much to be done. Care and training of horses,
relentless domestic chores, crafting and repairing of weapons,
grounds maintenance. In the months that have passed, Roan's
learned that each Brother has a unique schedule. He's adapted

to his own routine with remarkable ease. It distracts him from the sadness and anger and confusion that have plagued him since the destruction of Longlight. But there's no escaping his pain at night, when he's haunted by memories of his parents, Stowe, and all the other people he loved.

This morning, like every morning, is martial arts with Brother Wolf. Wolf spends much time showing his disciples "kill" points: spots on the body where a well-placed blow will cripple or slay the opponent. Roan has never questioned the instruction, though he doubts its intent is solely defensive. He works hard on his technique during the sessions with Brother Wolf, but early in the morning or late at night, alone in his tent, he practices his forms alone. This solo practice is part of another secret he keeps: what happens in his dreams.

The dreams come to him unexpectedly. Sometimes he's sleeping, sometimes he's awake.

THE MOUNTAIN LION PACES THREATENINGLY BEFORE ROAN.

A HOOK-SWORD APPEARS IN ROAN'S HAND. THE LION LEAPS, ITS CLAWS RIPPING ROAN'S SKIN. ROAN SWINGS THE BLADE, SLICING THE LION ACROSS THE SHANK. THE LION RIPS ROAN'S THROAT, LEAVING HIM A BLOODY MESS ON THE GRASS.

"DON'T HOLD BACK," THE LION SAYS.

"BUT I'LL KILL YOU," ROAN WHISPERS.

"YOU MUST DO WHAT IS NECESSARY. TRY AGAIN."

ROAN'S BLOOD FLOWS BACK INTO HIS BODY, AND HIS WOUND CLOSES UP. HE STANDS, HOLDING THE SWORD. THE LION LEAPS.

The dream comes again and again. Roan has learned to

strike hard and fast, managing to overcome the great beast as often as he himself is struck down. But he remains uneasy when it comes to applying these skills with Brother Wolf. He feels torn, keeping this secret from his master. Maybe one day he'll feel secure enough to show Brother Wolf how adept he's become. He would love to see the surprise on his master's face.

Every afternoon, Roan sand paints with Brother Stinger. He works contentedly now, but the skill was hard-earned. Initially he lacked the patience to sit cross-legged for hours, tapping out a few grains of sand at a time. Instead of focusing on the work, he would fidget, and his mind would wander to the terrible memory of the Fire Hole, or to the moment he lost his sister's hand, or to his fights with the dream lion. Inevitably, his funnel would slip, the red-brown sand would miss its mark, and Brother Stinger would gaze sternly at him with unblinking eyes.

But one day, as Roan fought to concentrate on the falling sand, the snow cricket wriggled in his pocket. Startled, he nearly dropped the funnel. But something had shifted. A deep feeling of repose came over Roan, and his eyes settled on the tip of the funnel. As he lightly tapped it, the sand flowed, and to his amazement, he could see each grain individually. It was as if the grains had grown larger, and Roan's eyes tracked them with such precision they appeared to stop in the air, floating. He felt he was using his eyes for the first time, actually *seeing*. That afternoon, when the bell rang ending the session, Roan was astonished. Three hours had passed in what seemed like five minutes. Brother Stinger looked at him with just the hint of a smile, and from then on, Roan was taken under his wing, receiving advice on how to further refine his concentration and focus. Stinger isn't a demonstrative man, but Roan can feel his warmth.

Most days, after sand painting, Roan is happy to while away the hours with Brother Asp. The man's mild temperament and interest in learning remind Roan of the adults in Longlight, and he has become Roan's favorite of the Brothers.

Saint had directed Roan to share his father's soil decontamination book with Brother Asp, and Asp had listened eagerly.

"My boy, we're blessed to have you. Others under our watch can benefit from the knowledge you provide."

Asp seemed almost too kind and gentle to be one of the brethren. He began to take Roan out into the bush to forage for healing plants, and their time together provided Roan with the opportunity to explore the outer edges of the Brothers' camp and get glimpses of what lay beyond.

Still, he hasn't been outside the defensive perimeter, and he's going a little stir-crazy.

One sunny afternoon, Roan sits guiding grains of sand onto the painting, feeling more peaceful than he has since before losing Longlight. The scent of new growth infuses the air, the cricket is quietly chirping in his pocket, and he is entirely engaged in his activity. But this idyllic moment is broken when Roan is unexpectedly summoned to meet Saint.

When Saint is not out of camp on one of his trade missions, Roan sees him often, but always at the end of the day. Roan will sup with him, then read aloud into the night. Months have passed, but they still remain with the history of King Zheng. Obsessed with the topic, Saint insists on going over each chapter again and again, committing many sections of the text to memory. With the aid of stones and roughly drawn maps, he delights in reenacting the battles described in the book, reviewing the errors the losers made. Roan, to his surprise, finds he also relishes the game. He's an inventive strategist, adept at deploying imaginary troops, anticipating attacks, and improvising lightning actions.

Approaching Saint's tent, Roan remembers how, one evening, after one of his more clever moves had eliminated half of Saint's "army," Saint had shaken his head in wonderment. "Where did you learn to do that? I didn't see that in the book."

"I played chess with my father, Roan told him. "This game doesn't seem much different."

Saint smiled. "Except that these pebbles are men. Men who died under Zheng. Men who could die under my command."

Roan went silent, recognizing the truth in the statement. He'd been helping Saint develop tactics to fight wars, to capture and kill the enemy. Human beings.

Yet despite understanding the deadly intent of the game, Roan feels compelled to keep playing, and today, if at all possible, he will win.

"You sent for me, Brother?" Roan queries as he enters the Prophet's tent.

"Today we finish the saga of King Zheng," announces Saint, handing Roan the book of Zheng's exploits. Roan can hardly believe the moment has come. He reads to the last page, closes the cover, and sighs.

Saint has been hunched over the rug, sharpening a long sword. He turns to Roan. "Read me the chapter about the building of the Great Wall again," he commands.

Roan winces. "I thought you had it memorized."

"I do, but I enjoyed watching your face when I said that."

Saint rises and lifts his sword, moving it slowly in the air. He looks gigantic, unstoppable. Lowering the sword and moving closer to Roan, he speaks with quiet intimacy. "If Zheng hadn't forced his people to build the wall and the nomads had invaded, his citizens' suffering would have been far worse, don't you think?"

"It's possible," concedes Roan.

"He acted in the interests of his people. Without a strong defense, everyone dies. You, better than most, should know that."

Roan broods silently.

"The man was cunning," says Saint.

Roan challenges him. "Then why did he need to burn books and have scholars buried alive or worked to death building the wall?"

"The Masters of the City did the same. Do you know of what I speak?"

"I know the Wars were fought with them. And that they won."

"Exactly. Like King Zheng, when they took control, they acted without hesitation. Thought breeds dissent. Eliminate the thinkers and you control the population. So they closed the schools, burned books, and executed anyone who had knowledge that was not in their service. That's the real reason no one knows how to read and why we live in chaos."

Saint pats Roan on the shoulder. "There's still plenty of light left. Come with me. It's time for you to spread your wings a little. See Barren Mountain."

He hands Roan a goatskin coat and they go outside to a smaller shelter behind Saint's tent. Saint throws back the oiled canvas door and wheels out his motorcycle. He motions Roan to get on, then revs the engine, and they roar away.

The first time Roan rode on the bike he was unconscious. This time he's wide awake, and the rush of wind and landscape is exhilarating. Saint drives to Barren Mountain and motors up a trail that's barely visible through the underbrush. The forest that was once here is long dead, and the broken stumps of ancient trees are overgrown with a voracious weed Roan recognizes. Nethervines. Their black thorns cause oozing, lethal wounds.

Roan and Saint disembark on a plateau high up on Barren Mountain.

"If we continued, and crossed to the valley on the other side of the mountain, we'd be entering the Devastation," says Saint grimly.

"I've heard the tales of what happened there. Is it still poisoned?"

"I don't know. No one has ever returned to tell."

Saint leads Roan to the edge of a precipice. In the wide expanse below, he points to a river that curls out for miles. Scattered throughout the landscape are dozens of tiny villages.

"Everything on this side of the river, from this mountain across that plain, the villages, the people, every blade of grass, is under the protection of the Friend."

"What about the other side?"

"That side of the Farlands belongs to marauders, brutes, killers for hire. The Lee Clan. Beyond them, in the south, the Fandors, the most crazed and bloodthirsty of all. Three other warlords, one more vicious than the next, hold the territory past where we can see. All of them are looking for booty or tribute. One of them destroyed Longlight."

Roan breathes, trying to calm himself, but he can't stop the strange heat burning through his body. "I want to know who it was."

The big man smiles grimly.

Roan's overwhelmed by images. Of the red skull man tearing Stowe from his grasp, of Longlight's broken gates, the shattered pots, the bones floating in the Fire Hole. The memories saturate him, feed his yearning for revenge. He shudders. Looking below, he sees in the valley a map of Saint's ambition. "You want to conquer them."

"The Friend teaches us we have an obligation to end chaos.

That means a central controlling order under one ruler. My duty is to ensure the Friend is that ruler. Your presence is a remarkable advantage on this quest, because through books you bring knowledge. Knowledge gives us the hidden weapon of strategy as well as insight into our opponents' tactics. Conquering the warlords will not be difficult. Zheng's story and our games have given me several excellent ideas. But taking the City, that is the challenge. The City is the true enemy, the heart of the evil that afflicts us all. The reason for Longlight's fall lies there."

"What is the reason?"

Saint doesn't take his eyes off the view below. "I don't have that answer yet, but I will, I promise you. I do know that the City takes what it wants, then destroys the rest. One of those clans on their own would not have obliterated Longlight. No. They'd enslave some people, rape some, but they'd leave the rest to rebuild and pay tribute."

"You think the murderers were working for the City."

"The Farlands are an irritant that the City wants subdued. The City never completely conquered these lands during the wars, and they are still trying to finish what they started so long ago. None of us is safe as long as the City rules."

"Didn't you get your motorcycle from the City? And the fuel for it? And your tents?"

Saint laughs. "We trade with the City. There is no choice; it controls all manufacturing. We acquire things, yes, but we also gain information. We find out how it functions, discover its weaknesses. When you see things more fully, you'll understand. Our final battle lies there."

"And how does a band of seventy-five take on a whole City?"

A strange, faraway look sweeps over Saint's face. "I was standing right here when it happened, Roan."

"When what happened?"

"I came to this spot in despair, feeling helpless before the City's power and ruthlessness. All of us in the Farlands were dispersed, lost, victim to petty warlords who never stopped battling with each other. I drove here ready to end it all, disgusted by everything around me. Just as my sword was set to my heart, I was blinded by white fire. I saw Him. The Friend. He stepped out of the flame and told me what I must do: build an army in His image. Free the people in His name. He promised that on the appointed day, I would lead His people to victory over the City."

"Was it a dream?"

"You see the villages there? They are full of thousands who have seen the truth of the Friend. They are ready to join us, when the time comes. If it had been a dream, it wouldn't have changed their lives. The tragedy of Longlight is that your people were lost before they could join the fight."

"I don't think they would have."

"No matter. I only need you. I believe He wanted me to find you, despite the peril."

"What peril do you mean?"

Saint sidesteps the question. "All great actions involve terrible risk. That is the nature of change. The Friend knows that even with all the support I have, I lack the strength to overcome the enemy."

"You're stronger than anyone I've ever known."

Saint turns, his eyes cloudy. "Roan, I was raised like an animal, scavenging for survival. Uneducated, ignorant. Before the Friend came to me, I was nothing more than a brute. The Friend raised me up, turned me into the Prophet. Yet I was still lacking in wisdom. So he pointed the way to you. With your knowledge and your growing talent as a warrior, everything now seems possible."

"What if I refuse to fight?"

"Longlight was exterminated. Brutally. Should your people pass with no one to avenge their deaths?"

Roan, chilled, cannot answer.

"What I say conflicts with your education. But I speak from a place of truth. I see you yearn to punish your parents' killers, and I see your shame in the face of this passion. Roan, there's no shame in seeking what is right. That's the glue that binds your mind, your soul, and your talent. Fight the desire of your spirit, and you are weakened. Stay one with it, and you will become an incredible force. I would be honored to fight by your side."

Why does he need me to fight the City? Roan wonders. What's the peril Saint faces?

Saint interrupts his musings. "You have a cricket."

Roan is startled. "How do you know about it?"

"Brother Wolf tells me the cricket sings during practice."

"I didn't realize anyone could hear under all the shouting."

"Never underestimate Brother Wolf. May I see it?"

Roan opens his pocket. The cricket lies perfectly still. Saint peers in and his eyes narrow. "A snow cricket."

"You've seen one before?"

"Not often. Never in someone's pocket. It allows you to carry it?"

"It does what it wants."

"It chose you?"

"I have no idea."

Saint shakes his head. "Roan of Longlight, you keep secrets from me."

"Not intentionally."

Saint smiles, then turns his back. The interlude is over.

The ride down the mountain is fast, and the chill in the wind so intense that Roan tucks his face behind Saint's back. When they come to the bottom, Saint brakes to a stop and jumps off the motorcycle.

"You drive," he says to Roan.

"Are you serious?"

"Should I change my mind?"

Without another word, Roan takes the driver's seat. Saint points out the pedals, hand controls, gearshift, accelerator, and brakes. "Go ahead, try it."

Roan carefully gives the machine some gas and slowly lets out the clutch. The bike lurches forward, nearly throwing him.

"Hit the next gear!"

Roan does, and the bike spasms, jolting him high out of his seat. He gives it more gas. The bike surges ahead. Roan revs the engine, and the noise helps drown out the sound of Saint's laughter.

The motorcycle gains speed. Once it is running smoothly, Roan raises the gears, feeding the machine more gas, and soon he's blasting down the road. The wind doesn't seem to bite like before, now that he's driving. The magical vehicle is in his grip, and it roars, it speeds, it flies.

As the rocks and brush sweep by, Roan realizes he's left Saint far behind. At a flat, clay-packed spot, he pivots the bike, throwing dust, then accelerates and blasts back the way he came, until he sees Saint standing there waiting. Only then does he realize it never even occurred to him to try to escape.


The sun is low in the sky by the time Roan and Saint arrive back at the camp. Ignoring the curious looks of the Brothers, and Raven's smirk, Saint drops Roan off and rides back to his quarters.

Saint's barely out of view when Feeder surreptitiously motions Roan into the cook tent. "First wine of the season. Time for a taste test!" Feeder announces. He pours them both a glass of dandelion wine, spilling a good portion of it on the table.

"I see you've already been into it," Roan observes.

"Have to make sure it's just right. I thought the golden boy should be next in line."

"Golden boy?"

"Cheers," Feeder says, gulping down another glass.

Roan tastes the wine. "Sweet. It's good."

Feeder scowls, slumping in his seat. "I'm sick of making wine, I'm sick of cooking food, I'm sick of everything."

"You're drunk."

Feeder shakes his head. "I'm not like you. I don't come from a special town. I didn't have parents who loved me and kissed my face all over."

"What happened to your parents?"

"I hope they're dead."

"No, you don't."

"You don't know anything about it. Guess what my parents did for my tenth birthday?"

"What?"

"Sold me to a farmer as a field-worker." Feeder takes another swallow of wine.

"That farmer was a mean bastard. There were six of us. He worked us too hard. After the third kid got sick and died, I ran."

"That's how you came here?"

"Eventually. When they accepted me as a novitiate, it was the greatest thing that had ever happened to me. It was Utopia, you know?" He picks up the bottle and pours himself more. "But I was no good at anything. I can't ride, can't fight, can't even sand paint. So now I'm the cook." He stares blearily at Roan. "I wish I was you."

With that, Feeder lays his head on the table and starts snoring. Roan puts the bottle and glasses away and leaves him to sleep it off. He wonders if everyone in this camp has some terrible story, some tragic event that brought them here. Maybe it's good that I'm here, he thinks. I belong.

# the giving of gifts

and the dream came to the prophet's
swordsmith. the horns of the great
bull fell before him, and they lay as
two crescent moons crossed. so
within the shape of his weapon was
laid the promise of peace.
— the book of longlight

THE WILD STRAWBERRIES that flourish on the southern
edge of the camp are the first crop of summer. Roan,
delighted by the fruit, forages at every opportunity, relishing
the berries' sweetness.

"You gobble those up like there'll be none tomorrow."

Roan, his mouth full, grins at Brother Asp. "You never
know."

Brother Asp smiles. "I have something else for you to try."
He hands Roan a carved wooden instrument. "I found this in
one of the villages. Thought you might like to play the cricket
some music for a change."

Roan accepts the gift, a little awestruck. It's been eight months since he's seen anything like this recorder. The craftsmanship rivals Longlight's. He's not sure he's worthy of it.

"What is it, Roan?"

"Brother Asp, how did you find the Friend?"

"I came to Him through my work. The Friend provided a shelter where I might thrive. In this way, I am better able to serve those who suffer. And now, thanks to the Friend, you are here with us. With what you have read to me, along with the experience you've related from Longlight, I'll be able to help many more."

Brother Asp smiles again, and leaves Roan to try a few notes on his new recorder. Asp's friendship fills Roan with guilt, for he has begun preparations for the day he will leave this place and these people. His Brothers.

Roan was just beginning to settle into camp life when he heard the old goat-woman while supping one night.

"PUT IT IN YOUR POCKET."

Roan looked up to see the ancient creature standing across from him. He glanced around fearfully to check if anyone else had seen or heard her, but the Brothers continued with their meal as if nothing at all was happening.

"PUT THE DRIED MEAT IN YOUR POCKET," THE GOAT-WOMAN SAID. "START SAVING FOOD. YOU'LL NEED IT WHEN YOU LEAVE. REMEMBER, A LITTLE AT A TIME, OR PEOPLE WILL NOTICE."

Before Roan could protest, the goat-woman was gone.

What he'd wanted to say was, I like it here. I like my tent, my talks with Brother Asp, my lessons with Brother Stinger and Brother Wolf. Saint treats me like a son. The Brothers care about me, they value me. With their help, I could exact revenge for Longlight and maybe even find Stowe. Apart from the repellent Brother Raven, this is a good place to be. Why should I leave?

On the other hand, Roan figured, there was no harm in being prepared. So he slipped the jerky into his pocket. From that moment on, he added food from every meal to his hidden stash.


Brother Wolf's practices have become more and more challenging as the days grow longer. He pushes Roan, working him harder than the others. But despite the heat, Roan is able to maintain whatever pace Wolf sets. Today's a particularly challenging workout, and Roan's muscles are quivering with exhaustion as Brother Wolf approaches him.

"Superb endurance. You're progressing exceptionally well, Roan."

"Thank you, Brother Wolf."

"You've mastered some of the most difficult sequences. You do not, however, test the limits of your speed and strength."

"I will seek to improve, Brother Wolf," Roan says. His tone is neutral, but he worries that his secret training may be starting to reveal itself.

Wolf extends a cloth-wrapped object. "This might help you improve in those areas." He signals Roan to take it. With mounting excitement, Roan removes the wrapping. It's a hook-sword, light and perfectly balanced.

"This is for me?" Roan asks, staggered by the enormity of the gift.

"My father was never a swordsman, but he was an unparalleled swordsmith. He made two of these, identical in strength and design. One was for me, he said. The other was for my greatest pupil. I've taught for many years. This sword belongs to you."

"I'm honored," says Roan, bowing his head.

"You've earned it," replies Brother Wolf. Without another word, he is gone.

Roan slices the air with the blade. It feels like part of his hand. But a pall is cast over his excitement when the only person he dreads crosses his path. Brother Raven, back again from one of his harvest excursions.

Roan's been overjoyed to be free of Raven, often for days at a time. Every week another wagonload of fresh fruits and vegetables arrived alongside a band of Brothers on horseback led by Brother Raven. It would take five Brothers over an hour to unload each wagon. To Roan's delight, some of the produce is served at meals, but Feeder supervised the brothers in preserving much of the haul: corn, snap peas, tomatoes, cucumbers, pears, apricots, and much more. The sheer bounty of it puzzled Roan, though. Could that much produce really be given freely, as Raven attested, by "friends and admirers"?

"Beautiful sword," Raven says, interrupting Roan's practice. "That must be one of Brother Wolf's prized weapons."

"It is."

"Well, then," says Raven, tossing him a yellow apple. "Here's another present for you, Roan. Best apple you'll ever taste."

Roan catches it and puts it up to his nose, savoring the fragrance. A yellow apple, just like the ones at Longlight. The smell's so familiar. Could it be from the orchard there? Is it possible? Does Raven know?

Roan looks up to see to see Raven eyeing him keenly. "Where does it come from, you're wondering?"

Concealing his thoughts, Roan bites into the fruit, the first he's tasted in a year. The last was one of a dozen his mother had given him to share with Stowe and their friends. Roan recalls how he and Aiden ran off with the fruit straight to Big Empty, with Stowe and the others screaming behind. At the treetop, Roan and Aiden pretended they'd eaten them all, and Stowe yelled bloody murder until he handed over the apples, not a one missing. He remembers her giggles and Aiden's laughter and the juice trickling down their faces, and he aches with sadness.

Tearing himself from the memory, Roan stares at the apple Raven has given him, hesitant to take another bite. It would be just like the Brother to taunt him like this. But how could he know?

Brother Stinger's voice breaks the tension. "You're required for a gathering of the Five."

Roan's startled to see Brother Stinger looking at him. Perhaps someone has discovered his stash of food or Raven has peeked in on a covert practice session. What kind of punishment would he face?

But upon arriving at the edge of the stream where Wolf, Asp, and Saint are waiting, Roan finds out he's been summoned for an altogether different reason.

"The time has come for a choice," states Saint solemnly.

Brother Wolf casts an discerning eye on Roan. "You are ready to begin your initiation into the Company of Friends."

Brother Asp asks the question: "Do you wish to join us?"

Roan glances Brother Raven, who smiles with transparent guile. For a moment Roan hesitates, then he looks at selfless Brother Asp; Brother Wolf, whose generosity belies his gruff exterior; Brother Stinger, so subtle and demanding; and Saint, who favors him above all others.

An unearthly silence descends over the Brothers. Roan hears the old goat-woman's voice, clear and certain.

"DO NOT HESITATE. THIS IS YOUR PATH."

Emboldened by her affirmation, Roan replies firmly. "I would be honored."

They move to a rise. Roan looks down to see that many of the brethren have gathered for the announcement. Saint places both of his hands on Roan's shoulders, nodding with pride.

"His initiation will begin!" Saint shouts out to the Brothers, who raise their arms in the air, "For the Friend!"

"Now you fast," says Brother Wolf.

Brother Stinger gazes at Roan with clear eyes. "Stay focused."

"I'm very proud of you," Brother Asp says, clapping Roan on the shoulders.

Brother Raven, grinning with all his rotting teeth, simply gives Roan a wink.

Roan accepts their goodwill with thanks, then excuses himself to attend to his duties.

It is the afternoon of a full moon, and Roan is anxious to return to the sand painting. The painting is over half complete now, and the central image is clear. It shows the Friend, his eyes blazing, his huge arms reaching down. The top of a bull's head is also becoming visible, its horns of sand poking at the Friend's skin. It's hard to imagine this rich portrait is simply sand grains sprinkled on stone. The artistry is exceptional. Roan can hardly wait to see the painting finished.

"Would you like a potato?" calls Feeder, trotting up to greet him.

"No thanks, can't eat it. I'm fasting."

"It's delicious. Fire-roasted."

Feeder's words are friendly, but Roan can see that he's scowling. "What's wrong, Feeder?"

"I suppose you're happy now."

"Yes, I am."

"You realize that once you join and learn the secrets, there's no turning back. The Friends will never let you go. It's forever."

"Nothing's forever."

"Yes, it is—for someone. One comes, one goes."

"What are you talking about?"

Feeder forces a smile. "Forget it, it's just poetry." He reaches to shake Roan's hand. "Congratulations. You deserve this."

There's something disturbing in Feeder's forced grin, and while Roan tries to penetrate the meaning of his words, the cook slumps away. Brother Raven is openly observing from a nearby grove. What does he hope to discover? Roan considers confronting him, but is prevented by a stream of Brothers approaching and offering their congratulations.

By the time the moon rises, bloated in the east, Roan is laboring at the forge with Brother Asp. Weapons and tools are made here; tonight Roan holds a piece of red-hot iron with tongs while Asp pounds the metal flat and bends it into the shape of a shovel. When their work is complete, Brother Asp turns to Roan with concern.

"You are troubled."

Roan phrases his response carefully. "I heard some Brothers talking after I accepted the invitation to begin my initiation…"

Brother Asp sips some water and hands Roan the flask. "Everyone is very excited about the joining."

"What does it mean, 'one comes, one goes'?"

"It's from our primary teaching story. The first initiate was the Friend. One of his final trials was to slay a bull. We use that phrase, 'one comes, one goes,' as a kind of blessing with new initiates."

"It didn't sound like a blessing."

"Perhaps that was because you had no context for it."

"Maybe," says Roan, deciding to speak no more about it.

"You have nothing to fear, Roan of Longlight."

But for the first time, Brother Asp's words are of no comfort.

Before dawn, Roan is shaken out of a deep sleep. He groggily opens his eyes in a halo of lantern light. Brother Stinger smiles.

"It's time for the first trial of your initiation, Roan."

A Brother lifts a veil and places it over Roan's head, plunging him into complete darkness. Shivering and disoriented, he is led out of his tent into the chilly air. Hands guide Roan, leading him forward. His bare feet stumble on the uneven ground. After a while, he hears the sound of running water. They're walking near the stream, he realizes. As the volume increases, he knows they must be moving toward the mountain, the stream's source.

The sound gradually crescendos to a roar. Brother Stinger's voice rises over the thunderous water.

"The world was nothingness. Then the great stone cracked and the Friend was born. He lifted the darkness and we could see."

The cloth is wrenched off Roan's head, leaving him blind in the glare of the newly risen sun. He turns from it to see seventy-five Brothers behind him. The waterfall that feeds the stream cascades down a cliff a few feet ahead. Each of Roan's hands is tied, a Brother controlling either rope. They lead him to the waterfall, then, pulling his arms wide with the ropes, hold him under it. Roan manages to grab a large breath of air just before the relentless torrent pours down on him. It pounds on his head, his shoulders, but he does not buckle. Minute after minute passes as Roan holds his breath, fighting the urge to panic. Finally the lack of air takes its toll and he can feel the inevitable pull, water dragging him down into itself. Suddenly the ropes slacken and he falls to his knees. With all his strength, he pulls himself from under the deluge, dragging in great gulps of air.

The Brothers unbind his wrists. Saint is above him, holding a long, shining sword.

"His love lights the world," says the Prophet. "His blade frees it."

Saint holds out his left arm, the ladder of scars glistening white. He pushes the blade between two of the scars, drawing blood. He takes Roan's sodden arm, making a similar cut, then lets his own blood drip into Roan's wound.

"We are Brothers. For Eternity."

The company of Friends repeats: "Brothers. For Eternity."

Each of the brethren, one by one, press their arms against Roan's, scars against his open wound, saying: "We are Brothers." When all seventy-five have finished, Saint hands Roan the sword.

"His blade will free the world. We serve the Friend."

Seventy-six voices join together. "His blade will free the world. We serve the Friend."

Roan feels himself being raised up by ten hands as the Five, smiling, surround him.

Saint gazes into Roan's eyes. "The Friend welcomes you."

"You are welcome!" shout all the Brothers, cheering him.

Roan's never felt so celebrated.

"THEY MAKE YOU FEEL POWERFUL."

He feels giddy, elated, extraordinary.

"THEY MAKE YOU FEEL LOVED."

As various Brothers shake his hand, pat him on the back, embrace him, Roan beams with delight.

"AND ARE YOU? ARE YOU REALLY?"

Roan sees the rat from his dreams sitting on the shore.

"WHO IS THE FRIEND? WHO ARE THESE BROTHERS?"

Roan looks at his new Brothers. He sees Feeder on the shore, watching jealously, doing his best to smile. Raven is grinning, but also scanning Roan's body, as if searching for the best place to slip in a knife. Saint, proud, triumphant, appears full of secrets.

It's true. Despite all his time here, Roan doesn't know anything about these men.

"NO. YOU DO NOT."

Roan is carried on the Brothers' shoulders back down the stream. His elation has faded. All the cheering and congratulations seem hollow. They enter the meal tent to feast on roasted eggs, fresh juices, and meats. All the while, Roan smiles and nods at the Brothers' good wishes. But the food is dry in his mouth.

# the red-haired woman

of the prophet's origins, rumors
abound. not born of woman but of ice
and fire. ice for the cold steel he
wielded to smite the warlords. and
fire for the new life he breathed into
the souls he freed from slavery.
—orin's history of the friend

"WE NEED to talk."

Determined to get to the bottom of Feeder's cryptic comments, Roan has sought him out. He's decided on the direct approach.

"About what?" Feeder mumbles, not looking up from the cabbage he's chopping.

"What did you mean, 'one comes, one goes'?"

"It's a blessing," he says, shrugging Roan off. "We say it to all the initiates."

Feeder looks past Roan when he hears the sound of Saint's motorcycle pulling up behind them. Without so much as a glance at Roan, he picks up his cabbage and retreats into the cook tent.

Saint, the bike still idling, motions Roan to join him.

"Do you have some business with him?" asks Saint.

"Not really," says Roan.

"Good. I have something special to show you."

Roan climbs on the motorcycle and they burn off, going down a trail that takes them onto the fertile plain. They pass flat sections of land where plants are being harvested by rugged farmers. As they pass, the people smile and wave at Saint, who lifts his hand in greeting.

"Over there!" Saint shouts back through the wind.

He points to a big parcel of land that's covered in the herbal plants Roan picked with Brother Asp.

"We're reclaiming all that, thanks to you!"

Roan gazes on the fields with pleasure. The farmers have implemented the plans he found for them in the book on soil decontamination. His father would have been proud.

Saint roars on, eventually coming to a village gate. Its wall is armored with a strange collection of flattened metal barrels, ancient car parts, and iron sheeting. A woman, red hair flowing past her shoulders, looks down from the guard tower and smiles broadly. She puts her fingers to her mouth, letting out a piercing whistle. The gate clanks open, and Saint and Roan motor in.

From up on the guard towers and beside the gates, a dozen

brawny women holding crossbows and spears shout greetings to Saint.

Saint shuts off the engine, and they step off the bike. Roan's surprised by the apparent strength of these women, the first females he's seen since joining the Brothers.

"This is my village," Saint says, as the red-haired woman strides up and kisses him hard on the mouth.

"Roan, this is Kira. Kira, Roan."

Kira is tall and muscular, roughly the same age and nearly the same size as Saint. She slaps Roan on the shoulder. "You *are* sturdy, aren't you? Saint's told me all about you, Roan of Longlight."

"What has he told you?" Roan asks.

"Oh, you don't want to know!" she laughs. Saint, blushing, laughs too. Then she pokes Roan in the ribs. "Only good things, kid! He can't stop bragging about you! C'mon, let's eat."

She puts her arm around Roan and guides him down a cobblestone path. As they pass rows of houses with salvaged metal walls and sod roofs, Roan marvels at how Kira speaks to Saint. Her joke made the great man blush!

When they arrive at Kira's house, Roan is astounded by its opulence. Solar heaters and lights, stained glass and polished wooden tables. He turns down a hallway, and through the beads that cover a door he sees a beautiful baby nursery. He continues on to the living room, where a huge mural shows an armored warrior bursting out of a stone, sword lifted to the sky. The Friend, Roan guesses. Roan looks up. A ceiling mural shows the same scene as the statue at Saint's altar: the Friend is slaying the bull, surrounded by the dog, the snake, the bird, and the scorpion.

"Do you like it?" asks Saint.

"It's beautiful. How long have you lived here?"

"No time at all. I'm simply a frequent visitor." Saint chortles. "No one possesses Kira."

"I could possess him, if I wanted," smiles Kira. "I like loving a Prophet, but I can't think of anything that would be more annoying than living with one!"

Laughing, Saint kisses her.

Saint's comfort around Kira, the way they joke together, reminds Roan of his parents. For a moment he allows himself the fantasy—then he notices the mantelpiece, on which sit two human skulls.

Kira steps over to them. "This one is my mother. This one is the man who killed my mother." Kira points out a hole in the second skull. "And this where my spear pierced him. That moment gave my life back to me." She looks at Roan with sad eyes. "Saint told me what happened to your people. I'm sorry you haven't had the chance yet to make your peace. The day you execute your parents' killers, that day the pain that strangles you will release its grip."

For a moment, Roan pictures his father standing beside him, looking at those skulls, silent, eyes brimming with tears. Roan longs to have him back, to embrace him, to ask his help.

Saint pats Roan on the shoulder. "You'll have your day, my friend, I swear it."

The aroma of a steaming casserole draws them to the table. Kira stands behind the chair at its head, lowers her eyes, and speaks.

"Friend who brings us this food, we thank you. Friend who brings us together, we thank you. We pray for the day you will rule."

"So be it," says Saint. The three of them sit, and Kira lifts the lid.

The meal is simple, a goat curry with potatoes and blue beans. Although Roan doubts he'll ever get used to the smell of meat, he has no trouble consuming Kira's spicy stew. She could teach Feeder a few things.

"Were both of you raised in this village?" asks Roan.

"No," replies Kira. A somberness weighs upon the word.

"You came here after your mother died?"

"Exactly."

"How old were you when you took your revenge?"

"Younger than you. But we'd been enslaved for years before I found my opportunity to strike."

"What was it like, being a slave?"

Roan immediately wishes he hadn't asked so rude a question. But Kira doesn't seem bothered by it. "I understand your curiosity." Her eyes bristle with intensity. "Before the Friend came into my life, I wished for my death every single day."

Roan looks over at Saint. The Prophet's jaw is clenched, the muscle in his cheek moving.

"It's a history we share," Saint murmurs.

Roan feels the cricket tickle the palm of his hand. He finds his eyes focusing deeply on Saint and Kira, seeing beyond their faces into the past. Beatings, endless drudgery, witnessing the murder of loved ones; nothing to cherish, everything to fear; hunger, pain, loneliness. They gained their dignity by denying their torturers delight in their suffering. They were raised in violence, and now they embrace it. Roan thinks of his life in Longlight. Every day a gift, every day designed to make him stronger. Love that continues to surround and protect him.

Kira pulls the thin recorder from Roan's pocket. "You play that thing?"

"I'm learning."

"Play something for me."

"I'm just a beginner."

"Please," coaxes Kira.

Roan sighs, lifts the recorder to his lips, and plays a simple tune of Longlight, one his mother used to whistle.

"What a lovely song," Kira says. "Who taught you to play?"

"No one. But a friend of mine took lessons. He started with three-finger tunes like this one."

"Did many play music in Longlight?"

"Yes, almost everyone. I was supposed to start learning guitar."

"You'll become accomplished at the recorder instead," Kira says.

"I suppose," Roan replies, saddened that the music of Longlight will never be heard again.

When the meal is over, Saint pushes his plate away.

"I have a few things to discuss with Kira," he tells Roan. "Why don't you explore the village?"

"Here," Kira says, handing Roan some candies. "Something to sweeten your day."

Roan steps outside, the sun warm on his face, rolling a candy over his tongue. Kira's house is completely covered in flattened metal. Even the roof is polished tin. Curious, he wanders around the side, examining the craftsmanship. In Longlight, there had never been access to the quantities of metal he's seeing here.

As he passes under a window, he hears Saint's low voice, and it is bristling with irritation. Quietly, Roan moves close to the wall, listening.

"I don't confide in Raven. He travels everywhere and knows no master."

There's a pause, and then Kira speaks, cheerlessly. "We lost the baby."

"Not another."

"We tried everything."

Saint sighs. "There will be more."

"And Roan?"

"I hope I get answers before they do."

"You haven't discovered why they needed them both?" Kira asks.

"No. He has many abilities. He reads and learns incredibly fast. He's as good as our best warriors, with only months of training. Stinger says Roan's focus is like none he's ever seen. He suspects there's more beneath the surface that Roan doesn't yet trust enough to show. But why is the City so desperate for both? My instincts say it's related to that cricket."

"Some say the snow cricket is a mark."

"The mark of a Dirt Eater."

There's a silence. Then Saint speaks, his words tentative.

"There must be a connection."

"What if..."

"*That*, we dare not even suspect."

"It's why the Friend brought you to him."

Saint sighs. "We will protect him."

"For how long? He will learn the truth."

"He will have what he wants, when the time comes. Now that you've met him, can you blame me?"

"No."

Silence. Roan strains to hear more, but they're no longer talking. He moves away, striding over the cobblestones, anxiously pondering what he's heard. He wonders if Kira and Saint knew he was listening, if they were speaking for his benefit. But does it matter? By "both," could they mean him and

Stowe, his sister? Does Saint know if the City has her? And what is a Dirt Eater?

"WE ARE DIRT EATERS."

"You?"

No reply. Roan devotes all his concentration to conjuring up his dream teachers, wanting to know more. He focuses, calling them with his mind. But they do not appear.

Roan's futile efforts are soon interrupted by the beating of a drum. He walks toward the booming rhythm. Turning a corner, he's struck by a cacophony of sights, smells, and sounds. A marketplace. People, brightly dressed in robes and dresses of vermilion, scarlet, and emerald, mill about the stalls. They haggle, some over the price of fruit and vegetables, others over stuff Roan's seen only in books, antiquities recovered from the Abominations.

He stares in awe at the displays. There are dozens of watches—round ones, square ones, silver and gold—and ticking clocks that all show a different time; yellow rubber ducks, green plastic frogs, red and blue fish, every size of plastic container, some melted around the edges; thousands of shiny discs, large and small, with strange images emblazoned on them; televisions, toasters, blenders, computers, telephones. Many of the appliances look as if they could be made to work, if only a power source still existed. Roan examines them all.

"Interested in rubber ducks?" barks a woman, big and strong like Kira. "I can give you a very good deal if you take more than three." Roan steps out into full view from behind the display. Seeing him, the woman retreats. "Pardon me, Brother, I meant no offense."

"None taken," replies Roan.

"You wouldn't happen to be the new initiate, would you?"

"Yes," nods Roan. The woman steps back and breaks out in a wide smile. "It was you, then, who taught Brother Asp!"

"No, no, he's my teacher."

"Weren't you the one who read the book to Brother Asp?"

"He reads!" says an eavesdropper, moving closer.

"I only read him the one book."

Within moments, several townspeople have joined them. A rotund man exclaims, "We're reclaiming acres of farmland thanks to you, Brother."

Roan, flattered, corrects him. "I'm not a Brother yet."

"Thanks be to the Friend for bringing you to our land," says the man.

"You know the Prophet?" asks a sad-eyed woman. She looks only a few years older than Roan, and she's obviously pregnant.

"Yes."

"You're blessed. We owe him everything." She looks at Roan's arm, admiring the blood-sharing scar. "Did it hurt much?"

"Not really," answers Roan, "nothing compared to what giving birth must be like."

The woman's face turns red, and she seems to be fighting tears. She steps away. Roan, thinking he's offended her, bows to everyone, taking his leave. But by the time he turns toward her, the woman is almost out of sight.

Roan threads his way through the curling lanes trying to find her and arrives at a playground filled with swings, slides, and climbing structures. She's gone. His village had a park, but it didn't hold a candle to this one. He's about to continue on when the cricket wriggles in his pocket. Roan pauses for a closer look. Only a few children are playing. He notices that one boy is limping, and another is missing a hand.

One little girl squats alone, intently drawing in the dirt with a stick. Something inside Roan trembles at the sight. She's small with hair like straw, and from this angle...He moves closer, then sighs with disappointment. The girl is at least a year younger than Stowe, and her features are completely different, a sharp nose and thin lips. He notices that she's covered the ground around her with drawings of the same shape. A triangle, inverted, with a circle on top of it.

"What is it?"

The girl, her eyes on her task, ignores him.

"I'm curious," he says. "What's that a drawing of?"

Seeing his feet, she follows his legs to his face. Her dirty face is streaked with tears. Roan reaches in his pocket, taking out one of Kira's sweets. The girl grabs it and pops it into her mouth.

"Why are you crying?"

She doesn't speak, just points at one of the triangles.

"Does it make you sad?"

She points to herself and shakes her head. It hits Roan. She's mute.

"Can you hear me?" he asks and points to his ears. "Hear?" She shakes her head no.

A shadow crosses over both of them. Saint. He towers over the little girl, his face grim. But when the child's face raises to greet him, he smiles.

"Hello, Marla," Saint says slowly, so she can read his lips. "Feeling blue today?"

She nods.

"Do you know what this shape means?" Roan asks Saint.

Saint shakes his head and turns back to the child. "Were you drawing a pretty picture, Marla?"

Marla frowns and draws it again. Saint picks her up, kissing her on the forehead.

"There was a power plant upstream. It was destroyed during the Abominations. Leached all kinds of poisons into the soil. Three generations later, and children like Marla are still being affected. But thanks to you, that will soon be a thing of the past."

"Brother Asp did all the work."

"You were book-learned in Longlight, and you had science to help you. Now, you help us." Saint carries Marla over to a sandbox, gives her another kiss, and sets her down.

It's well into the night by the time they make their way back to the motorcycle. Saint stops every few steps to bestow the blessings asked of him. Reaching the bike, he hands Roan a pair of strange-looking goggles.

"Ever seen anything like these?"

Roan puts the thick eyepieces up to his face.

"Night-vision glasses," says Saint. "Put them on. You're the lookout."

With a last farewell to Kira, Saint revs up the engine and they head back out the gates, everyone waving and shouting good-bye as they go.

Roan keeps his eyes peeled through the bulky lenses, but he sees nothing until he notices a familiar sort of structure in the distance. He taps Saint on the arm. Saint nods and accelerates to the spot. The bike's headlamp illuminates a large water-wheel attached to a building alongside a stream. They get off and Roan runs up to the wheel.

"It's a filtration wheel, just like the one I described to Brother Asp!"

Saint slaps Roan on the back. "I thought you might like to taste the water."

"I would," says Roan. He cups his hands under the outflow and takes a drink. "Not bad."

Saint has a swallow and nods in agreement. "Asp has a knack for these things."

"I wish I could have helped build it."

"You have other priorities," Saint tells him, and strides back to the bike. Before getting on, he turns to Roan. "So what do you think of Kira?"

"She's great," Roan replies, then asks, "Do you have children together?"

Saint doesn't answer.

"Kira has a nursery."

More silence. Roan is about to repeat the question but thinks better of it. Looking up at the star-filled sky, he changes the subject.

"There's Taurus, the bull."

Saint looks at him. "What are you talking about?"

Roan's caught by surprise. "The constellation. Taurus."

"Show me."

Roan points out the stars that make the bull. "You see that bright star? It's called Aldebaran. That's the bull's eye."

"Book-learning," Saint mutters. He looks uncomfortable. "When was it named?"

"Thousands of years ago. There's a band of stars up there, continuous. All the symbols of the Friend are in the sky. The dog, Canis Minor. Hydra, the snake. Corvus, the raven..."

"That's enough."

Roan is startled by Saint's tone. "What did I say? Why are you angry?"

"You must not speak of it again," warns Saint, bristling. "Some might take it as heresy."

"Why?"

"Because the Revelation came directly to me from the Friend. Not from stars given names an eon ago. From Him."

Saint kicks on the engine, and they motor off into the

night. As the cricket scratches in his pocket, Roan muses silently on why Saint is so upset. What does it matter if he knows nothing about the constellations, nothing about the stars? Then it comes to him: What Saint doesn't know makes him afraid.

# the trials

the badger digs. it digs and lives
unseen by day but in the night it
hunts. though small, it is abnormally
strong, and its prey seldom escapes.
 —Lore of the storytellers

THE DAYS GROW SHORTER, and though winter is still
months away, Saint makes a gift to Roan of boots and a
sheepskin coat, crafted by the brethren. Brother Wolf's training has become more detailed, difficult, and deadly. He
pushes Roan relentlessly, forcing him to his physical limit, so
Roan keeps getting stronger as his tactical skills improve. He
becomes accomplished at using his hands, head, feet, elbows,
and knees as weapons, directing his breath to focus power in
his bones and tendons. He masters the circle technique, which
enables a single combatant to escape a group of assailants.
Wolf also shows him ways to distract an opponent's eyes, how
to trick an adversary into reacting, and, when attacked, how to
yield, withdraw, and then strike with full force when least

expected. Roan is now adept at the how and when of striking soft and hard. Of being wind or mountain or tiger.

After one of their reading sessions, Roan borrows a book called *The Art of War* from Saint's library. He'd seen his father studying the book, but he'd never looked at it himself. It explains the importance of disguising your intentions, and Roan uses it as a constant reminder. He never tells anyone how he misses the smell of sawdust on his mother's skin, or the sight of his father's chalk-covered hands at the end of a teaching day, or the cheery voice of Aiden, calling to him from the street to play. Roan never divulges the terror he felt when Stowe's fingers were torn from his grasp that terrible night. Or how sometimes, after perfecting a new killing technique, he is so overpowered by exhilaration and self-revulsion he feels like retching. Masking his true feelings and abilities is a constant battle.

Though Saint never pressures him, Roan is sure the Prophet hopes to access some kind of information from him. Saint is relentlessly curious about Longlight, asking the most mundane questions about life in the village, Roan's parents' work habits, what family meals were like, the kind of furniture his mother most enjoyed building. Saint never tires of hearing about Stowe, the games she and Roan played, the tricks they sprang on their cousins, the stories they were told and loved.

When Roan questions this interest, Saint claims a shared history. His parents and siblings were also killed when he was young. This talk of family helps him remember.

Roan wishes he could discover what it is that Saint seeks. The more he thinks back to the conversation he overheard between Saint and Kira, the more he's convinced there is a connection between himself and Stowe and the City. If that's where she is, he will go there and find her, or die trying.

Brother Wolf's training turns out to be good preparation for Roan's second trial. One morning, at dawn, just after the raising of the sun, Roan is escorted by Stinger and three other Brothers to the streambed. There, he is given a pick and told to dig out a large stone. The hard-packed dirt doesn't give easily, so it takes Roan a great deal of effort to expose a substantial rock.

By now, many of the brethren have gathered around to watch.

"Pick it up," orders Stinger.

Roan squats down, squeezing his fingers around the rough stone. With a loud exhalation, he straightens his knees and lifts the rock. Saint steps through the assembly and approaches him.

"The Friend awaits this offering at the first summit of our mountain," says Saint. "It must not touch the ground until it reaches Him."

"The second trial begins!" announces Stinger with a yell. The Brothers cheer.

With Stinger in front and Asp behind, Roan walks alongside the stream in the direction of the mountain. The rock is heavy and makes Roan unsteady on his feet, forcing him to walk much more slowly than his usual pace. By the time they arrive at the waterfall, Roan is coated in sweat, and the rock is slicing into his fingers. His legs are sore.

Stinger squirts some water into Roan's mouth. Brother Asp checks Roan's eyes. "You're doing well," Asp mouths encouragingly.

Brother Wolf peers at Roan. "Now the real challenge begins."

The trail up the mountain is a clear path, but it's on a steep grade that zigzags in steady ascent. Roan keeps his breath stable, but it doesn't take long for him to feel lightheaded with the effort. He can feel blood dripping from his hands onto his bare feet. Sweat pours in his eyes. Blinking it off, he tries to remain focused, making one foot follow the other. Every step hurts, and the concussion of each footfall shudders through his body. Half-blind, his body aching, Roan stumbles, breaking his fall by lurching against the rock face. Pain flares through his side. The rock slips but he clings to it, hugging it to his stomach.

The Brothers begin to chant: "The Friend awaits. The Friend awaits."

Roan looks up but sees no end to the path. He looks down at the stone, wanting hurl it off the cliff. Then he hears the rat's voice.

"DON'T SURRENDER."

Brother Asp rushes to him. "Are you alright?"

"Yes."

"PAIN IS FUEL, ROAN. YOU MUST LEARN TO FOCUS IN EVERY SITUATION."

"Are you sure you want to continue?"

"Yes."

"USE THE PAIN. YOU WILL ACHIEVE THE SUMMIT. WE HAVE SEEN IT."

His cheeks burning, Roan pushes forward. Chest heaving, legs stiff and raw, he lumbers onward, not stopping until he reaches the summit—where a statue of the Friend stands looking down the mountain. At the statue's feet are dozens and dozens of large stones like the one Roan is carrying.

"The Friend arose from stone," Saint cries out.

As Roan struggles toward the statue, the Brothers chant, "Born from the stone, born from the stone." They do so until he drops the rock and collapses onto the ground. The Brothers applaud and Roan lies in the dust, gasping for breath, his flesh on fire. The cheers fade into the background at the sound of the cricket. Roan can feel the little insect in his pocket as it soothes his wounds with its song.

Roan is given a few days to recuperate from his second trial before resuming his regular schedule. Resting in his tent, he practices playing the recorder. The music he makes is nothing compared to that of the best musicians of Longlight, but he practices diligently. The cricket enjoys his efforts. Perched on Roan's knee, it appears to listen with rapt attention, feelers quivering. Unconsciously, Roan begins a tune from his past, his sister's favorite song—a tune she'd sing so often Roan would threaten to sew up her mouth.

"Then I'll sing with my nose," she'd say, and hum the old folk tune through her nostrils, grinning wickedly at Roan.

Now he is playing it, and thinking of her, praying she's alive somewhere, hoping she's safe. I'll find you, Stowe, as soon as I've finished these trials.

The third trial takes place a week later, at the daily sunset ritual. After the sun goes down, Saint calls Roan forward.

"Third trial. The novitiate communes with the Friend."

The Brothers nod in approval.

Brother Asp, leading Roan to the front, whispers: "The next few trials will be the most difficult of all. Are you sure you're ready?"

"Yes," says Roan. "I'm ready." Roan has turned to face the assembly when he hears a bleating sound. The Brothers part, and Roan sees Feeder walking toward him, leading a ram by a rope. Feeder and Brother Wolf tie the ram's feet, then lay the animal on a rock platform in front of Roan.

Brother Wolf addresses Roan. "Before communing with the Friend, an offering must be made to honor Him."

Brother Raven hands Roan a knife. "For the Friend."

"For the Friend," repeat the assembled.

Roan looks into the animal's dark eyes. To deliberately draw blood from living things was considered the greatest sin by the people of Longlight.

"YOU HAVE DRAWN MINE," SAYS THE MOUNTAIN LION.

Expectant eyes are on Roan.

"YOU EAT IT. YOU CAN KILL IT."

Realizing the futility, even the danger, of protest, Roan strokes the ram's head, whispering, "Forgive me." Trembling, he draws in air, holds his breath, and slices the blade across the ram's throat. As blood pours out, the animal spasms, then goes limp.

The ram's blood, collected in a vessel below, is lifted by Brother Wolf for all to see. Then each Brother dips in his fingertips and puts a streak of blood across his own forehead. Roan, shaking, does the same.

"The communion," says Saint, nodding at Roan approvingly.

Next a brightly colored casket is brought forward by two Brothers. Its panels are elaborately decorated with paintings of the Friend. The Brothers lift the lid off, and gesture to Roan to get inside.

"Remember your training," whispers Brother Stinger.

Saint puts his hand on Roan's shoulder. "Go to the Friend, Roan of Longlight. He awaits you."

Roan steps into the close-fitting casket and lies down on his back. All goes dark as the lid is replaced and screwed down. The only light comes from tiny airholes drilled in the wood. He hears the sound of footsteps as the Brothers leave the site. Within minutes, there is no sound at all. Roan is alone, captive in this box. He can move his fingers and toes, but not much more.

Roan's shin begins to itch. He tries rubbing it against the lid, but he can't reach the spot. He scratches his thigh, hoping to somehow satisfy the urge. That doesn't work either. He pinches himself, trying to distract his mind. But his efforts only make the itch stronger. I'll go mad, Roan thinks. Now he's itchy everywhere, inside and out, every part of him desperate to move or turn or squirm. His heart pumps wildly. He wants to scream, pound on the lid, claw his way out.

Fighting the panic, Roan tries to concentrate on his breath. He feels the air flow through his nostrils, move against his skin. The cricket shifts in his pocket, bringing its wings together, making a little series of chirps. Roan feels as if he's weightless, out of his body, no longer trapped inside the casket.

ROAN IS SITTING ON A ROCK IN A GRASSY FIELD. HE LOOKS DOWN AT HIS HAND AND SEES THAT HE'S HOLDING THE RECORDER. HE LIFTS IT TO HIS LIPS AND PLAYS. IT IS STOWE'S TUNE.

THE OLD GOAT-WOMAN APPEARS. "THAT'S NOT A GOOD IDEA."

"IT'S ONLY A SONG." HE PLAYS AGAIN.

"STOP."

"WHY?"

"SHE WILL HEAR YOU."

"ALL THE MORE REASON TO PLAY."

"SHE IS WITH THE DIRT EATERS OF THE CITY. THE TURNED."

"SHOULD I FEAR THEM?"

"ALL FEAR THEM."

"I THOUGHT YOU WERE A DIRT EATER."

"WE ARE DIFFERENT. AND YOU ARE EVEN MORE SO."

"WHAT ABOUT STOWE?"

HE HEARS A VOICE IN THE DISTANCE. HIS SISTER'S VOICE. "ROAN!"

THE GOAT-WOMAN LIFTS HER HAND, SEALING ROAN'S MOUTH. HE SCREAMS, BUT THERE IS NO SOUND.

"THE DANGER IS TOO GREAT. YOUR SISTER IS ALIVE. AND YOU WILL FIND HER. BUT NOT NOW. CONTACT HER BEFORE THE TIME IS RIGHT AND SHE WILL BE LOST FOREVER."

Roan's eyes peer into the darkness, his body still trapped in the coffin. He opens his mouth and speaks, testing his lips. "She's alive," he says aloud. "It's true, my sister is alive. The Dirt Eaters of the City have her. But who are they? What do they want?" But he calms himself, slowly sipping in air, counting his breaths until he drifts off to sleep.

He wakes to the sound of the screws being removed from the coffin. The lid is lifted. Roan, unsteady, eyes smarting from the bright sunlight, is helped to his feet, the Brothers all around.

Saint grabs his arms. "Did you meet the Friend?"

Roan, not wanting to lie, replies: "I felt a presence."

Saint embraces him. "Well done. Praised be the Friend!"

"Praised be the Friend!" the Brothers repeat.

Late that night, Feeder appears at the door of Roan's tent, looking wan and disheveled. "The painting's almost done. In a few weeks it'll be over."

"You've been watching?"

"After your next trial, you'll be baptized."

Roan nods. "The baptism will be blood."

"You figured it out."

"It should be the blood of a bull, like in the pictures. But that's not possible. All the cattle disappeared after the Abominations."

"No," Feeder mutters, "a bull's been found. They find one every year. A bull's blood will baptize you."

With that, Feeder turns to leave. Roan follows him outside only to see Brother Raven, as usual, standing by.

"He seems excited," Raven simpers.

"Does he?" Roan asks.

"I could have sworn I heard him talking about a bull."

"He says you found one."

Brother Raven sighs. "He should know better than that, speaking of the rituals to you. But I understand. He's jealous, of course."

"Why would he be?"

"You're a favorite of the Five. You take meals and motor-cycle rides with the Prophet. Through Brother Asp, you're a hero in the villages. Brother Stinger's convinced you have a gift of some kind. You received Brother Wolf's most prized weapon, and you have my undivided attention. While poor Feeder—well, let's just say he's been a disappointment. But don't you worry about it, I'll have a talk with him."

Brother Raven's words only add to Roan's concern. Why had Feeder come to see him? What was he trying to say? He'd seemed so...afraid. Roan needs to find out why.

The next night, on his way to read to Saint, Roan sees two figures silhouetted by candlelight cast on the wall of Brother Raven's tent. One sits. The other stands over the first, speaking close to his ear. The standing figure appears to be Brother Raven, and Roan is able to identify the seated figure as soon as he speaks.

"Yes. Yes. Yes," is all the person says. But Roan knows the voice. Feeder.

He can't make out the words, but it's clear Raven's manipulating the cook. Roan resolves to speak to Feeder about this strange incident the first chance he gets.

When he reaches the main room in Saint's tent, Roan finds it filled with candles. On the table, in front of the Prophet, is a bottle with a brown scorpion floating at the bottom.

"Sixteen years old today. Happy birthday, Roan of Longlight."

"How did you know?"

"Brother Asp told me. I think we should celebrate."

Saint opens the bottle, and Roan smells a familiar thick, tart scent. "Scorpion brew."

Saint fills two small glasses with the liquor and hands one to Roan. "This is an important moment. Today we toast your entry into manhood." He lifts his glass. "To Roan of Longlight, newest of our Brothers."

"I'm not there yet," Roan reminds him.

"In a few weeks you will be. But you already shine so bright it's fair to say those words. You are a huge asset to our cause."

Saint throws back his drink. Roan takes a gulp from his own glass, and his mouth explodes. Then he buckles over in a fit of coughing. Saint pounds him on the back, gasping with laughter.

"The brown scorpions are small, but their poison packs a punch," he says, handing Roan a pitcher of water. Roan drinks deeply, flushing the foul spirits from his mouth. "It's an acquired taste." Saint smiles.

Roan picks up his glass and swallows the remainder of its vile contents. He manages to keep it down by gripping the table. After a few minutes he exhales, surprised that his organs still seem to be intact.

"Nothing like it," says Saint.

"I think you're right," Roan replies, feeling a little dizzy.

"Take the bottle."

"Are you sure?"

"When it's finished, bring it back and we'll eat the scorpion together."

"It may take a while."

"We have plenty of time." Saint laughs gently to himself.

"What is it?"

"When I was sixteen, that bottle wouldn't have lasted a night."

"You'd drink a whole bottle?"

"I'd drink whatever I could get my hands on. I had a lot of demons. I was convinced drink would frighten them away." He looks hard at Roan. "But my demons were older and craftier than I was. I needed the Friend to help me cut them down. You see more clearly. You acquire knowledge and await opportunity. You are patient, Roan of Longlight. You lead by example."

A whistle outside the door announces a visitor. Saint calls him in. It's Brother Wolf.

"I'm sorry, Brother Saint, but we have some preparations..."

Saint curses, remembering. With hasty apologies to Wolf, he turns to Roan. "Go into the library and find us some new books. I'll be back in an hour or two."

As soon as Saint is gone, Roan wraps the bottle in a cloth and puts it in his carry bag. Scorpion brew could turn out to be useful.

In the library, Roan lights some candles and begins sifting through the books. He makes a small pile of volumes he recognizes from his father's library. He'll take them to his own quarters to study. Plato's *Republic*, a history of the French Revolution, Machiavelli's *The Prince*, the *Tao Te Ching*, *The Tibetan Book of the Dead*, and *Satyagraha in South Africa* by Mohandas Gandhi. His father often spoke of Gandhi. He called him "the warrior who never fought." Roan opens the book and reads about the word "Satyagraha," which is actually three concepts combined into one. "Sat" means truth. The commitment to see it and express it. "Ahisma" is the refusal to inflict injury on others. To practice Ahisma, you must genuinely love your opponent. "Tapasya" is the willingness for self-sacrifice—not in striving for victory, but in helping your opponent also see the truth. Roan's eyes sting. He wants to tear the book's pages out. These ideas killed his parents, killed Longlight. But what lay *behind* his people's self-sacrifice? There had to be more to it than the simple refusal to fight. Gandhi preached Satyagraha for freedom. What was the truth Longlight died for?

As he puts his father's books in his carry bag, Roan feels the snow cricket scrambling out of his pocket. Landing by the door, it bounds away. A little off-balance from the scorpion brew, Roan lurches out of the library and follows the cricket down the canvas hallway. After a few seconds, the little insect leaps out of sight.

Close behind, Roan enters what must be Saint's bedchamber. It's a simply furnished room, with only a woolen mattress and carpets to cover the floor. The cricket perches on a rug beside the bed. Roan hesitates. This is Saint's private place. Roan doesn't want to leave the cricket in here, so he moves toward it. The insect disappears beneath the rug. Roan, baffled, lifts the fabric, revealing the stone floor. The cricket sits motionless on the smooth rock.

As Roan reaches out his hand for the cricket, he notices a fine crack in the stone. Leaning closer, he follows it until a shape is discernable. An opening. Roan takes his knife out and slips it into the divide, prying up the rock. A metal box. He touches the box, feeling its cool surface. He wants to open it, but he hesitates. This is surely a private possession. He has no right to trespass. He puts his hands back on the rock, ready to close the secret compartment again. But the cricket jumps on the metal box, skidding brightly on the dark mottled surface, and Roan can no longer resist. He grips the lid and lifts it off. Inside is a book: *The Religions of Ancient Rome*.

Roan picks up the book and leafs through it. His eyes catch on an image of a bull being slain by a man, surrounded by a bird, a snake, a scorpion, and a dog. The chapter is called "The Cult of Mithras." It explains that the cult followed a religion practiced by the Roman army, and an illustration shows a group of warriors praying as a young soldier is baptized in a stream. Another illustration shows the god Mithras being born out of a rock, his sword raised high, fallen stones at his feet. There's another of a cave called a Mithraeum, a place decorated with depictions of Mithras. Soldiers sacrifice a bull to their god, its blood pouring onto an initiate.

Captivated, Roan keeps reading. He learns that thousands of years ago, the sun rose in the constellation of Taurus the bull every spring equinox. While Taurus ruled the sky, the celestial equator passed through the constellation Taurus, then those of Canis Minor the Dog, Hydra the Snake, Corvus the Raven. The same constellations Roan had pointed out to Saint the night they returned from Kira's village.

Over the years, according to the book, Taurus's position in the sky began to change, and the bull was gradually replaced by the constellation Aries. Mithras, whose name came from ancient Iran, was thought to have moved the universe, killing Taurus the bull and bringing in the age of Aries.

Roan is overwhelmed by what he's seeing, what he's reading, and he struggles to make sense of it. A hidden book filled with words the Prophet can't read. But he can understand the pictures. A bird, a snake, a scorpion, and a dog. Brother Raven, Brother Asp, Brother Stinger, Brother Wolf.

"Roan!"

Roan freezes at the sound of Saint's voice. He doesn't answer, he doesn't breathe. Making no sound, he places the book back in the box, replaces the lid, then starts to slide the stone cover back into place. The fit is too tight, it won't go in. He can hear Saint's footsteps.

"Roan!"

Heart pounding, Roan forces himself to calm. Shutting out everything else, he focuses completely on the lid, lifting it, then lowering it evenly into the slot. He replaces the carpet, sweeps the snow cricket into his pocket.

"Where are you?"

Roan glides out of Saint's bedroom. Thankfully, the canvas corridor is empty. He slips into the library, but not unnoticed. Saint is staring at him with narrowed eyes.

"What were you doing?"

Roan, maintaining his concentration, shrugs. "I was in the outhouse."

"I wanted to give you this," Saint says, holding up a small box. "A birthday present."

"Thank you," says Roan. Inside is a tarnished silver ring hewn into the shape of a badger. "What does it represent?"

"When badgers hunt, they don't stop until they get what they're after. Tenacious. We'll have to be that way to defeat the City. Badgers are also healing animals. They help us not lose sight of our purpose. Put it on."

"It's so light," Roan remarks. He can't help but be intrigued by this unusual token.

"Did you find me an interesting book?" asks Saint.

Is Saint toying with him? Has he been found out? Stomach lurching, Roan scans Saint's face. Not an inkling of suspicion. Relieved, he responds to the question. "I thought I'd read to you about the French Revolution."

"Good. Let's begin."

Keeping the clamor of his new knowledge at bay, Roan reads to Saint of intrigue, betrayal, and the death of thousands. Saint listens intently. As usual, Roan continues until Saint becomes drowsy. Then he walks back to his own tent, relieved for once not to see Brother Raven lurking nearby. Inside, he carefully empties his carry bag, hiding the bottle of scorpion brew and placing the books in his mother's rucksack.

Roan stretches out on his bed, trying to make sense of this new information. The more he goes over things in his mind, the more obvious and unsettling the truth becomes. Saint must have created the Brothers' religion based on the hidden book's pictures. He was lying about his Revelation on the mountain, about being given the Word by the Friend who appeared to him in a blaze of white fire. That would explain his fear when Roan pointed out the constellations. If the

Brothers knew about that, Saint's power as their leader would collapse. This is dangerous information. What if Saint were to find out Roan knows the truth about his God?

Roan still has one more trial ahead of him, and then the baptism of blood. Blood of a bull, just as he saw in the book. But there is no bull here. Roan knows that, and he's filled with dread at the thought of what might replace it.

Roan feels as trapped as he did in the coffin but much more afraid. At least then he knew there'd be an end to it. He breathes, trying to disperse the anxiety that's clutching at him, but it doesn't work. The fear builds and builds until a small shape crawls out onto his pillow. Roan, grateful, watches the cricket rub its wings together and begin to sing.

ON A FLAT YELLOW STONE, THE MOUNTAIN LION LIES SLEEPILY IN THE SUN.

"THERE ARE ANSWERS TO YOUR QUESTIONS IN THE CAVE WHERE THE RED ROCK TURNS BLUE," THE LION SAYS.

"HOW DO I FIND IT?" ROAN ASKS.

"LOOK IN THE SAND..."

# the cave

GREAT PAINTINGS THERE ARE THAT NO
ONE HAS SEEN OR WILL EVER SEE. THE
BROTHERS make THEM of SAND AND
WHEN THE FRIEND'S BREATH CARRIES
THEM away ON THE WIND, THE
VISITATION DESCENDS.
                —ORIN'S HISTORY OF THE FRIEND

WELL BEFORE DAWN, Roan stealthily passes the snoring Raven's tent. There are a few other early risers getting a head start on their tasks before being summoned to raise the sun. But as he expected, no one's arrived at the sand painting yet, and the canopy provides some cover from prying eyes. Until now, Roan's focus has been on his own tiny part of the painting. He's glanced at the progress of the larger picture but only to admire it for its artistic virtue. But now, under the torchlight, he stands before the huge painting, taking it in, studying it for clues.

He sees that the killing of the bull takes place inside a cave on the side of a mountain. The area around the cave teems with beautiful shades and shapes. He scrutinizes them, trying to make sense of the patterns, but he can't decipher the puzzle.

The morning bell rings; not much time. Roan breathes, calming himself, trying to concentrate on the whole painting in the same way he focuses on his minute grains of sand.

A long streak of blue meanders around the painting, ending at a waterfall near the cave. It's water. Of course. Roan understands. It's the same stream that comes from the mountain ridge about a mile south of where he stands. Follow the stream and he'll find the cave.

Roan ferrets out the large supply pot holding the sienna-colored sand, his sand, and empties all but a little of it into his bag. He conceals the bag of red sand by a cluster of trees near the streambed, and rushes off to the morning ceremony.

After breakfast, Roan heads to the food preparation tent. Raven has been intimidating Feeder, and Roan means to do something about it.

"You were in Raven's tent last night."

Feeder smiles mysteriously. Without a word, he picks up the carrots he's been chopping and turns to leave. Roan grabs his arm. As he does, he sees a raised cut behind Feeder's ear. He reaches to touch it.

"What's that?"

Feeder pulls away.

"Nothing."

"It looks as if something's been stuck in there. You've been hurt."

"No, I'm fine."

Feeder gazes steadily at Roan. He stands upright, almost proud.

"You seem different."

"Because I know who I am now. I do. I know who I am."

"What did Raven do to you?"

Feeder, never losing his crooked smile, ignores Roan's question and strolls out of the cook tent.

That wasn't Feeder's usual smile. He's not himself, Roan thinks. Feeder's mouth moves but the words aren't his. He's been changed, and it has something to with that strange wound. Why did Raven do that to him?

That evening, alone in his tent, Roan practices. Kicks, leaps, rolls, swordplay. In one year, his power and speed have become formidable, though no one else is fully aware of his progress. Once the sweat is pouring, Roan pulls the scorpion brew out from his pack, takes the cap off, fills his mouth with the liquor, swishes it around, and spits it out. Bottle in hand, he stumbles out into the night air, certain his watchdog will soon be upon him. Brother Raven, never one to disappoint, instantly appears.

"Sister Raven! Look what the Prophet gave me for my birthday!" Roan throws his arm around Raven for support and breathes heavily into his face. "Wish me a happy happy!"

Raven can't take his eyes off the bottle. "Happy birthday, Roan."

"Well, are you just gonna stand there? Have a drink!"

"I really shouldn't, it's late."

"Aw, c'mon, Raven, just one!"

"If you insist," says Raven. He lifts the bottle to his mouth and takes a long, deep swig of the harsh beverage. Savoring the aftertaste, he eyes the weaving Roan. "This is as fine a sting brew as I've tasted."

Roan leans against him. "Best you can get, I hear. Have another."

Raven swills again. "Exceptional."

"Enjoy!" says Roan. He sways and stumbles, nearly falling in the dirt. He pauses a moment, mustering as vacant a look as he can, then grins stupidly at Raven. "You know what? I gotta go to bed. G'night, Brother, you're a good man."

Roan trips on the way to his tent, then falls through the entryway. "I'm okay, I'm okay!" he calls out. As soon as he's inside, he turns to peek through a crack in his door. Raven has another long swallow, gasps, then stands there for a moment, bottle in hand, waiting to see if Roan's going to reclaim it. After a few seconds, he smiles and returns to his tent, greedily clutching the precious brew.

Next morning, Roan hovers outside Brother Raven's tent, listening. Even with Raven's large capacity, Roan calculates that drinking that much scorpion brew will keep the Brother snoring until well into late afternoon.

Brother Wolf's class has never been harder, since Roan's

mind is occupied with what he must do that day. Arriving at the sand painting area, he bows to the brethren, picks up his small crock of sand, and marshals his excitement by dropping the grains in place until the bowl is empty. He goes to the large supply pot, dips in his crock, then taps Brother Stinger on the shoulder. The supply pot is bare. Stinger, puzzled, checks for holes.

"Go to the streambed and fetch some more."

The words are few but what he hoped to hear. Roan leaves quickly, running along the streambed until he comes to the place where the sienna-colored sand has accumulated on the shallows. He stops for a moment to see if he's been followed. No one. He seizes the opportunity. In half an hour he arrives at the base of the mountain. Over the past year, Roan's seen the camp boundaries with Brother Asp. Saint has taken him far off into the townships and up Barren Mountain, but never anywhere near here. Why?

The stone here is multihued, the tones shifting from yellow to orange to red. But there's no blue, no color resembling blue at all. What was the mountain lion talking about? Roan searches frantically. The rock face goes on for miles, and there's no sign of a cave.

He pulls the snow cricket out of his pocket, hoping the insect will lead him to the right place, but the cricket does nothing.

Roan sits facing the rock wall. He estimates that he has a little over an hour before he must be back at the sand painting.

It's longer than he should be taking, but the Brothers are so entranced by their work they rarely notice the passing of time.

He stares at the mottled stone, shining in the sunlight, for the next half hour. Then, at the moment he is ready to rise in defeat, a cloud passes over, and Roan sees it. The shade on the rock shifts, bringing out darker hues. A hundred yards east, where a mossy green scrub grows up against the stone, the red tones in the rock turn blue.

Roan runs to the spot, and sees that the layer of moss isn't attached to the stone. He touches it, and it gives a little. The moss is woven into a camouflage blanket, similar to the kind that disguises the tents in camp. He feels around the edge of the moss and finds a kind of latch. As he lifts it, the blanket swings back, revealing a large opening in the rock. He steps in.

A torch and a fire stone are mounted just beyond the threshold. A piece of steel hangs from a chain. Striking the metal against the stone, sparks fly, lighting the torch. Road edges slowly into the shadows until he comes to an enormous carved stone. It's a figure of the Friend slaying the bull. Holding his torch overhead, he can make out a grate suspended by pulleys. They must tie the sacrificial animal to that, Roan reasons, then stand beneath it.

In the flickering torchlight, he notices color on the cave walls. Moving closer, he sees it's a group of paintings. Most are images he's seen before: the Friend, His birth from the stone, the slaying. But in one, a man is tied to the grate, suspended high in the air. His blood spills on the Friends gathered below. Roan's stomach churns. The sacrifice will be human.

Heart racing, Roan illuminates another painting, a burning village—and over it, a hand wielding a sword. The arm of the swordbearer is visible. It is covered in a ladder of thin parallel scars. Beside the painting hangs a cloth. Roan lifts it and slips into an adjacent cave. It's as if a hand had reached into his chest and wrenched out his heart.

The cave is full of masks. Masks of bone and tooth. Staring at him is the most grotesque mask of all, red and leering. The red skull mask worn by the person who stole his sister.

Roan backs out of the vault, gasping. Part of him had suspected this. Part of him hadn't wanted to believe. But now he knows. He knows.

Hatred and rage surge through Roan's body. He wants to burn the Brothers' tents, listen to their screams as they lie trapped in their beds. Stab them, spear them, slash their throats, crush their heads, let them bleed into nothingness.

*We watched revenge consume the world. And we turned away from it. We established this new community at Longlight, and we will never again raise a weapon, for fear of what we'll become. You cannot get peace from war. Remember, Roan, remember.*

But Roan no longer accepts his father's words.

He shouts into the darkness. "I will fight, Father!"

Yes—he will. But not until he's certain of victory. Until then, he will retreat. Retreat and wait for his opportunity. I have a goal, he thinks. I will find Stowe, and I will avenge the destruction of Longlight. I have no choice now but to hide my intentions and wait.

In the glare of sunlight, Roan feels raw, exposed. Sprinting back down the stream, he worries how he'll keep his vile discovery a secret. As he approaches the camp, he stops to retrieve the concealed bag of sand. No one even looks up when he returns. Resuming his place, Roan sprinkles sand on his appointed spot. He watches each grain fall slowly, controlling his emotions in this way. He must reveal nothing to the Brothers. And while the sand drops, he plans his escape.

At dinner, Roan sits beside a bleary-eyed Brother Raven as Saint intones the blessing. "His heavenly blade freed us from evil."

That heavenly blade brought evil to my door, thinks Roan, rage threatening to blister through his facade. How could Saint pretend to be my friend? How could he lie to me all this time? How could he oversee a massacre? Struggling to maintain his composure, Roan dutifully bows his head with the other Brothers.

Saint brings the prayer to a close. "With His love we will free the world."

"We are Brothers. We are Friends."

Silently, Roan vows: I am your enemy, and one day I will tear you down.

"The big day is coming is soon. Excited, Roan?"

Roan looks up at Raven with false cheer. "Very."

Observing Raven's puffy eyes, Roan has a revelation.

Images of Raven whispering to Feeder in his tent and the cut behind Feeder's ear flash through his mind. Suddenly he knows without a doubt the person in the grate will be Feeder. Roan is meant to be baptized in Feeder's blood.

Raven smiles back at him. "How do I know you'll pass the last trial with no trouble at all?"

Roan shrugs amiably.

Once dinner's finished, Roan finds a spot of high ground, and in the muted light of the setting sun he contemplates his escape route. To the south is Fandor, ruled by a clan still unconquered by Saint. But if he can believe anything Saint says, they're crazed and bloodthirsty. East is where Longlight once stood, and all the lands around it are controlled by the Friends. His only choice is to go west, over the Barren Mountain, into the Devastation. He'll need time, perhaps a week, to gather what he needs for the journey. And he'll need the motorcycle.

"The most beautiful time of day, isn't it?" Saint's voice is warm behind him.

"Without a doubt."

"You're getting very close to the final joining, Roan. Your next trial is imminent. If you are successful, you will be baptized into the Brotherhood." Saint puts a hand on his shoulder. "You know you will never find peace until you've seen justice for Longlight. It's a situation that must be resolved."

"I agree."

"I want you by my side, Roan. But I need you looking forward, not back. As soon as you complete the trial, I want you to take part in a Visitation."

"A Visitation?"

"You know Brother Wolf and I lead groups away from time to time. You were told they were trade missions. But now that you've attained the third level, you may know the truth of it. One day we will unify all the lands and take the City. To do that, we must be strong at our core. The Visitation is our way of achieving a perfect balance. In it we transform ourselves. Through it, we become the purifying Wind of Fire. The Visitation passes like a dream. We do it for the greater good."

*During the Madness, they called genocide holy, a cleansing.*

His father's voice echoes as Roan bows his head humbly. "I'd be happy to be part of it, Saint. Thank you."

"You make me glad, Roan of Longlight."

Everything Saint does is calculated, Roan realizes, to bind me to him. Because he thinks I have some kind of special power. Something the City wants. Something they could use. Something I can't see. What?

Back in his tent, Roan takes out his mother's pack. Inside is a bedroll, a water bag, some scraps of dried food. He'll need more provisions. Clean water. Feeling two lumps in the outside pockets, Roan looks inside. His father's shoe. His sister's doll. He grips them both, imagining their owners' faces.

ROAN FLOATS ON A PAD OF TWIGS ON THE WATER. ALL HE SEES ARE WAVES.

"ROAN!" IT'S STOWE'S VOICE. "ROAN."

"I'M COMING, STOWE! I'M LEAVING HERE SOON!" ROAN CRIES, BUT A HIGH-PITCHED SCREAM OBSCURES HIS WORDS.

THE OLD GOAT-WOMAN IS SITTING ON THE EDGE OF THE RAFT. "COME TO ME FIRST," SHE SAYS. "YOU MUST COME TO ME."

# the final test

it comes at night, it has a bite,
and leaves its stinger in you.
you will not cry, you will not die,
but one wrong word will kill you.
    —Lore of the storytellers

THE MOON PULSES FAINTLY behind a luminous haze in the orange-black night sky. Outside Brother Raven's tent Roan smiles at the loud snoring he hears. Raven is still recovering from the previous evening's binge. Roan treads lightly to the opposite side of the encampment to find Feeder also sleeping. He gently nudges the cook awake. Feeder's eyes snap open, and he sits up abruptly.

"What're you doing here?"

"Sh!" Roan commands in a whisper. "You tried to tell me what was going to happen. 'One comes, one goes,' you said. I know what it means now. There are always seventy-five Brothers in the camp. One Brother is sacrificed for the new one. This year, you die for me."

"I won the lottery." Feeder smiles. "It's the first time I've won something in my whole life."

"You don't have to die. We could run away."

"We can't do that."

"It would be hard, but we could try."

Feeder shakes his head. "I'm staying."

"Why?"

"I've finally found my purpose."

"What?"

A beatific expression spreads over Feeder's face. "I didn't understand before. I was afraid of everything. But then something wonderful happened. Brother Wolf spent hours talking with me. Brother Raven invited me to his tent. They helped me see who I am. Helped me find my destiny. You see, I'm not going to die. I'm going to live. Forever."

"They did something to you, Feeder. Put some kind of drug in you, maybe. In that cut behind your ear."

"Before, most of the Brothers thought I was a fool, stuck in the kitchen, too weak to fight, afraid to go on Visitations. But everyone thinks I'm important now. You should see the way they look at me. The respect."

"Feeder, they want to butcher you."

"You're jealous. You liked me better weak, so you could lord it over me. But I'm strong now, and I'm no longer afraid."

"Then come with me."

Feeder stares at Roan with wild, glazed eyes. In the shadowy light, the cut behind his ear seems to be throbbing. "I'm staying. And so are you. If you go, you'll ruin it for me. I'll lose everything. You can't go. I won't let you."

Roan, bent on preserving his own escape, improvises. "You're right, Feeder. Forgive me. I didn't realize you wanted this."

"I do, more than anything."

"Then you'll have what you want. But you mustn't tell anyone that I suggested leaving. If you do, they'll lose faith in me. They'll cancel my initiation and you'll miss your chance."

Feeder winces. "They can't do that."

"They won't. Not as long as they're sure I'm committed. But if there's any doubt in their minds, you know that will change everything."

"I won't say a word."

"Thank you, Feeder. I needed to be sure it's what you wanted. Sleep well."

There's no time to spare. Roan must leave at once. He'll have to get more provisions, without Feeder's help. He pads his way to the cook tent and gingerly negotiates the dim interior. In the wavering half-light of the torch at the entrance, he loads the pack he brought with dried goat meat and fruit and fills his water sack from the cistern. Then—a sound. He ducks behind the chopping block.

Two voices, slurred with drink.

"Be right there, I'm just gonna to grab a handful."

One of the Brothers enters the tent.

Roan watches the man's shadow glide to the chopping block, his hand reach into the jar that holds the dried fruit.

Roan doesn't breathe. The Brother drops a piece of fruit. It hits Roan on the head, and bounces onto the clay floor.

"Damn!" The Brother bends over to pick up the lost tidbit, inches from the frozen Roan.

"Hurry up!" growls the voice outside.

"One second!" the Brother hisses, still reaching. Roan is poised to spring.

"C'mon, or I'm finishing this bottle myself!"

The Brother sighs and saunters out.

Roan exhales, then takes in some more air. When he figures the two Brothers are out of earshot, he puts on his pack and looks out the entrance. They're gone. He winds his way behind Saint's tent to the small enclosure. He lifts the canvas door, ready to leap on the motorcycle. His heart sinks. The bike is gone.

Saint took it. Where did he go? What do I do now? Roan's head buzzes with questions. There's no escape without the bike; Roan wouldn't get more than a few miles. The only reason for leaving tonight is his fear of Feeder talking. He'll have to wait. And pray that Feeder stays silent.

After the wake-up bell next morning, Roan strolls by Saint's tent.

"He's not back yet," says Raven, appearing behind him.

"Where did he go?" asks Roan casually.

"Come, come, he didn't tell you?"

Raven touches Roan's cheek. Roan jerks back. "It makes

you nervous, doesn't it? How different your life would be without Saint. You know, the last trial is both the simplest and the most difficult. But don't worry—soon you'll truly be one of us. "

"Is that where Brother Saint's gone? To prepare my trial?"

"Be ready. He could return at any time!"

Roan's relieved: clearly Raven hasn't spoken to Feeder yet. Roan heads off to Brother Wolf's class, only to find out it is cancelled. Brother Wolf and many of his classmates have been called away. Preparing himself for what is coming, Roan returns to his tent and puts his sand-painting furs in the top of his pack to conceal his supplies. Then he picks up his hook-sword, goes to the practice area, and works out until the bell. By the time it rings, he has mastered some of his growing anxiety. Taking what he hopes looks like his sand-painting gear, he fastens his weapon in its sheath and heads for the midday meal.

Roan sits far away from the others, observing. Feeder is serving the soup, and it's clear that everyone's attitude toward him has transformed. They no longer ignore him or act as if he's invisible. Instead, they talk and joke with him and compliment him on his fine cooking. Whose soup will you eat once Feeder's blood is on your hands? wonders Roan.

Brother Asp joins Roan at the table. Roan looks at him, trying to understand how he could be so wrong about a person.

"You seem bothered, Roan."

"Saint told me about the Visitations," Roan says in a low voice. "I wondered how you feel about these events."

Asp sighs. "The Visitations are an important part of the Friend's work."

"But you're a healer."

"I heal the brethren and those who worship the Friend."

"What about the others?"

Brother Asp looks down at his plate. "If they fall outside the Friend's light, they are not visible."

A blast of horns shatters their dialogue. High, wailing trills and the roar of Saint's motorcycle capture everyone's attention. Clambering up onto a table, Brother Raven announces, "Everyone to the Assembly. A joyous victory for the Friend. Come!"

Surging with excitement, all the Brothers are out of their seats within seconds. Brother Asp grips Roan's hand. "This is the moment you've been waiting for, Roan. Come!" Roan puts on his pack and tightens it on his back as they join the throng.

Just as the brethren settle onto the tiered benches, Saint rides to the center of the arena, gets off his bike, and addresses his followers.

"Brothers! The Friend is great!"

"The Friend is great!"

"For years the renegade leaders of Fandor have eluded us, a blight in the eye of the Friend. Today, with a handful of our best, and with the Friend's blessing, we went to Fandor and liberated their chief and his lieutenant."

The brethren stomp their feet and cheer as Brother Wolf,

his tunic torn and bloody, enters at the head of the band of battle-worn Brothers. Pulling on coarse hemp ropes, they lead two hard-looking men, battered and bruised and limping from their wounds, across the rough wooden floor.

"Roan of Longlight!" Saint calls. "Join us. Meet the ones who murdered your people and destroyed Longlight."

Roan, heart racing, walks down to Saint and the prisoners, all eyes upon him.

"I promised that you would find justice, Roan. It stands here for the taking."

Pain and fury boil inside Roan. He stares at the accused killers. "You attacked Longlight? You killed my people?"

The taller of the two looks at Roan, dazed. "Yes," he says in a flat voice, "we killed everyone."

"Why?"

The prisoner speaks with difficulty. His teeth are broken, and blood oozes from his mouth. "The City paid us. Take the two, they said. Kill the rest."

"Who are the two?"

"You and the girl."

"For what purpose?"

"That's all I know."

"For what purpose!" shouts Roan.

"I don't know," the man repeats. He looks down at his feet.

Roan spots the bulging wound just behind the captive's ear. The same as Feeder's. Whatever that thing is, the Friends use it to make people say and think what they want. But Roan knows the truth. These two men are innocent. The real killers are all around him.

"Are you satisfied?" Saint asks him.

Saint is so sure of me, so sure, Roan thinks. That is his weakness.

Roan nods ever so slightly. He looks at the Assembly, at the expressionless faces of the Brothers. They are unified in their desire to obscure the truth, to keep Roan happy so that he will become one of them.

"The time has come for your final trial," says Saint. "Though it will be more of a pleasure than a pain. You are being given the honor of making the offering."

"Use your weapon," Brother Wolf says, nodding at the beautiful hook-sword crafted by his own father. "For the Friend. For your family."

Wolf unsheathes the sword from the side of Roan's pack and puts it in Roan's hand.

Saint smiles at Roan. "It's what you've been waiting for. Justice. Take it."

Roan doesn't move.

The Prophet whispers in Roan's ear. "The thought of killing is hard for you. That's why this is your final trial. Do not hesitate. You swore to kill the people who destroyed Longlight."

"I did."

"This is your chance. Use your sword. Take them."

"Take them! Take them! Take them!" chant the Brothers.

Roan stands still, clenching his sword.

The Prophet whispers again. "Now, Roan. Do it!"

Roan looks at the brethren, their faces twisted with blood lust. Their chant has changed now, to "Kill, kill, kill!"

"Roan!" yells Saint. Roan looks into the Prophet's eyes, and for a moment time stands still. Roan places those eyes, he remembers them at last. They are the eyes that lay behind the red mask of bone. This is the man who stole his sister, the man responsible for killing everything Roan loved.

"I have seen you!" cries Roan. He leaps at Saint, swinging the blade, slashing Saint's head, his ear, his neck.

The Prophet falls without a word, blood pouring. Brother Wolf flies at Roan, but Roan dodges him at high speed and drops the master with a smash to the chest. The other Brothers converge on him, but Roan sees the path between as clearly as if the men are slowly falling grains of sand. Slipping through his assailants, he leaps onto Saint's motorcycle, kick-starts the engine, and is gone.

# the devastation

this is the way of the blood drinkers.
on the third day of their thirteenth
year, their every tooth is filed and
sharpened, their ears cut off and
burned at the root, and from that day
forward they are sustained by blood.
——the war chronicles

As the sun casts its last light of day, Roan starts climbing the trail up Barren Mountain. All around him are delicate amber blossoms. Their sweet fragrance entices, but it is a deception, for these are flowers of the deadly Nethervines. He rides with care. The touch of even one of the black thorns can be fatal.

Roan doesn't stop until he reaches the summit. By then, storm clouds have rolled in over the peak. He scans below. There's not enough light to see through the downpour. But the rain will erase his tracks, and maybe wash some of the evidence of his crime from his clothes. He tilts his face into its wet sharpness and allows the impact of what he's done to penetrate him. He has drawn blood. He has attacked another person in anger. In one blind moment, he lost all self-control, broke every rule he had ever been taught, and mortally wounded another human being. He's become one of them. They are all the same monster.

Tomorrow he'll enter the Devastation, and he'll probably wander there until he dies. The worst that happens, he'll deserve.

Soaked, Roan pulls the bloody hook-sword from its sheath. He winds back his arm to hurl the weapon over the cliff. But the cricket stirs. It scurries out of his pocket, leaps down his arm, and sits on the sword.

Roan tries to coax the cricket off, but it doesn't move. Finally he surrenders. He wants to throw the sword away so he can forget what he's done. But the cricket seems to be telling him to keep it. To remember.

Pulling a blanket from his pack, he throws it over the bike, creating a shelter. Under the makeshift roof, he wraps himself in his bedroll. Trembling with wet, cold, and terrifying emotions, he waits for dawn.

He runs through it again and again. The feeling of the sword in his hand when it struck Saint. How easily it cut through his flesh. And Saint falling. Did I kill him? I hope I killed him. Roan feels his finger. Saint's ring. He's revolted at its touch, but then he thinks, I should wear this. To remind me of what I did, what I am. He wants to cry, but his rage stops the tears.

When first light breaks, Roan gets up and looks over the precipice at the lands below. In the distance, riders. The Brothers. Like a swarm of mad hornets, they'll be after him, hungry for vengeance. His trail will have been washed out by last night's rain, so they'll have no leads. He feels sure they'll head to the other side of the river, to the Lee Clan lands. They'll suspect he's joined their enemies there. But once they've scoured the Farlands, they'll try the Devastation. How long does he have? A week, maybe two if he's lucky. Nothing more.

Roan walks the bike to the other side of the mountaintop. Eventually he finds not so much a trail as a sliver of a dried-out creek, water-eroded stone. He kick-starts the bike, plummets over the ridge, and bounds down the scarred, rocky path. It's still morning when he reaches the annihilated valley. There's not a tree in sight, not a bird. On either side, steep charred mountains. Before him, as far as the eye can see, are festering craters filled with a putrid blue-black froth. Roan's been told stories about this place. Here, the last of the Resistance had its secret camp. They were well hidden, but also trapped. The planes that came dropped poisons as well as explosives, turning lush meadow into moonscape. Every last member of the Resistance was massacred, and the land was made toxic. No matter where Roan looks, he sees the twisted skeletons of long-dead rebels. No one could enter to bury the dead and survive.

But someone has come back, and recently, for scattered throughout this abysmal graveyard are tiny, ragged shrines of ripped fabric and dead flowers. Someone cherishes these people, he thinks, keeps their memory alive. He hopes the visitors are friendly.

There's no time to pay his respects to those who died here. He once knew their cause, but what was their fight for? Simply to oppose the City? It's not clear to him anymore. So he accelerates. The craters go on, the stench grows worse, and Roan's anxiety increases. The sun is past its peak in the sky when the motorcycle sputters to a halt.

At first Roan refuses to believe it, trying again and again to turn over the engine. Finally he has to admit it to himself: he's out of fuel. From this point on, he'll have to go on foot. There's nowhere to hide the bike, so he strips his gear off it, pushes it to the edge of a crater, and rolls it in. The brackish waters come to life, crackling and bubbling. Saint's cherished motorcycle dissolves into nothingness.

By the end of the day the last fetid crater's behind him. The air smells better. Grass grows on the flats. He turns, searching in the twilight. Listens. No one in pursuit. Not yet. He searches for a protected place to settle, eyes looking every-where. The ground suddenly gives way under his feet, but the fall is shallow and the cavity just deep enough for him to lie down in. He'll be difficult to spot from a distance. He lays out his bedroll, sips some water, eats a bit of Feeder's goat jerky, and opens Plato's *Republic*, a vision of a perfect society and the philosopher-kings who reluctantly rule it, scanning its first few words in the fading light. Roan hopes that his escape cancelled the final sacrifice, that his erstwhile friend is still alive, though Feeder would never forgive him for ruining his claim on eternity. Straining to keep his eyes and his mind on his book, he drifts to sleep.

THE RAT'S BLACK EYES MEET ROAN'S. "YOU'RE TROUBLED."

"I KILLED SOMEONE."

"AND IF ONE PERSON DIED SO TWO COULD LIVE?"

"IT'S MURDER. HIS BLOOD IS ON ME."

"NO NEED TO FEAR. HE STILL HAS MANY LEFT TO KILL."

"YOU MEAN HE'S ALIVE?"

"THAT'S SOMETHING YOU MAY REGRET."

Roan snaps awake as the sun breaks through mud-yellow clouds.

Saint alive? If he is, nothing will stop him, nothing.

The snow cricket, nearby, feeds in the turf. Slipping the precious book safely into his pack, Roan lifts himself from the cavity and surveys his surroundings. To the west, the orange-tipped grass goes on for miles. Behind him, Saint and the brethren are sure to appear. His only hope is to gain as much distance as he can. He moves swiftly, packing up his bedroll and obscuring any trace of his presence. After he eats and drinks a little, he cups the cricket carefully into his pocket and ducks into the cover of higher grass. The going won't be easy, but he'll be well hidden.

By early afternoon, the valley opens into a great plain and he sees smoke. A village? Should he risk shelter? The cricket, agitated, wriggles in his pocket. Roan looks again at the smoke.

It's moving their way. Dust. It can't be his pursuers—they'd be coming from the opposite direction. Taking no chances, he dives into the long grass and waits.

Within a few minutes the ground's trembling. Fast approaching is something unlike anything Roan's ever seen. The creatures, completely hairless, have hoofed feet, short curved horns. Their hides are sagging, blistered, and scabbed. Eight of them are stampeding in his direction.

Then Roan hears a shrill whistle. Coming up behind the beasts are half a dozen men on horseback. As they draw closer, he sees their skin is waxen, their eyes pink. Their mouths hang open, revealing sharp fangs. None of the men seem to have ears. They are a vision of horror. Albino riders, swinging weighted ropes over their heads.

With a screech, the riders throw their ropes. The rigs make a hissing sound as they fly end over end through the air, entangling themselves in the beasts' legs. One by one the creatures topple until the entire herd is lying in the grass, panting and wheezing.

The ghoulish riders are immediately off their horses and upon the exhausted animals. Roan shudders with revulsion as he watches each man pick a beast, place his arms around its neck and sink his fangs into its throat. The attackers gulp mouthfuls of blood as the animals lie heaving, eyes bulging.

One of the Blood Drinkers is so close Roan can see the scars where his ears once were. The man sucks intently on the trembling animal, then raises his head, blood splashed across his torso, his mouth a gash of red. He sniffs the air. Roan, perfectly still, thinks nervously of his own blood-splattered clothes. But after an excruciating moment, the drinker goes back to his meal.

Finally, the riders are sated. They go to their horses and pull large plastic bottles out of their saddle bags. Roan knows bottles of that size are hard to come by; it's been many decades since the last plastic was manufactured. Unless the Masters of the City have found a way.

The fanged men drain more of the animals' blood into their bottles. The beasts passively accept this further insult. Then the men untie the beasts, return to their horses, and head off. The injured animals slowly get back on their feet and walk unsteadily away.

Roan waits until both riders and beasts are long gone before he dares move again. He is deeply shaken by what he's witnessed, and the sight of the blood-sodden ground fills him with pity.

Keeping as fast a pace as he can, he travels until his feet are sore, his eyes so exhausted from constant vigilance that he has no choice but to stop. Tomorrow, he promises himself, he'll parcel out his energy more efficiently.

Scouting a place to camp for the night, Roan trips over what he assumes is a log. But where would a log come from, when he hasn't seen a tree for miles? Warily, he bends down and peers through the grass. It's the desiccated remains of a man. Noticing the puncture wounds on the victim's neck,

Roan guesses that the vampire riders have an appetite for two-legged prey as well. The dead man looks about the same age as Roan's father.

Without warning, all that Roan has been spared overtakes him. He pictures his father's anguished face, imagines what he must have felt as he watched Saint and his fevered brethren sack the village, then turn on the houses. Did his father hold himself over his weeping mother, attempting to shield her from the death blows that rained on them? He sees his friends, Aiden, Rolf, Esta, and the others, run screaming from the masked intruders, but they find no escape from the Fire Hole. This was the Visitation. Saint's Holy Quest. Roan feels a hate so dark, so rich, he can taste it. As it rises from his stomach, he hears his father's voice.

*That's not our way; that way is for others.*

But I am other now, Father, Roan thinks. My hands are stained with blood. I can never return to what I was.

Roan finds a soft place in the tall grass a few yards from the dead man. He lies down and closes his eyes. He will sleep with the dead. The dead are his brethren.

"ROAN! ROAN!"

STOWE IS FAR DOWN THE ROAD, ON A HORSE-DRAWN WAGON. SHE'S LOOKING FROM SIDE TO SIDE, SEARCHING FOR ROAN. ROAN RUNS TOWARD HER, BUT THE GROUND TURNS TO QUICKSAND, SLOWING HIM DOWN. HE HEARS STOWE CALLING FOR HIM.

"ROAN? MOMMY AND DADDY ARE DEAD. THE BIG MAN KILLED THEM, DIDN'T HE, ROAN? DIDN'T HE? ROAN?"

ROAN TRIES TO SHOUT AN ANSWER, BUT HIS MOUTH IS FILLED WITH SAND.

"I KNOW YOU'RE THERE, ROAN. I CAN SHOW YOU. TOGETHER WE CAN DESTROY THE BIG MAN. WE COULD KILL HIM, ROAN. WE COULD KILL HIM."

HER WAGON BEGINS MOVING.

"ROAN . . . ROAN?"

SAND RISES IN A WAVE, CARRYING THE WAGON AWAY.

"ROAN? MOMMY AND DADDY ARE DEAD. THE BIG MAN KILLED THEM, DIDN'T HE, ROAN? DIDN'T HE? ROAN?" SHE CONTINUES SAYING THE SAME PHRASES OVER AND OVER.

TROUBLED, ROAN OFFERS NO RESISTANCE AS THE WAGON AND HIS SISTER, HER CALLS BECOMING MORE AND MORE MUTED, DISAPPEAR FROM VIEW.

Roan wakes in a cold sweat. It's still dark. The moon's a burned husk in the sky; even the darkness seems charred. Roan sits up and listens. The snow cricket is singing. Roan can't understand why he's crying, but tears keep falling and will not stop.

I never buried my father. I never buried my mother. But I can bury you. Roan sits in the bleak darkness and mourns the dead man. For all they both have lost.

When the muted light of predawn comes, Roan looks for stones to cover the man, but there's only grass. He takes the hook-sword, cuts into the ground, and pulls up sod.

Roan takes his father's shoe, places it beside the man, and

rolls the sod over him. He kneels to say the prayer that choked in his throat at the Fire Hole. The Longlight prayer of passing. For this man, for his parents, for his people.

*That the love you bestowed might bear fruit*
*I stay behind.*
*That the spirit you shared be borne witness*
*I stay behind.*
*That your light burn bright in my heart*
*I stay behind.*
*I stay behind and imagine your flight.*

Then it's time to walk.

All that day, and the next, and the next, Roan stops only to eat, drink, or relieve himself. When he sleeps, he dreams of the drowning sand and his sister's anguished cries. Always, he is consumed by dread.

At the eighth sunset, he reaches the end of the grasslands, glad to see the sun go down. He's been told that once autumn days were cool, leading into winter. But since the Abominations, the climate's unpredictable and extreme. The heat often continues late into fall, making first snow impossible to predict. Today the sun burned hot. But the weather is bound to turn. Roan squeezed out the last of his water this morning, his food the night before. A sudden blizzard would finish him. He wonders how long he's got.

He's been using meditation to control his thirst, but Roan

is grateful to arrive at a low, moss-covered stream with a few trees growing at its banks. The water runs a little, a promising sign. Roan puts his nose close to the surface and smells. Fresh and delicious. The luscious water is just a trickle, which is good, because he's parched and might drink too fast. He rests his face on the muddy bank and sips, luxuriating in the cool liquid's flavor. Better yet, he sees it's safe to rest here, hidden by the sloping banks.

In this tranquil state, Roan loses track of time. He's dozing when he feels the first bite. He bolts upright and slaps his neck hard. An insect tumbles to the ground. Roan looks down. A black-winged fly, its wings still beating. He groans with pain as he feels another bite, on his hand. Ten more bugs swoop down on the same spot. He's being swarmed. Hundreds, thousands, of slow-flying, black-winged flies.

Roan runs, flailing at his ears, his eyes, but there are too many of them. Biting and biting again. Half-mad with pain and fear, he trips, landing in the stream. Mud fills his mouth, and he gasps for breath. Then he realizes the mud is his salvation. Frantically digging into the bank, he covers himself with it. It soothes his wounds, stops the biting. And when the hole is big enough, he crawls inside, burying himself until only a bit of his mouth is exposed.

Cocooned in his mud tomb, Roan worries about the snow cricket. He thinks he feels it wiggle in his pocket, but can't be sure. It could be one of the black-wings that got into his clothes.

Roan guesses where the flies have come from. The out-of-season heat probably hatched them from eggs in the stream that's protecting him now. They emerged at dusk to feed. Roan's timing couldn't have been worse. His only hope is to wait it out until morning.

Willing himself to stay relaxed, he sips the air slowly and counts each time he inhales. His heart rate descends, and he drifts.

THE MOUNTAIN LION LICKS ROAN'S FACE. ITS SANDPAPER TONGUE IS WARM AND DAMP.

"WHAT'S HAPPENING TO MY SISTER? WHY DO YOU KEEP ME FROM HER?"

"WE KEEP HER FROM YOU. IT IS THE ONLY WAY YOU CAN REMAIN SAFE."

"THE CITY WANTED US BOTH, SAINT SAID. WHY?"

"THEY HAVE THEIR REASONS."

"WILL THEY KEEP HER ALIVE WITHOUT ME?"

THE MOUNTAIN LION IS SILENT.

"WHY DON'T YOU ANSWER?"

"ALIVE, YES. THEY WILL KEEP HER. ALIVE."

Roan gags suddenly. A fly is crawling into his mouth. He coughs and spits it out. Have they found a way in? Is he being swarmed again? He listens, trying to hear through the caked mud. Nothing. He calms as he senses there are no others. What would Stowe think of him now, buried alive, stalked by raiders and flies? He falls back to sleep, dreaming of fire and insects and red skies.

# Lumpy

THEY WILL RUN TO YOUR GATES. KEEP
THEM SHUT. THEY WILL PLEAD FOR YOUR
MERCY. DO NOT RELENT. AND IF THEY
EMBRACE YOU, BUILD THE PYRES HIGH.
——THE WAR CHRONICLES

THE SUN BEATS DOWN on the creek, and Roan bakes inside his mud encasement. Aching from lack of movement, he listens for sounds, but all he hears is an angry stomach. His.

Without warning, he's jolted by something leaping onto the surface of the bank. Sharp claws dig into the clay. Roan bursts out of his cocoon with a shout, hoping to scare whatever it is away. He scrapes at the dried mud in his eyes, and in the blur he sees a brown mangy dog.

"Go!" Roan commands. The dog bares yellow teeth, snarling.

Eyes darting, Roan sees his pack and hook-sword are out of reach. A long branch is closer at hand. He feints, grabbing the branch as the dog leaps. With a twist, Roan catches the dog on the side. The animal lands hard on the ground. Before it rises, Roan scrambles up the bank, hoping his one blow is enough to dissuade the animal. The dog barks, a hard yelp that tears through Roan's ears.

Roan speaks firmly to it. "I'm going now, friend, so stay put." He slowly steps backward, his heart pounding, hoping the worst is over. But in an instant, five other wild dogs appear, snarling around him.

One mongrel snaps at his feet. Roan kicks it hard, and as the dog comes back, Roan smashes its foreleg. Two others charge and Roan whirls with the branch, catching one with a glancing blow on the back and smacking the other on the snout. Then the biggest of the pack leaps, sinking its teeth into Roan's calf. He swings the branch, but there are too many of them, ripping at his coat, lunging for his gut. Soon he'll tire, and the dogs will leave no more of him than bones scattered across a wasteland.

An ear-piercing whistle slices through air. The dogs freeze. A cloaked, hooded figure appears, a silhouette before the blinding sun. The dogs snarl as the intruder lowers his hood and hisses. The leader of the pack backs up, then skulks off, and the others follow. That's the end of it. The dogs are gone.

Roan eyes the figure for weapons, but it's difficult to make him out in the glare of sun. All he can see is the outline of a big knapsack on the figure's back.

"Are those your dogs?" Roan asks.

The faceless figure laughs, then speaks in a deep, raspy voice. "Anything but."

"I'm grateful. But if you have any intention of eating me yourself, that whistle of yours won't do you any good."

"I don't eat humans," says the figure and turns to go.

Roan calls out. "Are you traveling alone?"

"Always."

"Maybe we can walk together for a while."

The figure snorts.

"This territory's new to me," says Roan. "I could use the help of someone who knows his way around."

"You don't want my help," advises the figure, lowering his hood and stepping out of the glare.

Roan gasps. He sees the face of a boy his own age, but this boy's face is covered with lumps and deep open pits, some of the edges rising an inch above the skin, with a thin green mucous seeping over. The boy's eyes are barely visible through the craters and mounds.

A crooked little half-smile quakes across the landscape of hills and pits. "You haven't run."

"Should I?"

"Most people think I'm contagious, so they either run or try to kill me."

"I owe you my life. Let me fight by your side."

"I never fight."

"Then I'd fight for you."

The boy puts his hood back up.

"You don't have to cover yourself on my account," says Roan. "I've seen too many dead people to be bothered by the way you look."

The boy lets loose a wild giggle. "He thinks I look better than a rotting corpse!" He turns again to leave, but unaccountably stops, staring at Roan's chest.

"Where did you get that?"

Roan, puzzled, looks down to see the snow cricket perched on his top button.

"It's from my village. Way on the other side of Barren Mountain."

"It stays with you?"

Roan nods. "It found me the morning after my people were killed. It's been with me for months."

"Snow crickets don't take to people easily, but once they adopt you, it is said they never leave."

In the silence that follows, Roan can see something's changed in the stranger's attitude toward him. After a moment, the strange boy speaks again.

"Any bites?"

It takes Roan a moment to understand what he's being asked. He'd almost forgotten the wild dogs. In that moment, the pain flares, coursing through him.

"Any bites?"

"My leg."

The boy nods. "I can help you."

He bends down, gathering a black moss growing along the

stream bank. Roan winces as he crouches to join him, pulling up handfuls of the dry, springy turf. The stranger moves to a spot in the stream where the bank overhangs making a half-roof. He takes off his heavily patched knapsack and pulls out a piece of flint and a scrap of steel.

"My name's Roan, what's yours?"

"Lumpy," says the stranger, lowering his hood. That odd smile again. Scraping the steel against the flint, he makes a spark that lights the moss. "It may not burn hot, but it makes almost no smoke. Which is good, if you're avoiding someone."

Lumpy takes a small bowl and an old glass jar out of his pack. He places the bowl on the fire, heating it. Then, scooping the remains of a salve from the jar, he melts it in the bowl and dresses Roan's wounds with it until there's none left.

"Where did you get this stuff?" asks Roan.

Lumpy doesn't answer, just takes a small handful of what looks like dried meat out of his pack and gives a piece to Roan.

"Chew it slowly," Lumpy says. "This is the end of it."

Roan thanks him and chews. The burst of rich, spicy flavor makes him feel lightheaded.

"Where do we get more?"

"I was headed that way before you and the dogs distracted me."

"I have no food. I could use some."

Lumpy lays a goatskin bag on the surface of the water, dipping the neck gently in. As Roan does the same, Lumpy warns, "If we don't leave this place before the sun sets, the black-wings will eat us alive."

"I noticed," says Roan. He grins, brushing off some of the crusted mud still all over his clothes, face, and hair.

Their water sacks full, they load their packs and set out, moving past the creek and grasslands onto a rocky terrain. The injury to Roan's leg seems superficial, and the salve has made the pain manageable. They walk for hours, staying close to the boulders for cover, neither one speaking. Roan is filled with questions about this strange, mutilated boy. Lumpy saved him, fed him, and salved his wounds. But Roan's been treated well by others who turned out to be anything but trustworthy.

After sunset, the two come to a stand of scraggly pines. The trunks are twisted and bulging. Lumpy takes off his pack and throws it on the ground.

"Cover," says Lumpy. Yanking a blanket out of his pack, he plops down. "I love the smell of pine." Lumpy shuts his eyes, and soon he is snoring.

Roan pulls out his bedroll and sits down, hook-sword close at hand. He is tired, but he's too dubious about this new acquaintance to sleep. Lumpy could be working for Saint, leading Roan into an ambush. He might have given him the last of the medicine to trick Roan into seeing him as an ally.

Determined to stay awake, Roan props himself up on his pack. He attunes his senses to the environment around him, focusing on every sound and smell, keeping his mind alert.

But his fatigue prevails. Eyelids sag, head drops forward, and his body slowly folds itself onto the ground.

Roan wakes with a start to see Lumpy gone, as well as the packs. Furious with himself for falling asleep, he bolts to his feet. Too quickly. He feels the scabby tissue on his leg split apart. Ignoring it, he bursts out of the stand of trees, ready to hunt the thief to the ends of the earth.

Thump. Roan whirls at the sound. His pack is at his feet.

"I thought you'd never get up," says Lumpy.

"What were you doing with my stuff?"

"Feel your face."

Roan does. There's a spot of sticky-sweet sap on his cheek.

"It was getting on the packs, so I moved them. Do you have a problem with that?"

"No," says Roan. "Thanks."

"You're welcome," replies Lumpy. "Let's get some break-fast. Fresh and delicious. C'mon."

The terrain is dry, speckled with sparse stands of stunted hemlock. This was once dense forest, Roan guesses, but the Devastation and subsequent erosion wasted it. As he and Lumpy dart between patches of trees, taking whatever cover they can find, Roan's appetite grows from a whisper to a scream. The promise of a hearty meal has wrecked his ability to concentrate and his mouth waters in anticipation. Lumpy stops at a pointed mound rising six feet out of the ground.

"What's this?" asks Roan.

"Breakfast," says Lumpy, giving the mound a hard kick. From a hole in the side, hundreds of two-inch termites rush out to defend their home. Lumpy grabs one, breaks off its legs, and pops it, still wiggling, into his mouth.

"Dig in," Lumpy yells, grabbing another.

Roan stands and stares at the wriggling bugs. "This is the dried meat you fed me?" he asks, feeling queasy.

"Didn't you like it?"

"Yeh."

"Even better fresh!"

Roan takes a breath, then plucks a fat termite off the hill and pops it straight into his mouth. Before he can bite down, the insect jumps out and scurries away on the hard-packed ground.

"Break the legs off first," Lumpy advises.

The next termite squirms in Roan's grip, but he manages to break off the legs. The extra step means he has to look at the insect, which makes it harder to then put the bug in his mouth. But he won't back down under Lumpy's scrutiny. He bites, chews, and swallows. He doesn't exactly like the sensation, but it isn't as bad as he feared. And the live bug has the same rich, spicy flavor as the dried version.

"I thought the shells would be harder," says Roan, grabbing another termite and gobbling it up.

"Best part," Lumpy says.

After they've gorged themselves, Roan sits back and watches Lumpy pull the empty salve jar out of his pack. He's filled it since Roan saw it last.

Lumpy takes a flat stick and starts to trail the contents of the jar across the cracked clay to a clump of hedges against a stony rise, where he smoothes the bulk of the sticky treasure. "This sweet tree sap is their favorite."

Within seconds, a worker termite crawls from the hill, goes to the sap, tastes it, and rushes back to the hill.

"Get ready!" shouts Lumpy. In a blink, a wave of termites explodes from the hill, pouring across to feed on the delicacy.

Lumpy starts squashing the bugs with his feet.

"What are you doing?" Roan asks, mystified.

"Making dinner!" he yells. Roan joins in, pounding the bugs tentatively at first, but soon smashing with gusto.

After a half-hour of this grisly work, Lumpy gathers up the dead. Under cover of the hedge, he shows Roan how to make dried "meat" by smashing the bugs into a paste with a little honey and molding it into strips. Taking some black moss out of his pack, he lights it and shelters it with his cloak, and then dries the jerky by the fire.

"Bugs eat us, we eat bugs. Nice balance, isn't it?"

It takes until well into the evening, but now they have enough food for a few weeks. Sitting in the hedge, the blue darkness closing in around them, Lumpy rubs a soft stone from his pack against one of the mounds on his face, massaging it. His dark eyes lock on Roan. "Who are you running from?"

Roan's stomach churns. "Why do you want to know?"

"I like to know who I'm up against."

Roan hesitates, still unsure of Lumpy. He steels himself, then meets the other boy's gaze. "Saint."

Lumpy lets out a low growl.

"Saint murdered my people," Roan whispers. "And captured me."

"You escaped?"

"Not exactly."

Lumpy stands. "You were one of *them*."

"No. Never."

"Explain."

"He had me read to him."

"You're a reader? Where did you learn?"

"In my village. Longlight."

Lumpy looks skeptical, but he sits back down. "Longlight?"

"You've heard of it?"

"You're telling me you come from Longlight?"

"Yeh."

"You think I'm going to believe that? Everybody knows it doesn't really exist."

Roan looks curiously at Lumpy. "It did. Until the Friends destroyed it."

"Why are you trying to sucker me? I may look bad, but I'm no dupe."

"It's the truth."

Lumpy sighs, not sure what to believe. "What else did you do for Saint, besides read?"

"I was an initiate with the Brothers."

"How far did you go?"

"Third stage."

Lumpy whistles. "And then you left?"

"That's right."

"They wouldn't like that. There'll be a price on your head, dead or alive."

Roan points to his hook-sword. "Are you interested in finding out the price?"

Lumpy laughs. "I've seen what those Friends can do. I have no interest in making contact."

Roan nods somberly. "It might be better for us to go our separate ways."

Lumpy reaches for his pack, and pulls out his blanket. "It's your choice. I'm heading west, whatever you decide."

Roan eyes rest on a moonlit sky thick with stars. His hook-sword near his hand, he keeps a sharp eye on his companion. Lumpy baffles him. How long has he been here, wandering alone in the Devastation? What was it that disfigured him so horribly? And why does Lumpy think Roan's lying about Longlight?

As a yellow mist obscures the stars, Roan's startled by a gasping sound. Grabbing his hook-sword, he sits up, ready to take on the threat. But it's only Lumpy in a restless sleep, wracked by sobs. As Roan's breathing returns to normal, the snow cricket wriggles out of his pocket and scrambles over to the weeping Lumpy. Crawling onto a mound on Lumpy's hand, it rubs its wings together. Its song has an odd lilting quality that Roan has never heard before. As it sings, Lumpy's tears stop, and soon he's returned to a deep, peaceful sleep. Roan's never seen the cricket sing to someone else before. Perhaps he was meant to meet this unusual guide. Comforted by the thought, his eyes grow heavy, and he gives himself over to the night.

After a breakfast raid on the termite hill, Roan and Lumpy get underway.

"Where exactly are you heading?" asks Roan.

"All you need to know is that this route takes us farthest from Barren Mountain, which is where the Friends will be coming from."

The hard-packed flats make for easy hiking, but as the sun rises there's no escape from the heat. Roan wraps his blanket around his head to avoid the blistering rays. But Lumpy welcomes them, taking off his cloak to let the sun bake his blighted skin. Roan tries not to stare at the state of Lumpy's body, but it's impossible to ignore.

"Fascinating, isn't it?" says Lumpy, catching Roan's gaze.

"How did you get the disease?"

"You mean you've never seen it before?"

Roan shakes his head.

"I thought Mor-Ticks were everywhere."

"Not on my side of the mountain."

"You mean in Longlight?"

"That's right."

Lumpy chuckles. "At least you keep your story straight."

Roan ignores the jab. "What are Mor-Ticks?"

"They're little bugs with a shiny green shell, like emeralds. They crawl on you, sparkling, hundreds of them. For a second it's like your skin's turned a beautiful green. Then they dig in and make these mounds. It was the second worst pain I've ever felt."

"What was the first?"

"When their eggs hatched and the larvae exploded out of my skin. That's why some mounds have the craters. Most people don't survive for more than a few days."

"But you did."

"Yes, I'm a freak of nature." Lumpy's arm shoots out, and he points at Roan's foot. Roan jumps, but there's nothing there. Lumpy laughs bitterly.

"Don't worry," he tells Roan. "We've passed some Mor-Ticks, but they won't hurt you. You've got protection."

"You?"

But Lumpy falls quiet, withdrawing into his thoughts.

Over the next two days, Roan and Lumpy trek on a dried-out riverbed, its high banks providing cover. Lumpy walks in silence. From time to time, Roan tries to make conversation, but Lumpy won't bite. He simply picks up the pace, walking so fast Roan can do nothing but increase his own speed and maneuver the terrain, evading the little lizards that scurry among the stones. His hand remains close to the hook-sword, always vigilant.

Towards the end of the third day, Lumpy stops abruptly and glares at Roan's hook-sword.

"What do you take me for?"

"What do you mean?"

"You might be a reader, but I'm not stupid. Longlight is a myth. I've heard the stories, everybody has."

"What stories?"

Lumpy snorts. "Don't play with me."

"I'm not. Tell me what you've heard."

Lumpy sighs. "Just before the end of the Abominations, a group of rebels left the war and went east to find a place where they could create an oasis of peace and learning."

Roan nods with recognition. "Those were the First Ones."

Lumpy eyes him. "That's right, they're called the First Ones. So you have heard these stories."

"My great-grandfather was a First One."

"Then what is somebody from the legendary village of peace doing with a hook-sword?"

"I told you, I was captured by Saint."

"Well, you're carrying the sword now, aren't you?" snaps Lumpy, stomping away.

Roan tries to catch up, wanting to explain, but Lumpy won't have it. He merely walks faster. Roan's only consolation is knowing they're increasing their distance from the Friends.

For another five days they keep up their pace, constantly on the lookout for pursuers. They speak only as necessity requires. Every night, while Lumpy sleeps, Roan practices his martial movements, in preparation for whatever threat may come. When he's ready to rest, the cricket sings him to sleep, and Roan dreams the same dream of Longlight.

THE VILLAGE IS RUBBLE, THE FIRE HOLE SMOLDERING. THE STREETS ARE EMPTY. THEN ROAN HEARS SOMEONE SINGING. A MELODY HE KNOWS. IT'S HIS MOTHER'S VOICE.

HER SONG COMES FROM THE OTHER SIDE OF THE SHATTERED TOWN HALL. HE RUNS TOWARD THE BUILDING AND GLIMPSES HER BACK, HER LONG BRAIDED HAIR AS SHE DISAPPEARS INTO THE RUINS.

HE RUNS THROUGH THE DOOR. THE HALL IS EMPTY. HE LIS-TENS. HEARS FOOTSTEPS. BEHIND A FALLEN PILLAR, HE GLIMPSES HIS MOTHER MOVING TOWARD THE OUTSIDE. HE CHASES HER INTO THE APPLE ORCHARD, WHERE RIPE FRUIT IS HEAVY ON THE BRANCHES. HE SEES HER STEP OUT FROM BEHIND A TREE.

"I'VE BEEN WAITING FOR YOU, ROAN. I'VE MISSED YOU SO MUCH."

ROAN STUDIES HER FACE, HER DARK EYEBROWS, HER BEAUTI-FUL LIPS CURLED INTO A SMILE. HE TAKES A TENTATIVE STEP TOWARD HER. IS IT REALLY YOU?"

TEARS RUN DOWN HER FACE. "HOW CAN YOU DOUBT IT?"

"MOTHER, I'VE MISSED YOU TOO." HE TAKES ANOTHER STEP FORWARD, BUT A STRAND OF WEB CATCHES HIS ARM, WINDING ITSELF AROUND HIM. AS THE THREAD COVERS HIS FACE, HE

SEES HIS MOTHER'S FACE CHANGE. NOW HER FACE IS THE FACE OF STOWE.

"ROAN! DON'T GO, PLEASE. WHERE ARE YOU? I NEED YOU!"

THE WEB THICKENS AND HE'S HIDDEN FROM STOWE, THOUGH HER ANGUISHED CRIES STILL PIERCE HIS HEART.

Every morning Roan wakes tormented from this dream, as if the web barrier still binds him. The real Stowe is trying to reach him, he knows. But in the dream he can sense the malevolent force behind her. It alarms him. What's happening to his sister?

Roan keeps his troubling dreams to himself and walks each day lost in contemplation. But this morning his thoughts are interrupted when he and Lumpy come to a clear running stream. Lumpy eyes it suspiciously and sniffs.

"What do you think?" asks Roan.

Lumpy starts gulping it down, and Roan joins in. It's the deepest stream and the freshest water they've yet encountered. After they've filled their water sacks, Roan sets the cricket on a rock, strips, and jumps in. It's so cold he has trouble catching his breath, but the feeling of fresh water on his filthy skin is exhilarating.

"Come on in!" he yells.

With a crazed screech, Lumpy leaps into the stream with his clothes still on, soaking in the shallow water. Roan grabs his own clothes, and rubs his shirt and pants on the rocks.

"Blood doesn't wash out."

"I'm working on the stink," replies Roan, wishing Lumpy

was wrong, that somehow the dark blotches of blood would disappear.

At midday, as they round a bend, they see a village in the distance. Lumpy scrambles up the riverbank and into the brush, heading away from the town.

"What are you doing?" calls Roan.

"Avoiding trouble."

Roan's incredulous. "But we can get fresh food there."

"We can live without it."

"I have some old coins I can use to buy supplies."

Lumpy's eyes narrow. "What if Saint's put a bounty on your head?"

"I won't tell them my name. I won't say where I'm from. I'll just use my coins to buy us some fresh bread and vegetables. Wouldn't you like to eat some real food for a change?"

"If you want to go, go by yourself," says Lumpy, with finality. He holds out his hand. "Maybe we'll meet again."

Roan hesitates, feeling the pull of the village, the chance to visit with other people, to have a roof over his head. He's still unable to completely trust Lumpy. How can he, after all that's happened? But who's to say the village will be safe? Lumpy's helped him and guided him. He's clearly no ally of Saint's.

Roan stands a moment, then grips his companion's scarred, disfigured hand and smiles ruefully. "You're right. It's a stupid idea. Let's get out of here."

Lumpy offers his crooked half-smile in reply.

That night, as Roan and Lumpy sit chewing their dried food by a glowing moss fire, Roan muses about the village they passed.

"Why did you want to avoid that place? The price on my head's reason enough for me, but what were you afraid of?"

"I told you. Everyone this side of Barren Mountain knows what Mor-Ticks can do."

"But there are no Mor-Ticks on you."

"Would you bet your whole village on it?"

Roan is silent.

"When people are afraid, they do terrible things," says Lumpy gravely. "Have you ever been stoned? Beaten with sticks? Thrown down a ravine? That's what happened to me in the first three villages I went to for help."

Roan shakes his head in disgust. "Didn't you fight back?"

"Is that the way they taught you in Longlight?"

"No, and they're all dead because of it." Filled with a frustration he doesn't understand, Roan spits into the moss fire, making smoke and a few sparks that fly up into the air.

Lumpy glares at him. "Idiot!"

Roan, realizing his mistake, throws dirt on the fire.

"Too late," mutters Lumpy.

"Do you think anyone saw it?"

"Let's not wait around to find out."

They grab their packs and stumble off into the moonlit night. Through the long dark hours, weary as they are, they don't stop even to drink. Lumpy noiselessly slips through the brush, careful to not break any fallen sticks that might leave a trail. Roan follows, shamed by the thoughtless act that has put them at risk. Twigs fly back as Lumpy pushes through, and Roan allows branch after branch to slap against him. It's a penance he feels obliged to pay.

"ROAN, YOU'RE GOING THE WRONG WAY."

ROAN GLIMPSES STOWE, PEEKING THROUGH A BLUE LACE CURTAIN. THE CURTAIN FLUTTERS.

"TURN BACK."

ROAN TURNS. THE BROWN RAT IS LOOKING AT HIM.

"KEEP MOVING WEST."

"TURN BACK, ROAN, TURN BACK!"

"IT'S A TRAP," THE RAT SAYS. "KEEP MOVING. WEST."

"What are you doing? Wake up!"

Roan, surprised, sees Lumpy's face inches from his own.

"You were walking like you were in some kind of trance."

"I was—"Roan stops himself. "Sorry, guess I'm tired."

"Yeah. We've been pushing pretty hard."

Lumpy sits, leaning against a tree. The first light of day is filtering through the leaves. Roan looks down at him. "Why won't you tell me where we're headed?"

Lumpy picks up a stick, mumbling, "It's nowhere special."

"I'd like to know."

"I've heard rumors."

"Of what?"

Lumpy, embarrassed, turns his face away from Roan. "A healing place. A storyteller came to our village years ago and talked about it. Physicians and rebels gathered there after the Abominations."

"You think they can help you?"

"Probably not. It's a long shot, likely a myth, but if Longlight is... *was* real, then maybe..."

"And you know where this place is?"

Lumpy nods.

"What are we waiting for?" Roan exclaims. Wrapping his coat around his head, he trots off, Lumpy close behind.

# the Labyrinth

oasis exists. i know it does, though i
myself have never seen it. but anyone
who pays heed to tales of immortals
thriving in caves of light is a fool.
—Lore of the storytellers

Fired with enthusiasm to reach the healing place, Roan and Lumpy push themselves to their limits, sleeping little and resting less. They drink what water crosses their path and feed on tree sap and grubs, which to Roan's relief are much easier to eat than termites.

As they near their destination, the terrain changes abruptly. The ground is torn up where bombs once blasted the roads. Huge pieces of concrete and steel lie scattered like scraps of paper. They've arrived at the ruins of what appears to have been a small, prosperous city. Hollowed-out, half-collapsed buildings, some standing ten stories high in sections, line the broken sidewalks. The rusting relics of smashed cars and overturned buses, the first Roan has ever seen, litter the ruptured streets. There's no sign of life apart from a few weeds and vines that thrust up from the shattered remains, but there are many shadows, and the travelers become more and more apprehensive.

"This is the place?" asks Roan.

Lumpy nods his head. "This was the last city the rebels held. Bombs were dropped on it for four weeks straight, night and day. If what the storyteller said is true, some rebels came back to keep the healing place alive. The building must be here somewhere."

They weave through the crumbled concrete, searching block after desolate block. Lumpy doesn't say a word, but Roan can feel his companion's tension, his growing desperation. Just as Roan begins to doubt they'll ever find it, there, in tatters, is a white flag with a bold red cross hanging over a large, damaged entranceway.

Lumpy points at some broken letters above the threshold: H...P...T...A...L. "Do you know what they mean?"

"Some of the letters are missing, but I think it once spelled hospital."

"What's a hospital?"

"A place people went to be healed. They had medicines there, and special machines and doctors and nurses. The red cross on that flag means first aid. This must be the place you heard about."

"Let's go!" shouts Lumpy. He squeezes through the entrance, followed by Roan.

Inside, the hospital is all walls and rubble. They pick their way through hallways blocked by dead ends where the ceiling has fallen in or floors have collapsed. It's obvious this structure had once been filled with beds where people were healed; countless skeletons lie entangled in the rusting frames, fragile wisps of cloth still clinging to the bones.

"This might not be the place," says Roan.

"It's a hospital," Lumpy replies, a quaver in his voice.

"It was once."

Through a gaping hole in a wall lies what must have been a clinic. This area is in much better condition than the rest of the hospital. There are a dozen beds, the cabinets are intact, and the floors are dusty but free of rubble.

Lumpy rifles through the cupboards. Roan joins him, but most of the cupboards are bare, and the few jars they do find are empty. Lumpy slams the last cupboard shut and slumps down on a dust-covered bed. Roan can see tears clouding his dark eyes.

"Raiders must have gotten to this place. Let's go," Roan says gently.

Lumpy shakes his head. "I've staked a lot of hope on this place. I'm not ready to leave yet."

Roan nods sympathetically and squeezes back through the dark corridor, planning to wait outside. Pondering his companion's dilemma, he distractedly steps out into the light of day. For one critical moment, the bright sun blinds him. In that instant, two spears push against his ribs. Behind them, five horses but only one rider. Brother Wolf.

"We don't intend to harm you, Roan of Longlight. The Prophet lives. He wishes to see you."

Hearing his former teacher's voice has a galvanizing effect on Roan. He empties his mind, completely focusing on the threat. Four Brothers are off their horses, two with spears. Where are the other two? A quick glance doesn't reveal them, so he deals with the immediate danger. He feints, pushing one spear aside and grabbing the other with his free hand. He pulls hard, dragging the Brother off balance, and knocks him against the wall. Roan turns to the other assailant, blocking the man's spear thrust. Leaning in, he grabs his opponent's arms and hauls him down. Jumping on the fallen man, he whirls to face the other Brother, who is now back on his feet. The two of them leap into the air, but Roan is faster. Grabbing the Brother's arm in midair, Roan yanks it toward him and deals a precise blow to the vital point below the armpit. The Brother groans, falls. Roan reaches back, grabbing his hook-sword from his pack. But Brother Wolf has already dismounted.

"You've improved," says Wolf, aiming a kick at Roan's neck and swinging down with his own sword. Roan blocks the kick and deflects Wolf's weapon with a crash of his hook-sword. But Wolf's fist lands a ringing blow to Roan's ear. Momentarily stunned, Roan can't stop his teacher's next sword stroke. It hits Roan's hilt with such force that his hook-sword flies from his hand, out of reach. "Surrender," orders Brother Wolf.

In pain, Roan clutches his sword hand and kneels to the ground. But it's a ruse. He suddenly bursts up, attacking Brother Wolf full force. Retreating from the flurry of kicks and punches, Wolf backs toward the building, faltering against the wall.

"Drop your weapon," Roan orders breathlessly. Wolf nods and drops his sword. Roan catches the flicker in the Brother's eye too late. A net drops on him. The other two Brothers have been perched on the roof. Roan fights to free himself from the webbing, but they hold the net tight. He's caught, and struggle is no use.

"Very, very impressive," says Brother Wolf. "But you lacked the foresight to anticipate complications." Wolf stares Roan down, Roan's betrayal hanging heavy between them. For a moment Roan expects retribution, but Wolf just smiles and turns to the Brothers. "Pack him up."

The men start to pull on their quarry, but they freeze at the sound of a shrill, agonized wail. The horses fidget, and the men's mouths drop open at a horrible sight.

Lumpy, stark naked, his volcanic skin utterly exposed, runs toward them, waving his arms, howling as if mad with pain.

"Mor-Ticks, Mor-Ticks!" he screams. "Please! Please help me! Mor-Ticks!"

The brothers let go of the net, backing away in terror. Roan disentangles himself just in time to see Brother Wolf aiming his spear at Lumpy's heart.

"Let me put you out of your misery," Wolf shouts.

Roan erupts at the thought of yet another murder, this

time of his only living friend. He dives for his hook-sword, then leaps up. With one swing, he slices through Brother Wolf's spear. He throws his teacher to the ground and presses his blade against Wolf's throat.

Wolf stares down at the sharp metal. "So you would cut my throat with a blade my own father fashioned."

But Roan only means to use Brother Wolf as a shield. He signals Lumpy to disarm the other Brothers.

"You were my teacher, and you always treated me with respect. Take the Brothers. Get on your horses and go. Tell Saint to forget I exist."

Brother Wolf nods. The Friends climb slowly onto their horses.

"I'll tell him, Roan of Longlight, but he will not heed. Wherever you stand he will find you. You are a Brother, and no Brother stands alone."

Roan releases Brother Wolf, who signals his men to mount their horses. With one final nod to Roan, he slides his own hook-sword into his saddle, and leads the others away. Roan, battle sore but not wounded, remains vigilant until the riders are out of sight. Then he turns to the naked Lumpy. Bursting with triumph and relief, they laugh.

Throwing on his clothes, Lumpy snorts. "Well, it worked, didn't it?" Then he motions for Roan to follow him. "I found something in the clinic." He charges inside with a curious Roan close behind.

"What did you find?"

Lumpy grins slyly. "Look at this!" He runs to a large cabinet at the rear and opens the door. It's empty.

"There's nothing there, Lumpy."

"Exactly." Lumpy lifts a shelf, then places his weight against the back of the cabinet.

Roan hears a click. He watches with fascination as the cabinet moves, revealing a flight of dilapidated stairs.

"How did you find that?"

"When you've been scavenging as long as I have, you develop a way with these things. Besides, the storytellers talked about it. I thought it was a legend at the time—you know, like Longlight. Storytellers wouldn't last very long if they said exactly what they meant, but then I met you, so I decided to look a bit harder here. Come on. At the very least, it will be a good place to hide. And the Friends are bound to be back."

Even after they pull the cabinet back into position behind them, enough light stabs through the cracks in the walls to allow them to pick their way down the stairs. At the bottom, there's nothing but a narrow crevice in the floor. Lumpy starts to squeeze into it.

Roan grabs his arm, stopping him. "Wait. We don't know what's down there."

"It's a tunnel. I was coming to tell you that when I heard the ruckus."

"Do you know where it leads?"

"I bet it's some kind of escape route the healers set up. Maybe the tunnel leads to them."

"Or maybe the tunnel leads nowhere."

"It's our only chance. The surface isn't safe anymore."

Lumpy pushes through the opening in the floor and Roan follows, grimacing as he presses behind. Every muscle in his body aches from the battle, and his ear is throbbing. But as Lumpy promised, the crevice leads to an underground passage that opens into a tunnel. The walls of the tunnel glow; the stone seems to be naturally luminescent. It's not bright, but they can easily find their way.

"I say we stay down here, wander around a bit, hope like hell your friends get bored, and pop back up when our water runs out," Lumpy proposes.

"You really think we might find the healers?"

"Yes. But even if we don't, we're still better off."

"We could get lost down here."

"We'll mark our way."

The tunnel twists and turns. It is sometimes so narrow they can barely make it through, sometimes so high they can't touch the ceiling. From time to time, Roan scrapes a large X in the glowing stone with his hook-sword, a mark that can be clearly seen from a few feet away. After what seems an hour or two, they reach a point where the tunnel branches off in three directions.

"Crossroads," announces Lumpy.

They take a few steps in each direction. The first branch is very dark and seems to go straight down. The other two curve away but don't look any more inviting. Lumpy sniffs the air in each. "This one seems the freshest. What do you think?"

Roan takes a whiff. They all smell exactly the same to him. "I'll trust your scavenger's nose."

As they walk, Roan's senses quiver. He says nothing to Lumpy, but he has the unsettling feeling that they are being observed, as impossible as it seems in this narrow tunnel where the slightest sound reverberates. Roan keeps his sword close at hand.

Before long, they encounter another fork. Lumpy sniffs the air, picking the path, and Roan makes his mark. They press on until they find a spot with a smooth floor that seems a reasonable place to rest.

Roan sits stiffly, his sore spots starting to flare into bruises. Lumpy opens his goatskin bag and has a swallow, then offers it to Roan, who also drinks sparingly. The snow cricket emerges from his pocket. It sips from a few spilled drops of water, then begins to sing. The song has a beautiful resonance as it echoes through the tunnels. Within moments, Lumpy nods off. Roan, exhausted, allows his own eyes to close.

A voice, seeming to emanate from the air, mutters irritably. "There was to be only one."

"Well, now there are two."

"One was all that was spoken of."

"Two are what we have."

"Perhaps he is not the one."

"He is the one. He carries a white cricket."

Roan snaps awake. Did he dream the words? No, he's certain he heard voices. But now there is nothing but a weighty silence. He wakes Lumpy and, after chewing a little bug stick, they move on. Roan is paying the price for his exertions fighting the Brothers and every one of his muscles burns in protest. Although he has to steel himself to continue, he walks without complaint.

The narrowness of the passageway discourages conversation. Lulled into a trance-like state by the rhythm of their footfalls, they're both startled when Roan stumbles over something that rattles, then scatters in front of him. Fearing it's some kind of trap, Roan pulls his sword. Lumpy reaches down and picks up one of the objects. A human skull.

"At least we're not alone down here," says Lumpy, doing his best to make light of it. But his smile fades as they discover more human bones and scraps of clothing scattered around them.

"They look old. Maybe from when the hospital was bombed," Lumpy says.

"They're not that old." Roan is filled with unease, certain something terrible awaits them in these bleak channels. "I say we go one more long stretch. If we haven't seen daylight by then, we head back to the hospital."

"Under the circumstances," replies Lumpy, eyeing the skull, "I have to agree."

Within moments, they come to another fork in the tunnel, where a narrow passageway juts off.

"Feel the air?"

"Dry. Cold."

"Very cold."

"What do you think?"

"Why not?

They sidestep along the corridor, the walls so close they can see their breath condensing on the glowing stone. Granite tears at their skin as they struggle for each claustrophobic step. Finally they emerge into a large cave, sighing with relief. Their respite is short-lived. They stand rigid at a terrible sight. All around them lie mummified human bodies. The rock's luminescence casts an eerie glow on the hollow eyes and gaping mouths strung with skin like weathered paper. Some of the bodies are sitting like grotesque, wrinkled dolls.

"There are dozens of them," whispers.

"How'd they get like that?" Lumpy wonders.

"The cave's really dry. No water to rot them."

"They could have been here for centuries," says Lumpy.

"Maybe they're recent."

"From the Abominations?"

Roan grimly shakes his head. "Some of the bodies don't look nearly as dried out as the others. Look at the clothing. They may only be a few years old."

"Maybe they were sick, or couldn't leave because of the bombs, and then ran out of food and water..." Lumpy thinks for a second, then blurts, "Let's get out of here."

"Good idea."

At first it seems their route back will be simply a matter of following the scratches Roan made. The initial few forks are well marked with his Xs, but when they come to the third forked passage, there's no mark at all.

"It doesn't make sense. I marked each one," Roan says, mystified. Finally he spots a chip in the rock, so they hesitantly pick that path and carry on. But soon Roan stops.

"This is the wrong way. We're doubling back. We were curving a little to the east, then we turned south."

"How could you know that?"

"I don't know it, I just feel it," is all Roan says. But he's aware that the deeper they've penetrated this labyrinth, the more acute his senses have become.

They reverse direction. Their pace is rapid, triggered by mounting anxiety. But they arrive at a dead end. The passage is blocked. Lumpy stares, disbelieving.

"This is the way we came. It wasn't blocked before!" Roan says.

Lumpy gives Roan a worried look. "You're sure?"

Roan drinks his last few drops of water. Then he breathes slowly, settling himself, and gazes at the wall. After a moment, he hears the faint murmuring of voices.

"He knows how to use his eyes."

"He is formidable."

"The enemy taught him. He may be tainted."

"Not possible."

"I've seen it before."

"This one is different."

Roan scans the rock, detecting small holes. He puts his eye

up to one and looks in, trying to see who's talking. He whispers to Lumpy. "Did you hear that?"

"Hear what?"

"The voices."

Lumpy looks at Roan like he's lost his mind. "It's dead quiet in here. There hasn't been a sound."

"There were two people. Talking. A man and woman."

Lumpy shudders. "We need to get out of here. Now."

They turn around again, and after a brief time they arrive at another fork.

"This wasn't here before," moans Lumpy. Then his eyes light up at the sight of one of Roan's marks. He eagerly sets out down the passage with Roan behind, moving more quickly than ever.

As they pass through more sets of branches, Roan grows increasingly certain the path is wrong, that they're circling back. Whoever or whatever has captured them is forcing them to go this way. He debates telling Lumpy, but his companion is already so nervous, Roan worries the information would send him into full panic. Suffering from thirst and fatigue, they push on through the serpentine tunnels until they find the narrow passage in front of them again.

"We're going to die down here, aren't we?"

"The voices I heard. I know it seems impossible, but somehow they've been moving the walls," Roan whispers. "Somebody's playing with us."

"That doesn't make any sense."

"I'm not saying it does. But there's no other explanation."

A look of terror crosses Lumpy's face. "What do you think they want?"

"I wish I knew."

Lumpy kicks a wall and yells at the unseen captors. "Let us go! LET US GO!" His voice echoing through the caves, he sets off running. Roan follows, but it doesn't take Lumpy long to slow down. Their feet have become leaden, fear dragging on them like a sinkhole. Lumpy groggily bumps into the sides of the passage, trying to chatter his fear away.

"Maybe we're close to something. Maybe they heard my voice. Maybe they'll take pity on us. Soon maybe the tunnel will take us out, and then it's just a matter of finding some water and a little food, whatever we can get, it doesn't matter, because at least we'll be outside."

His words stop, interrupted by the sight before them. Roan would cry if there were enough liquid in him to generate tears. They're back with the mummies.

"How did we get back in here?"

Roan starts tremble. "I have no idea."

A low rumbling sound makes them jump. Behind them, the entryway is closing. Lumpy rushes to it, tripping over one of the desiccated corpses. Roan charges the wall just as it closes in seamlessly, stone against stone.

Lumpy presses on the walls, frantically searching for some secret button or switch that will release them. Roan puts his hand on his companion's shoulder.

"Come on, let's sit down. We're prisoners. Either they'll let us go, or they won't."

Lumpy stares at the withered bodies. "I wonder what I'll look like. Not like them. Different."

Fighting his own panic, Roan takes Lumpy firmly by the shoulders. "Sit."

Lumpy slides down the wall, moaning. In the silence, Roan can feel him growing calmer. Roan's pocket shakes, and the white cricket crawls out. As Lumpy holds out his finger, the cricket leaps onto it. It sings, soothing both of them.

"It likes you," Roan says.

"A cricket like this gave me my life, or whatever's left of it," says Lumpy. "It's probably wondering if there's anything to eat on me."

"Snow crickets eat ticks?"

"After we were kicked out of our village, my family headed to your side of the mountain. They died one by one, and I started wandering in the foothills. I was sure death was just a step behind. When I saw a white cricket, I thought I'd had it. Instead, the cricket sang. The Mor-Ticks that were buried came out. Their eggs hatched and the larvae crawled to the surface of my skin. It ate them all."

Roan is beginning to understand. On his side of the mountain, people weren't bothered by the malady because of the snow crickets. That was the reason Lumpy had told him he needn't fear the deadly ticks.

"Where is your cricket now?"

Lumpy's voice is weak. "A few weeks after it saved me, I went to the first village I could find to beg for food. They beat me with sticks and threw me back out the gate. I survived, but not the cricket."

"You were afraid I'd lose my cricket...at that village. Lumpy?" But Lumpy is crumpling onto his side.

"Lumpy, wake up!" Roan yells. He tries to lift his companion, but he has no strength left. "Please, Lumpy, c'mon!" It's no use. Lumpy is in a deep stupor. Gravity pulls on Roan's hurt, spent frame, and he sinks to the rock floor, weariness washing over him. He sits beside Lumpy and puts his arm around the person he realizes is the best friend he's ever had.

Through bleary eyes, Roan sees what must be angels. There are four of them, all with white translucent skin and long gray or white hair, wearing snow-white robes. Roan supposes he must be dead, but curiously, he can feel the warmth of their hands as they touch his forehead.

"Do we take them both?"

"Of course."

Roan tries to speak, but his mouth can't form words. A female angel leans over him and takes his hand.

"Welcome, Roan of Longlight. We've been expecting you."

Darkness descends on Roan, a blissful escape.

# the forgotten

imagine the unthinkable, said roan
of the parting, but no one could. the
devastation will come, he warned.
but no one listened. no one believed.
no one but for a very few, who
became the keepers of the light.
—the book of longlight

Roan awakes, bathed in a dazzlingly bright light. An angel holds his head, putting a glass of water to his lips.

"Sip," she says. "A little at a time."

Roan sips. The water tastes sweet, ambrosia to his parched mouth.

"Why is it so bright?"

"Amplified sunlight."

"What's—where's my friend?"

"You'll see him soon."

"What is this place?"

"Oasis."

"A refuge in the desert."

She nods.

Roan notices that he's wearing a clean white robe, and that the cricket is sitting beside him on his pillow.

"I thought you were angels."

"We are the Forgotten."

She has strong hands, like Roan's mother. He struggles not to be lulled, remembering the false image of his mother in one of his dreams.

"I'm Sari."

Roan hesitates, wondering how much he should reveal to this stranger. But Sari does not wait on his decision.

"Rest. Your body needs to heal."

She guides Roan's head back to the pillow. He drifts, questions floating like dust.

When Roan next awakes, Sari is there again, this time with a bowl of yogurt. Roan can't help but grin when he tastes it.

"You like it?" she asks.

"Much better than termites," Roan replies.

"You're feeling stronger. Are you up to meeting the others?"

Suddenly a wild, angry cry rips through the air. Lumpy.

"Easy on your feet!" warns Sari, but Roan jumps off the soft bed and runs out, stumbling as he reaches the doorway. He feels Sari's strong hands steady him as he peers across a large cavern to see Lumpy atop a large rock, brandishing a stone.

"Get back! Back! Murderers!" Lumpy warns the mass of people who surround him. But they don't appear very threatening. Most of them look old, hair turning white, garbed in robes.

"You're alive, aren't you?" says one of them mildly.

"Well... You kept changing the tunnels on us... You forced us into the cave with your other victims."

The man nods. He's tall, straight-backed, with deep-set eyes. "You entered our defense system."

"What are your plans for us?" demands Lumpy, slowly lowering the stone.

"My name is Haron. You're free to leave now if you wish," the man says. "We offer our regrets for any discomfort you may have suffered. You're welcome to stay as long as you want. With winter coming, you might find things more comfortable here."

Lumpy eyes him suspiciously. "Where's my friend?"

"Here I am, Lumpy!" Roan calls out from the other side of the cave.

"Let me through," Lumpy says, and the crowd parts, giving him free passage to Roan. Sari respectfully steps away, as do the others, giving Roan and Lumpy a wide berth.

"What do you think?" Lumpy whispers. "They almost killed us."

"If we leave, the Friends will be waiting for us."

Lumpy rolls his eyes.

"You have to admit these people *do* have a pretty good defense system," adds Roan.

"Good point," says Lumpy.

"And they've had a good look at you and haven't tried to stone you yet."

Mustering as much dignity as he can, Lumpy announces, "We'll stay for a while."

"Come, I'll show you around, if you're feeling strong enough," says Sari. "Look up." The brightness makes him squint, but Roan can see that among the stalactites that hang high above them are numerous polished mirrors. "Our caves are riddled with cracks that let in sunlight. These mirrors capture and amplify the light."

Throughout the cavern, people are busy at a variety of tasks, polishing mirrors, making furniture, weaving cloth, but each takes the time to nod to the newcomers as they pass.

"About three hundred of us live here," Sari tells them. "We came toward the end of the Abominations. We'd had our fill of the brutality, bloodshed, and fear, and we agreed that cooperation was the key to our survival."

"Where are the children?" asks Roan.

Sari grows somber. "We have none. There is a chemical that permeates the rock. It gives us health and very long life, but we discovered to our regret that it also prevents us from having children."

At the edge of one wall, Sari presses on the stone, and a barely visible crack appears in the granite. It opens further under her touch to reveal a dim tunnel. Roan and Lumpy struggle to keep up as Sari moves dexterously through the winding passage. But they're brought to an abrupt halt when confronted with a blinding shift in the light. As his eyes adjust, Roan is amazed by the sight of a gigantic garden. They'd had a few small greenhouses in Longlight, but nothing on this scale. Dozens of gardeners work in long rows of tomatoes and peppers and cucumbers. Sari explains that fruit and vegetable scrap is recycled into fertilizer. In an adjacent cave, another composting system reclaims human and animal waste.

"Deeper in our caves are mines, where we retrieve the silver for our mirrors." Sari's fingers brush another opening, and the wall again gives way before them. "And as you've already seen, our stone sculptors are exceptionally talented."

Roan examines the threshold, admiring the nearly invisible stone work and extraordinarily close fit. He swings the rock wall the other way, and it creates a barrier on the opposite rock face. "This is how you trapped us."

"It took many years for us to perfect the technique, but when your survival depends on it, almost anything is achievable," says Sari.

Lumpy grimaces as they turn a corner. "Argh. I can't stand that stink!"

Roan's puzzled. "I don't smell anything."

"I hate the little bearded devils!" groans Lumpy.

The cave ahead of them is rife with bleating goats. The animals immediately swarm Lumpy, nibbling on his clothes.

"They like you," chortles one of the goatherds. Lumpy scowls.

As the herders wrangle the animals into a long procession, Roan notices that a number of them are armed with long bows and finely crafted arrows.

Sari follows his gaze. "We never know when a roving band of brigands or mercenaries might appear," she explains. "The tunnel from this cave leads to a hidden valley in the outside world. There the goats can graze while we tend our wheat and our apple orchard."

"Why don't you live in the valley?" asks Lumpy.

"After the last rebel stronghold was destroyed, our parents argued about whether to live in the valley, which seemed secure, or to stay hidden in the caves, which we had discovered but still had much to learn about. The majority chose the surface. We chose the underground. At first we envied the valley-dwellers. Despite the poisoned land all around, the prevailing winds had protected the valley's soil from contamination. It was rich, and their crops grew high. But at the end of the summer, an army of mercenaries attacked. Many perished, and the fruits of their labors were lost. Those who remained realized the open was unsafe and joined us in the caves."

As the last few goats are led outside, Lumpy gasps. One of the archers is a girl of about sixteen. Her skin is covered in Mor-Tick scars. Their eyes meet for a moment, then one of the goatherds calls out her name: "Lelbit!" The girl turns and disappears down the passage.

"Lelbit was brought to the old hospital when she was a

child," explains Sari. "Our healers worried many months over her survival. Her spirit is very strong."

"You used the healing place?" Lumpy asks.

"Until it became too risky for both the patients and the healers. But we're grateful Lelbit found us. She's our finest archer, and she has developed a great number of other useful skills as well. Perhaps our healers can help you as well."

A look of yearning crosses Lumpy's face, but he doesn't speak. Sari calls out and one of the Forgotten appears, and motions for Lumpy to follow.

Lumpy whispers to Roan. "If this is some kind of trick..."

Roan gives Lumpy a pat. "This is what you came for. I think it's safe."

"Hope you're right, but if I don't come back, save yourself," mutters Lumpy as he's led away.

Sari turns to Roan. "We have a place you might find interesting."

The cavern is enormous. It's filled with shelves, every one of them jammed with books. Librarians on ladders tend the hundreds of volumes, and on long, sturdy tables below, dozens of scholars write and study.

"You read!" Roan dashes to the book stacks, running his fingers over the spines. A long-nosed, broad-bellied man joins Roan.

"It's nothing, really, much less than a small public library used to contain in the old days."

"It's fantastic."

"I'm Orin, Head Librarian."

"Roan of Longlight."

"You possessed a fine collection of books there, I'm told."

"Not as big as this. You know about Longlight?"

"Yes, we heard the sad news."

"How?"

"We have not lost our eyes and ears."

"Then you might know that many of the books, at least my father's collection, survived."

Orin's eyes open wide. "Really? Where? We do venture out sometimes on missions of that sort."

"I believe a large part of his library is still in the house. The rest of the books were taken by Saint."

Orin frowns at the mention of Saint's name. "'And he went up the mountain and was changed forever. There the Friend appeared to him out of the darkness and gave him the Word.' Oh, dear. Saint and his Friends. What an ambitious crowd." Orin shudders.

"I spent a year with them. And I read to him from his library."

"And you left his company. I don't suppose it was an amicable parting."

"Far from it."

"You'll be safe from his reach while you're with us." Orin clamps his hand briefly on Roan's shoulder. "If you like, you could help me out here in the library."

Roan smiles. "I'd like that." In fact, he thinks, nothing could make him happier than spending time in this room.

At supper, the meal table is loaded with vegetable stew, salad, cheeses, crusty breads and fruit. Apple tarts and cookies for dessert. This is the kind of food Roan's family lingered over in Longlight. But after filling his plate, he anxiously looks around. Lumpy still hasn't turned up, and Roan's beginning to doubt his instincts about this place. He's finally sitting before the meal he's dreamed about for months, and he cannot eat it.

"Don't worry, they didn't kill me," says Lumpy, surprising Roan from behind.

Turning to greet his friend, Roan can't help but stare at Lumpy's skin, trying to discern if there's any improvement.

"Don't wear your eyes out," says Lumpy. "The change is inside, not out. They gave me this salve for the pain."

"Does it work?"

Lumpy grins. "It's the first relief I've ever had. They said I'm suffering from a low-grade infection under the scars. If I apply the salve every day for the next six months, the pain will be gone for good."

"But not the scars?" asks Roan.

Lumpy shakes his head. "Believe me, I've already gotten more than I hoped for."

Their new sleeping quarters are in a small, comfortable hollow with clean-smelling woven beds. The walls in the room have been painted to darken the luminescent stone. Roan closes his eyes, but he can't sleep. He feels the cricket crawl across his hand. His eyes open to see the little white insect scurrying onto his pack. Roan reaches into one of the pockets and pulls out Stowe's doll, the cricket riding on top. He's relieved to hear Lumpy's voice.

"Can't sleep?"

"No."

"Me either. I haven't slept in a bed in years. Or without pain."

"So you still think we should stay here for the winter?" Roan whispers to his friend.

"Of course," says Lumpy. "Besides, I can't stop wondering about that girl, Lelbit. I've never seen anyone else like me who wasn't dead. How about you?"

"I'm willing to stay. I feel safe here. Still..."

"They seem sad."

"It's true," says Roan. "There's no real sunlight, and no children."

"Eventually they'll all die off. It must be hard to know that."

A searing loneliness consumes Roan, and he falls silent. In the darkness, he strokes the straw hair of Stowe's doll, making a scratching sound.

"What was that?"

"Something of my sister's."

"You had a sister?"

"I was escaping with her. I was beaten down. She was taken."

"She's dead, then."

"No, I don't think so."

"Why?"

"Dreams."

"You've seen her in your dreams?"

"She calls me. But there's something different about her. Changed. I can feel danger and I'm worried it might be coming from her."

"What are you going to do?"

"I don't know. I think I'm supposed to be here. It feels right. Somehow this place is connected to it all."

Roan wakes refreshed the next morning. Curiously, no dreams or visions disturbed his sleep, but a rollicking appetite prevents him from considering the matter. When Sari joins them at breakfast, Roan's slightly embarrassed at the mountain of biscuits, jam, and yogurt he and Lumpy have piled before them.

His mouth still full, Roan looks at Lumpy, then back at Sari.

"We'd like to accept your offer to winter in Oasis. Orin invited me to work in the library while I'm here. Are there any other tasks we can help you with?"

A wicked smile breaks out across Sari's face. "Wonderful. You can help Haron harvest the radishes! You should be even hungrier by lunchtime."

While Sari leads them through the labyrinthine passageways, she explains, "Haron is the oldest of all of us. Over a hundred."

"He doesn't look that old," says Roan.

"Not a day over ninety," adds Lumpy, with a smirk.

She takes them into the garden, and waits with quiet patience while Haron, in a single graceful gesture, pulls up a radish and places it in a sack.

"Roan and Lumpy are here to help," Sari tells the old man.

Without so much as a glance at them, Haron pulls himself up and reaches high over his head, stretching. Then he walks over to a storage shed and gathers for each a small wooden trowel and a large woven bag.

"Fill these up. That section over there," Haron whispers hoarsely.

"Good luck," Sari says, an amused look on her face, and leaves.

"What was she smiling about?" Roan asks Lumpy.

"I don't want to think about it, but I'm sure it's something good for us. At least, *she* thinks so."

On the other side of the garden, Roan and Lumpy begin yanking up radishes. Their energy flags only after their bags are half full and their faces are covered in dirt and sweat.

As they inch over to the water cistern, nursing aching backs, they observe Haron still languidly harvesting the crop.

"Bet you he hasn't finished a quarter of a bag," says Lumpy.

"Let's find out."

Filling a mug with water, Roan walks across to where the

old man is harvesting. He's surprised to see that Haron's large bag is nearly full of radishes.

Haron nods his thanks for the water and drinks deeply.

"I knew your namesake."

Roan looks at him, confused.

"Your great-grandfather Roan," Haron says. "We fought together in the Last Battles. I saw him for the final time at the Parting. He was an extraordinary man. Greatest leader I've known."

"The Parting?"

"That's what we called our decision to quit the war and split up. Your great-grandfather went one way and started Longlight. My group came here."

"There are others?"

"Yes. They went farther away and even deeper into cover."

"Do you think they survived? I mean, could Oasis be all that's left, now that Longlight is gone?"

Haron doesn't answer. After a look that penetrates Roan to the core, he hands back the mug and returns to his work.

Adrift in a sea of unknowns, Roan is relieved to find Lumpy still awaiting the word on Haron's radish status. It's more fun than it should be wiping the smile off his face.

"Haron's bag is almost full," Roan solemnly reports.

Lumpy charges back to work, tugging up radishes at an impossible clip. Roan matches him pull for pull, but soon their hands and fingers are throbbing, and their spines feel as if they'll never straighten again. Bags only two-thirds full, they collapse in the dirt, too sore and tired to go on. At that moment Haron passes by, leisurely lugging his bag, which is overflowing.

"Don't worry, boys, the first time's always the hardest," he says, biting into a radish.

Determined, Roan and Lumpy remain until they've finished filling their bags. Delivering their radishes to the kitchen, exhausted and wanting only rest, they are then swept off to the community bath.

The bath is a pool of water heated by a steaming fissure in the rock. It's big enough to accommodate ten people, and when Roan and Lumpy arrive, both men and women are soaking naked in the waters. Lelbit, the archer, is among them.

Lumpy hesitates. "Maybe we should come back later."

"You're not the only one who's lost his skin," one of the men says as he stands. His own skin is horribly scarred. "I was caught in the Red Rains; a lot of us here were. Come in. You're in good company."

Lumpy looks at Roan and shrugs. They strip off their robes, then step into the water. It's very hot, with a slight scent of sulfur. A far cry from the cold streams they've been splashing in.

The steaming water makes Roan buoyant. It would be easy to enter into a blissful state here, but he has something else in mind. He signals Lumpy to start up a conversation with Lelbit, who's resting her head on the pool's edge, eyes closed.

"Not now," Lumpy whispers.

"Go on." Roan nudges Lumpy.

Annoyed, Lumpy nudges back, but he loses his balance and bumps into Lelbit. Her eyes open, and Lumpy grins nervously.

"Sorry. Did I hurt you?"

She shakes her head. Lumpy keeps going. "This bath is amazing, isn't it? Everything here is amazing. The mirrors are amazing, the goats are amazing…"

Lelbit puts a finger to her lips. She closes her eyes again and lies back to enjoy the bath. Lumpy slides Roan an irritated glance. They both take Lelbit's lead and surrender to the soothing waters.

Looking for a place to set down their overloaded lunch plates, Roan and Lumpy notice Lelbit at a table by herself. Shyly, Lumpy heads over to ask if they might join her. She pulls out a chair beside her, and Roan sits down across from them.

"Sorry for disturbing you before," Lumpy says.

Lelbit shrugs and has a bite of her bread.

"I heard you found this place the same way we did, looking for the old hospital," Lumpy says.

Lelbit holds out three fingers, and makes a gesture with her hands of things falling. Then holds up the three fingers again, and pushes down one. Then another.

"Three of you, but only you made it to the infirmary?" Lumpy guesses.

Lelbit makes the falling gesture again, this time over her head. Then points to her mouth. Lumpy shudders.

"The Mor-Ticks got in your mouth," he says.

She smiles wanly and pours Lumpy a glass of water.

He takes it from her. Their eyes meet, sharing a thousand hurts Roan can only begin to imagine.

# winter in oasis

the parting was not the ending but
the beginning. our beginning. the
beginning of new hope.
—the book of Longlight

THE DAYS TURN TO MONTHS as Roan and Lumpy enjoy
the pleasures of Oasis. Lumpy and Lelbit have become fast
friends, and Lumpy has even taken to goat herding, an activity
that Roan knows his companion finds malodorous. But oversee-
ing the animals while they graze on the winter grasses is a small
price to pay for afternoons in the sun with his new friend.

Roan is happiest in the library. He spends long hours
painstakingly reconstructing the text of a damaged book. For
some unknown reason, Orin has given him the task of accu-
rately gleaning the meaning of each sentence. The book is
about the raising and education of children, and Roan often
finds himself lost in memories of his own childhood. In
his spare time, he pores over modern history texts, trying to
better understand the events that led to the Abominations.

Assisted by the library's map collection, he's able to track the geography of the Last Battles as well.

Roan's curiosity about the past is matched by Orin's interest in the present. The librarian is fascinated by Roan's experience with the Friends, and he has no end of questions about it.

"The Friends claim they limit their Visitations to one a year. Is that what you've observed?"

"That didn't stop them from raiding the Fandor camp," Roan replies.

"So there are inconsistencies in their belief system?"

"There are inconsistencies in Saint," Roan says, still struggling to make sense of what he knows. "He's not completely his own master."

"Because he's beholden to the City?"

"It's not just that. He's bound to this faith he's created. I found a book on Roman religions he keeps hidden in his bedroom, and the pictures in it seem to be the source of the religion of the Friend. Once I told him how each symbol in his faith was connected to a constellation."

"He didn't know?"

Roan shakes his head.

"And your observation threatened his authority as the one Prophet."

"Yes, but that wasn't all," says Roan. "I can't explain it. I could feel his fear. It frightened him that he didn't know, I think. And maybe that he'd never been told. Sometimes I wonder if he found that book, or if it was given to him."

Roan's jolted by a wild laugh. "What's the difference? Saint's a fraud, and we'll use it against the butcher!" The speaker's a young man with black curly hair and blazing eyes, dressed in a torn, multicolored shirt and ragged trousers. Not exactly what Roan's come to expect of the Forgotten.

Orin is obviously irritated by the intrusion. "Good day to you, Kamyar. So glad to see you're back," he grumbles.

"I'm happy to be back too," nods Kamyar, not taking his eyes off Roan. "How could I miss the opportunity? I had to see him for myself."

"I don't suppose I can blame you," sighs Orin.

"So," says Kamyar. "I hear we nearly killed you."

"Things have turned out just fine," says Roan.

"Hmm. I think the verdict's still out on that," Kamyar replies.

Orin breaks in. "Roan, Kamyar is part of a secret we guard. You see, some of the Forgotten venture out of Oasis from time to time as storytellers."

"I've heard of them," says Roan.

"You don't say," Kamyar interjects, a mischievous grin on his face.

"Then you know the storytellers travel from village to village in the guise of beggars, offering a tale for a bite to eat."

"And in return, we do a bit of feeding ourselves. Of the mind," Kamyar elaborates. "Each story's a seed, planted to get people to question the lies of the City. To stop for a moment and ask why. Something you might consider doing."

Orin harrumphs in protest, but Roan's curiosity is piqued. "And you told the story of Longlight."

"An excellent tale that was," says Kamyar. "The people loved it. They did. It gave them hope. Now, unfortunately, it's turned tragic."

"But they think it's a myth."

"Nothing's more powerful than a myth."

"It was real," Roan says angrily. "It was my home, my family."

Kamyar smiles. He moves so close to Roan their noses almost touch. "So naïve. The only thing that makes them real is you. And you have no idea who you are."

Roan bristles. "What does that mean?"

"Enough!" snaps Orin. Kamyar backs off.

"I'll come back at a more opportune time, Orin, to consider the stars." And he's gone.

Orin is apologetic. "Forgive him. Storytellers live in constant danger, and they become a bit outspoken and, well, let's not mince words—rude. But you've been so generous with your answers. Perhaps you have a few questions of your own."

"What do you know about the Dirt Eaters?"

"Oh, the Dirt Eaters, ha!" the old librarian chuckles and scratches the bald patch on his head. "Not enough, my friend. They are fascinating, though very secretive. We have no facts about them, only rumors."

"Do they actually eat dirt?"

"Apparently. Well, many medicines are made from dirt of one kind or another. But it is said they ingest a rare kind of soil that allows them to enter into an alternate reality, one that transcends time and space."

"Does anyone who eats this soil become a Dirt Eater?"

"I don't think anyone who wasn't a Dirt Eater has ever had access to it, or even really knows what it is. But I imagine a Dirt Eater would need to possess a combination of genetic propensity and specialized training. We believe their numbers are quite small. We suspect they are very powerful. Perhaps they can even see the future and travel with their minds." Orin clears his throat. "At least that's what I've come to understand. Well, I'll leave you at your work now."

Orin shuffles off, but Roan is given no time to reflect on their conversation.

"Beware the Dirt Eaters," Kamyar mutters.

"You were spying on us?" Roan says irritably.

"A wise man learns to keep his ears open."

"And what do you hear of the Dirt Eaters?" Roan asks.

"They believe they know the future," Kamyar says disdainfully.

"What's so bad about that?"

"What if they're wrong? What if there are other possible futures they don't want the rest of us to know about? What if dirt doesn't make you see at all—what if it makes you blind? Ask yourself, Roan of Longlight, is there only one good story in you?"

"I don't know what you mean."

"I think you do," Kamyar smirks. "Here's some free advice.

Ask many questions. Accept nothing at face value. Create the future as you go." With that, he turns and vanishes into the catacombs.

Kamyar's a bit overbearing, Roan thinks, but there's nothing wrong with his counsel. Be cautious. Be careful who you trust.

As the days pass at Oasis, Roan often shares a quiet meal with Sari, who takes a deep interest in him and his journey. She's fascinated by his tales of Longlight and his family. When he tells her about the masked invaders and what he found at the Fire Hole, she lowers her eyes and speaks with quiet ferocity.

"This injustice is a terrible blight on us all."

A sharp desire for vengeance surges through Roan, annihilating his sadness.

Sensing his distress, Sari speaks firmly. "There was nothing you could do."

"No, not then. I was raised not to fight. Never to hold a weapon. Never to strike out in anger. But I could do something now."

"You struck out at Saint. Many have tried. You're the first to succeed."

"I wish I had killed him," Roan mutters. Then he sighs. "My father would be devastated to hear me say that."

"You don't know that, Roan. All you know are the beliefs Longlight practiced. You may not fully understand the reasoning behind their purpose."

"They refused to fight. Just as you do."

"We carry weapons. We have no qualms about defending ourselves. Or even killing when necessary. In the Parting, those who chose Longlight embraced a philosophy of complete non-violence."

"Why?"

She takes a long look at him before speaking. "Their vision has left an indelible mark you cannot escape. You will always question the ways of violence and power."

"What good will that do me?"

"You have tools to defend yourself against terror and domination. With what you know, you can defend others. Your father would not be ashamed of you for doing that."

"I don't think he'd understand it."

"I suspect he might," Sari says. "And I'm sure he understood that this ability bestows power on those who exercise it. You will never use or accept this power easily, Roan. Your integrity will make you a great leader."

Roan chews slowly, thinking on her words.

Later, in his room, Roan sharpens his hook-sword, honing its edges razor sharp. He holds the sword in his hand, feels its weight, and swings it into the air. He focuses, meditates, contemplates, but nothing comes to him. Is there some truth embodied in his weapon? What did Sari mean about him becoming a leader? What does she know? He senses that she wants something from him, but he can't figure out what it might be. All he can do is follow his instincts and hope they lead him well.

That night and every night after, before Lumpy comes to bed, Roan practices his fighting exercises. He reviews Wolf's lessons on stance and strategy and hand-to-hand combat. He relives his war games with Saint, and their discussions about battle tactics and the politics of conquest. If he has to use these skills, he'll be ready.

The peaceful months at Oasis work their restorative powers on Roan. He slumbers deeply, without dreams, or at least any dreams that he can remember. Each morning, he awakens more and more revitalized. Something deep inside is healing, he realizes. Whoever these people are, whatever their expectations, he knows they wish him well.

When he's not in the library, Roan sometimes gardens with Haron. It brings back memories of many similar moments with his father. Good memories.

"Tell me about Longlight's garden," Haron says to him one afternoon.

"We grew carrots and peas and cabbage and corn, potatoes and herbs, all kinds of beans and tomatoes in a little greenhouse."

"Those seeds came from the old gardens we kept in the valley near Heather Mountain."

"Where the Devastation is now?"

"That's right. The gardens there were big enough to feed a thousand people. One day your great-grandfather woke in a high dudgeon. He insisted we get right to preparing seeds, start sorting and drying them. He pushed and pushed, so everybody got on with it, even though it was a good month before it would usually be done. The second those seeds were ready, the announcement was made. We had less than one day to evacuate. The new Masters of the City had located us."

Haron pauses, revisiting memories of that day.

"It seemed impossible. Our camp was secluded, secret. The other leaders demanded to know where Roan, your great-grandfather, had got that information. His explanation was met with skepticism, frustration, and anger. He insisted we stop fighting. We were to break up into groups and form new societies based on a plan he'd laid out for us. There were many who trusted him; the man was wise as well as perspicacious. Some of us decided to do what he said. Those who did not accused us of being cowards. They stayed, convinced they were safe. This was the first Parting. Those who left split into four groups, each going separate ways. Our group was only two days away when we saw the airplanes. It was our grief to witness the clouds of noxious smoke released over the valley."

"Where *did* my great-grandfather get his information?"

"It came to him in a dream. He said the instructions were given to him by a brown rat."

Roan, unnerved by Haron's words, sits heavily.

"Are you alright?"

"Yes. I think so. Just tired." But Roan is filled with excitement, and as soon as he can he excuses himself, his head spinning.

With each step, new questions swirl into Roan's mind. A brown rat! Was it the same one that visited Roan in his dreams? Did his great-grandfather also see the mountain lion and the old goat-woman? But his musings are halted by Lumpy's voice in the distance. There's a quality in it he's never heard before.

"Show me again."

In the archery cave, Lumpy is taking target practice from Lelbit. As Roan peeks in, he sees her put one hand on Lumpy's shoulder, then use the other to guide his pulling hand back to draw the string and arrow. Lumpy lets go, and the arrow flies straight into its mark, a painted circle a hundred yards away.

"Did you see that!"

Lelbit hugs Lumpy, and he picks up another arrow, stretching the bow back and firing again. This arrow splits the first one. Lelbit kisses him. Roan turns away, not wanting to interrupt them. It's been a long time since Lumpy was touched so tenderly by anyone. He's gone too long without being loved.

Now that spring's arrived, Roan's intent on leaving Oasis. He'd taken Lumpy's companionship on the road ahead for granted. Now he wonders if he'll be making the journey alone.

That night, for the first time in months, Roan dreams.

HE'S LOUNGING COMFORTABLY IN A ROOM FILLED WITH HUGE, SOFT PILLOWS, SIPPING ON A COOL DRINK, WHEN HIS SISTER'S VOICE BLISTERS THROUGH HIM.

"ROAN! ROAN! ROAN!"

ROAN DROPS THE GLASS AND LIQUID SPILLS, POOLING AT HIS FEET.

"THEY'RE HURTING ME, ROAN. HELP ME. I HAVE TO FIND YOU, PLEASE. IF YOU WON'T COME TO ME, I'LL GO TO YOU. TELL ME WHERE YOU ARE."

FEATHERS FLY INTO ROAN'S MOUTH. COUGHING, RETCHING, HE LOOKS FOR A WAY OUT OF THE ROOM, BUT A STORM OF FEATHERS FILLS THE AIR, BLINDING HIM. HE FEELS A HAND, GUIDING HIM THROUGH THE FLURRY. THE OLD GOAT-WOMAN.

SHE PLACES HER LIPS NEAR ROAN'S. AS SHE EXHALES, A GUSH OF SWEET WATER CLEARS HIS MOUTH. "THE ROAD TO ME IS THE ROAD TO HER."

SUDDENLY THEY'RE SITTING IN A FOREST OF THIN, UPRIGHT RED STICKS. BEHIND THE GOAT-WOMAN IS A BUBBLING LAKE.

"I'M WAITING," SHE SAYS AND SMILES.

Roan wakes to see Sari sitting by a candle on the floor, the white cricket on her hand. She looks up at Roan.

"It's been a long time since I held a snow cricket in my hand. Pardon me coming in here uninvited. As I was passing, I heard you cry out in your sleep."

"Where's Lumpy?"

"With Lelbit and the herders. You've slept quite late."

"You know I'm leaving."

"Where will you go?"

"I had a dream. Tall red sticks everywhere. And a steaming lake. Is there a place like that?"

"Orin will know. You're certain you're ready?"

"I've accepted your hospitality for too long."

"As you wish," she says, her face inscrutable.

Roan breakfasts alone. He walks most of the morning, clearing his mind, preparing himself to leave this haven and head into the unknown. He's learned to navigate the tunnels of Oasis, and when he comes to a narrow threshold, he knows exactly where he's going. The mummies have not changed in any way since he first sat down among them. Gazing at their shriveled bodies, he contemplates the mystery behind who lives and who dies. A few months ago he came to Oasis having survived flies and wild dogs and Blood Drinkers and deprivation. He should be one of these withered corpses. What right did he have to live when everyone else from Longlight was gone, nothing but bones floating in the Fire Hole?

"I thought I might find you here."

He had thought he wanted to be alone, but Roan welcomes the sound of Haron's voice.

"I often come here myself, to contemplate fate. You know, the hardest part of living this long is witnessing so much death. I've lost them all, parents, brothers, sisters, friends. Some went easily, but most suffered in ways I don't like dwelling on. Often, working in my beautiful garden, I think, 'What right have I to be happy, when they suffered so?'"

Roan keeps his eyes on the stone floor, his face flushing. "It all happened so fast...I never said good-bye." He stops, fighting the mass of unresolved grief welling up inside.

Haron puts his hand on Roan's shoulder. "What your family shared didn't require good-byes. They were proud of you, I'm sure, and understood you loved them. They knew you better, Roan, than you know yourself."

Roan looks at the old man, uncomprehending.

"Your great-grandfather, Roan of the Parting, was a visionary. He could see it would take a long time to rebuild the world, generations. And Longlight was set to a purpose. You are the culmination of that purpose. Your parents knew it. That's the reason you were given his name, the name of your great-grandfather and my old friend."

"Why was I never told of this?"

"These are things best left unexplained. None of us is certain what the future brings. We make plans, we have hopes, we suggest and perhaps even urge a little. Beyond that, we can do no more. All will become clear to you through experience."

"Winter's over. I feel it is time to leave, Haron."

"You're on a path, Roan. You carry *our* dreams, too."

In the dinner cave, those at Roan's table eat quietly.

"I heard you were going. Leaving without telling me?" asks Lumpy, looking at his food.

"You've wandered alone a long time, Lumpy. I understand why you'd want to stay."

"You do?" Lumpy asks, his face a mask.

"Yes. I do."

In the hours since making his decision, Roan's determination has hardened. He knows the road will be difficult, but he's learned some lessons along the way. Lumpy has taught him how to survive in the outside world. And he will.

Roan catches Sari's eye. "In the morning."

"You're prepared?"

"Yes." But the goodbyes to come are a burden on his heart.

Next morning, Roan finds that Sari has left out a set of travel clothes for him. When he goes to the library to take his leave of Orin and the librarians, they all shake his hand gravely and wish him luck. Orin presents him with what looks like an old, weathered book. But when Roan opens it, he sees that the pages are blank.

"Where did you get this...how did you find it?" Roan stammers. Paper itself is difficult to find, but an old unused journal is impossibly rare. "I can't accept it," he says. "It's too valuable."

"Then make the words count," Orin says. "Tuck it safely away. One day you'll feel the need to fill up those empty pages."

Relenting, Roan grips the librarian's hand. "Thank you, Orin. I'll often think about you, and our talks here."

Roan adds the gift to his well-stocked rucksack, hook-sword bound to its side. Then he pulls out two of the books he's been carrying with him since leaving the Friends. "I'd like to add these to the library," Roan says.

Orin fingers through them. "Machiavelli! Plato! What treasures! Oh!" He enthusiastically sits down with them and buries his nose in the pages. Roan gives him a pat on the back. With a last look around the library, he steps into the stone corridor, where Haron waits to bid him farewell.

Haron cups a fire stone and a piece of steel into Roan's hand. Roan looks into the old man's eyes. "Thank you for being my friend."

Haron smiles, and as he slides his fingers over the wall, it opens. Sari, Lumpy, Lelbit, and a few guards wait on the other side. The group's mood is somber as they weave their way through the intricate passages. When they arrive at their destination, Sari pauses before the final doorway.

"This leads out onto a mountain thirty miles east of the place you seek—the bubbling lake. We've packed rope for your trek down. It will be difficult, but it's the least exposed route. At the foot of the mountain is a dead forest. Its southern edge is overgrown with Nethervines, which you know to avoid. Follow the sun west across the forest. Some poison left from the Abominations still haunts the wood. Do not pause: you will not survive it. You must arrive at the old road before sunset. Continue west along it, and the way will be clear."

Roan turns to her. "I'll miss you."

Sari's eyes are clear and strong. She puts her hands on his shoulders. "You journey for us all. Go straight and true, and never doubt we are with you."

"Thank you," says Roan.

Sari lays her hand on the fracture that marks the threshold, and the door to the outside world opens. A wall of plummeting water, fed by the spring runoff, thunders before them, sun glimmering through its mist. Blinking in the bright light, Roan follows Sari across a ledge. The others follow. At the far side of the ledge, Sari leaps and kicks a jutting stone. To Roan's astonishment, a stone bridge slides out from the rock face. As Sari crosses onto it, she blazes with sunlight, again the angel Roan first imagined her to be. He follows her and his lungs fill with fresh, crisp air. He marvels at the expanse of snow-capped peaks, sheer rock cliffs and, far to the west, barren flatlands dappled with melting snow.

"The trail begins beyond the bluff," says Sari, pointing.

Roan turns to Lumpy, arms open, dreading this farewell. But Lumpy's turned away.

Lumpy clears his throat. "I'm going with you," he says as he hoists a pack over his shoulder.

Roan can hardly believe it. "What about Lelbit?"

"She figures you wouldn't last a week out there without me."

Lelbit nods in agreement, a slight smile on her face.

"I can manage fine, really."

"Wild dogs'd sniff you out in five minutes."

"You've taught me a few things."

"Not enough."

"The place I'm headed, there's a town there. It might be dangerous."

"Good. I was starting to get too soft."

Lelbit takes Lumpy's hand and presses it against her heart.

Then she follows the others back into the waterfall. Sari waves a final good-bye before the threshold closes behind them.

Roan pulls the snow cricket out of his pocket, and they both let the sunshine warm them. The cricket rubs its wings together and sings. Roan turns for one last look at where Sari stood. There, before the waterfall, is the mountain lion.

"TRAVEL WELL, ROAN OF LONGLIGHT."

Roan blinks, and the lion's gone.

# the WOUND that WOULD NOT HEAL

the SCARLET CLOUDS BEGAT the
RED RAIN that BURNED aLL that it
toucheD. anD the RED RAIN BEGAT
the DEADLY netherVINES anD their
seDuctiVE fLOWERS.
—the WAR CHRONICLES

"THIS LOOKS LIKE the way down," says Lumpy. He takes a step and slips on the moist orange fungus that covers the rocks. Unscathed, he hops back up.

"Wait!" Roan breathes, steadying himself, and peers at the slope below. "This way," he says, and begins carefully stepping down the hidden trail.

"How do you know?"

"I'm not sure. When I focus I can just see it."

Lumpy gives him a curious look, then shrugs. "I'm right behind you."

They travel in silence until they find themselves on the

brink of a precipice. Lumpy inches his face over the edge, then immediately pulls back, looking dizzy.

"There's got to be another way."

Roan shakes his head. "The rocks are too slippery for us to make it back up. Our only choice is down. Let's use the rope. We can anchor it around that tree."

"You call that a tree?" Lumpy tests the small, scraggly growth by grabbing around its gnarled trunk and pulling with all his weight. "I guess it'll do."

"Do you want to hang over and have a look?" asks Roan.

"I'd like to keep my breakfast," says Lumpy. "Please, be my guest."

Roan binds the rope around his waist. Lumpy sits by the tree, digs his heels into a small outcropping, and grabs the rope for extra security. Roan moves to the ridge, energized by the vast landscape, the bracing air, and the endless sky. He looks down at the sheer drop and grins.

"You actually like this?" clucks Lumpy in disbelief.

"In Longlight, we had this tall tree, Big Empty. I was the first to climb it. After that, I was always looking for something higher and harder to climb," says Roan. He lowers himself over the edge. Dangling in the air, he spots a shelf. He swings his legs forward and lands, pressing his chest to the bare rock face, fingers lodged into a crack in the stone. "Come on," he shouts up to his partner, "hang your legs over!"

Lumpy leans over the edge. "I was afraid you'd say that."

"Don't you trust me?"

"You, yeah. It's the sheer cliff with nothing but air for support I'm not sure of," calls Lumpy. He grabs the rope and lowers his feet, letting Roan guide them into position. When he's within reach, Roan secures him on the shelf and Lumpy stands, breathless. He peeks cautiously over his shoulder. "Great view," he gasps.

"This ledge keeps going down the rock face," Roan tells him. "With any luck, it will take us right to the foothills."

The footing is tricky , but they're able to follow the abutment until they arrive at a platform of granite overlooking the land below. Roan and Lumpy sit for a drink of water and take in the view. Gigantic tree stumps stretch as far as the eye can see, tantalizingly out of reach. Infesting their eastern edge, as Sari warned, is an overgrowth of Nethervines.

"This forest must have been incredible. Look how wide the stumps are. Those trees took centuries to grow," Roan says sadly.

"They were cut down in the days before the Abominations," Lumpy explains. "Some people say the trees would have died anyway, when the Red Rains came. But how can they know that would have happened? A storyteller came to my village and told the tale. Funny learning the truth in Oasis about who the storytellers really are and why they do it. It's a good idea, using stories to change the way people think. It worked on me. You start figuring out things for yourself. After I heard those stories I never trusted the City or the Friends. Hardly any of us did."

"Well, the storyteller I met certainly tried to make me think about things."

"Like what?"

"The Forgotten have expectations of me, but they're vague about what those are, exactly. Kamyar seemed to be saying I should get some concrete answers."

"He's probably right. Think about it. Everything from those dreams to the way you use your eyes. There are things you've got to do, Roan, and I'm going to help you do them if I can."

The idea of fulfilling some kind of destiny makes Roan nervous. How does he begin to tell Lumpy about his great-grandfather and the brown rat, to discuss what it all might mean, when he knows so little himself? Besides, Sari said they must be out of the forest by sunset. Better to deal with the problem at hand.

"First things first," Roan says. "As far as I can see, there's only one way to go. Once we're down this lip, we'll be on those slopes, and they'll take us right to the bottom."

Roan leans over, resting his gaze on the seemingly sheer rock face. After a minute, he sees the way. Bending down, he squeezes his left fist into a large fissure in the rock. "We use the cracks." Gripping his fist tight to hold his position, he shifts his body and stretches out his left leg, finding a tiny toe-hold. The fingertips of his right hand slip into a small crack. Once his right leg finds a toehold, he's facing the rock and ready to go.

"You have to be kidding," shudders Lumpy, hanging back.

"I'm stable. Use me," Roan commands. Lumpy reaches out, braces his left hand on Roan's shoulder, and turns his body. Pressing his front against the stone, he lowers his toes onto a slight outcropping.

"Keep going!" shouts Roan, who's already begun spidering down.

Lumpy obeys, making a steady descent. He moves with increasing confidence, finally pulling even with Roan. "We're doing it!" he grins.

In that moment of broken concentration, Lumpy's toehold crumbles. As Lumpy falls, Roan grabs his friend's wrist with his free hand. Fist aching, barely able to maintain his grip, he shouts, "Find a toehold!"

Lumpy feels with his toe, detecting a ledge. "Got it," he yells. But just as he releases his full weight, it crumbles. The sudden jolt is too much for Roan. His fist bursts out of the safe hold, and the two of them plunge down the steep slope, rolling all the way to the edge of the forest.

Lumpy's up first. He's limping, but seems to have eluded major injury. His pack has burst open in the fall, and as he retrieves his things, his eyes and Roan's settle on a jar that's rolled into the Nethervines, far out of reach. The healing salve.

"You need that stuff every day," says Roan. "Let's get it."

Lumpy shakes his head. "Leave it. Getting poisoned by one of those thorns would be a lot worse than what I'm facing."

Roan looks at him. "Are you sure?"

Lumpy nods. Then he sees a drop of blood on Roan's sleeve. "You're cut!"

"No, we stopped before we hit the Nethervines."

"Not quite." Lumpy points at a narrow branch of Nethervine that curls past the spot where Roan landed.

Lumpy has a closer look at Roan's arm. Just below Roan's elbow is a small thorn. "We've got to get it out," says Lumpy urgently.

He picks up two small, sharp stones, then delicately grips the thorn between them and removes it. The area around the tiny wound's already inflamed. "Lie down," Lumpy orders. "Movement spreads the poison."

"I can't even feel it," Roan protests.

"You will, I hope. Get down."

Lumpy cuts a length of rope and ties it around Roan's bicep, above the scratch, making a tourniquet. Then he pries some wood off an old stump and starts a fire. Taking a piece of cloth, he coats it with an unguent he was given in Oasis, heats it, then presses the cloth against Roan's wound.

"Do you feel it now?"

"Yeh," moans Roan. "I do. It's burning."

"Good. It's when you can't feel the pain that you're in trouble. The more poison there is in your system, the more it numbs you. Stay still."

Roan is overwhelmed by a tidal wave of fire. He steadies himself, rising to the assault, mustering every cell in his body to battle the invader.

Lumpy repeats the extraction treatment four more times, then throws the cloth into the fire and watches as it bursts into flame.

Looking up weakly, Roan rasps, "Can we take off the tourniquet? My fingers are going numb."

Lumpy checks the wound. "The inflammation's gone down."

As the rope is released, Roan flexes his fingers, feeling the blood rush back into them. The sun is still high in the sky.

"Time to go."

"I'm not sure you're up to it," Lumpy says.

"Sari said we have to get across the forest by sunset."

"There's probably still poison in you."

"We have to risk it."

Lumpy reluctantly acquiesces, but first sets out some food. Roan woozily eats and drinks a little, then gets himself up and pulls his pack on. But the ordeal's weakened him. Keeping his mind fixed on the wound and mentally fighting the Nethervine toxin prevents him from moving quickly. He feels Lumpy close behind. He can sense his friend's concern at his every caught breath, every stumble.

Their footsteps are the only sound in this forest graveyard. No crows or sparrows. No insects buzzing. No rustling of animals or leaves. They are the only living things here, and that dawning realization fills them with dread.

"There's got to be at least a bug. This would be a perfect place for grubs," says Lumpy. Prying off a piece of bark, he exposes nothing but decay. "It doesn't make sense."

Roan feels in his pocket for the snow cricket, but the insect is still.

"What's wrong?"

Roan looks at Lumpy, worried. "It isn't moving."

"Let me see."

Roan cautiously lifts the cricket from his pocket and holds it in his open palm. Lumpy touches it lightly with his finger. Nothing. Lumpy looks at Roan, grief-struck.

Roan's heart sinks. The cricket's been with him from the beginning. Its song has woven itself into his very being, kept him safe, warned him whenever danger was present...

"We have to get out of here!"

Lumpy nods. Roan slips the cricket back into his pocket, and they take off at a swift clip, following the sun. But Roan's unable to keep up. The vibration of every footfall rips through his arm. Drenched in sweat, moving only through sheer force of will, he notices that Lumpy has also slowed his pace, wincing in pain. Without the Mor-Tick salve, the discomfort he was once accustomed to has come roaring back. But the two of them plod on as the sun dips perilously close to the horizon.

"ROAN? ARE YOU HERE?"

STOWE PEERS BLINDLY THROUGH A THICK MIST, THEN DISAPPEARS INTO THE VAPOR.

Lumpy looks blearily at Roan. "We're almost at the end. I hope."

Though Roan knows it's a bad idea, he lets himself crumple to the ground. "I need to rest now. Just for a few minutes."

"No! We've got to keep going," says Lumpy. But once he's spoken the words, he collapses next to Roan.

Drifting into unconsciousness, Roan feels hands gripping him below the shoulders, pulling him to where the air feels safe and good. He drinks it in as the dark mists of slumber overtake him.

Stirred by the warmth of the sun, Roan groggily opens his eyes. Slowly, painfully, he sits up, his arm aching. Lumpy, beside him on a clump of speckled grass, wakes at the sound. A hundred yards behind them is the dead forest. Snow-capped mountains lie beyond.

"Thanks for pulling me out of that forest."

Lumpy smiles. "My pleasure. Just wish I could remember doing it."

"Well, what matters is that we're out."

Lumpy helps Roan up, and they have a look around. Just up a ridge is an old asphalt highway. Weeds have split its surface, and in the dried dirt scattered over the road, Lumpy points out an unsettling sign—hoofprints. Then Roan spots something worse: a sole tire track.

"Have you ever seen one of these?" Roan asks his friend.

"Motorcycle. I've only ever heard of one person having one."

Roan nods.

"You think it's him?"

"He must have found another one. All things come to those who serve the City."

"Which way do you think those tracks are going?" asks Lumpy.

Roan focuses his eyes on the tread mark, searching for any minute trace that will give him a clue. Then he sees it. Bits of soil thrown off by the tires. Roan's eyes follow their trajectory.

"We may be in luck. He's headed east."

"Still, he may have left some men to go the opposite way," Lumpy says, examining the hoofprints. "We have to get off the road and stay under cover."

They move to where a brush-covered ditch runs parallel to the road. Roan feels the cricket shift in his pocket. Using his good arm, he reaches in and brings it out. "Welcome back," Lumpy says to the insect. "I guess he was doing some kind of hibernation to get through those woods."

Whatever the explanation, Roan's relieved the cricket has survived. As he bends to set the precious insect down on the grass, the ground tilts and an icy wave sweeps across his whole body. He shivers. It's a snowstorm, he's trapped. Trapped, floating on frigid water, the snow falling, falling, falling…

"Roan!"

He opens his eyes. Lumpy's standing inches from him, looking anxious.

"You're sweating."

"I'm cold, the snow."

"You have a fever."

Lumpy takes his arm, and Roan cries out. "Don't, please, don't touch it!"

As Lumpy gingerly rolls back Roan's sleeve, they see his arm has grown huge and purplish.

"It's swelling," says Lumpy, alarmed. "I should have tried to get more poison out when I had the chance. Roan, I have to take your ring off."

Roan nods blearily. Lumpy slowly removes Saint's ring, every movement marked by Roan's labored breaths.

"Hey, it's not that bad," Roan says, his eyelids heavy.

"We need to get you help."

"I just need some rest."

"It'll have to wait." Lumpy looks far out in the distance. "There's some smoke. A village."

"Just sleep a little more...," murmurs Roan.

"No! We have to go now," Lumpy insists. Tucking the ring into one of his own pockets for safekeeping, Lumpy clutches his friend by the waist, and they begin their trek.

In a haze, Roan puts one foot ahead of the other, barely seeing the red-raw bark on the stick trees that shift in the breeze, or the ebony beetles whose thick webs span the spindly branches. Lumpy guides and coaxes him, always driving them on.


"How's the pain?" Lumpy asks.

Roan breathes heavily. In a haze, he glances down. His arm is swollen to twice its natural size.

"There is no pain," Roan murmurs.

Lumpy dribbles a few drops of water over Roan's parched lips.

Through the fog that shrouds him, Roan can see that Lumpy is afraid.

"Hang on, Roan, you've got to hang on till I get you there."

Roan's eyes waver as the white cricket sings to him. They settle on something in the distance.

"What is it?" Lumpy asks.

Something unusual stands twisted in the bracken behind some trees. Going to investigate, Lumpy pulls out what looks like a harness, roughly constructed, woven from the same red wood that surrounds them. He turns to Roan.

"Look. We can use this. Stay still and I'll get it around you."

Roan feels Lumpy bind the harness around his waist. He tries to focus, to concentrate on his breathing, but he can't.

"ROAN?"

STOWE IS HOLDING A LONG STICK, PROBING WITH IT INTO THE FOG.

"ARE YOU THERE? TAKE HOLD OF THIS. ROAN?"

"Stowe," Roan mutters.

Lumpy leans in close to his face. "Stay with me, Roan. Open your eyes. Roan, I'm gonna carry you."

Roan gazes at him, the face shifting into view. "Lumpy."

"I'm going on the other side of you to put my arms through the other straps. Stay awake, Roan, you gotta stay awake!"

Lumpy disappears from Roan's view. Then Roan feels a bump and he's lifted up, his weight on Lumpy's back, his legs dragging behind. They slowly start to move. Roan hears Lumpy's labored breathing as he drifts in and out of consciousness. Through red wood. Red trees. The goat-woman's forest. "Are you here?" he calls out to her.

But only Lumpy answers. "I'm here," he pants. "We're gonna be okay."

Roan's back is hot and wet from Lumpy's sweat. His eyes dully scan the stick trees, searching for the old creature, trying to summon her. Then Lumpy's voice bursts into the reverie. "Talk to me, Roan. Say something!"

"Red trees."

"You've seen them before?" asks Lumpy, his voice quavering with each heavy step. "Keep talking to me! Roan! Have you seen them before?"

"Yes," Roan mumbles.

"Where?

Roan drifts away.

Lumpy's voice calls him back. "Roan! Where?"

"In...in a dream."

Roan feels his body lurch as Lumpy stumbles, falling to his knees on the ground.

"Sorry, sorry." Lumpy mutters. "Are you alright, Roan?"

"Alright."

"I tripped, that's all. Everything's okay," Lumpy tells him, but he's slow to rise up again and, once straight, he stands without moving. "Are you with me, Roan?"

"With you."

Lumpy starts to plod ahead again, one step tottering after another.

A foul odor taints the air. "Smell..."

"You're right, something stinks. It's in front of us!" As Lumpy moves faster, the stick trees grow thicker, and Roan feels Lumpy push through deepening clusters of web.

"Look, Roan, look at it!"

Roan blinks his eyes at a strange vision. Before him is a lake so enormous he can't see the other side of it. Its waters teem and bubble, brackish brown. The only sign of life is crusted yellow seaweed. The lake he saw in his dream.

Roan's fevered eyes follow the shoreline. There are buildings wavering in the distance, set far back from the shore.

"Do you see the town?" Lumpy asks.

Roan's eyelids flutter.

"Keep breathing," Lumpy begs.

But it seems easier not to. Easier to just close your eyes. But something crawls on Roan's cheek. He lifts one eyelid and glimpses something white. The cricket. It chirps, and Roan involuntarily sips in some air.

"Just another half-hour or so. Don't worry, we're almost there."

Lumpy trudges forward. Roan drifts in and out until suddenly the footsteps stop. Roan feels himself being set down on hard ground.

Someone is shaking him. "Roan, Roan! Talk to me, come on, please!"

But Roan's eyes won't open.

"Please don't die on me, please!"

The cricket creeps across Roan's brow. Roan's eye opens a little. He sees Lumpy's face.

"We're here, Roan, we're here!"

Roan can see red-gray clouds looming large overhead.

"Roan, listen to me. I have to leave you here. If they see me, they'll think you're infected. They've got to help you, it's your only hope."

A tremor begins in Roan's hand, spreads up his arm, and into his chest. Soon his whole body is convulsing.

In the distance, he hears Lumpy's voice. "Roan...Roan!"

All at once, Roan is weightless. A cloud of tiny stars flickers around him. He is part of the sparkling ether, floating high above himself. Everything is glowing, but through the brilliance he can see the village, see himself and Lumpy, see a man in a watchtower shouting down at them.

"Identify yourself!"

"I found him caught in Nethervines," Lumpy calls up, his face hidden by his hood. "Take pity on him."

"Why should we?"

"He told me he has gold."

"We got a healer."

"Take him and get rich," yells Lumpy as he escapes back into the forest.

Two tall men cautiously emerge from the gates, holding battle-axes. They lean over Roan's body and pick him up. Roan's ether-self drifts after them, following them through the gates, down a street, into a house with deep blue ceramic tiles.

# tHe BLesseD viLLaGe

all thanks to governor brack.
his people were poor but now
they're rich. they despaired but
now they have hope. all thanks
to governor brack.
—Lore of the storytellers

Through the bright, flickering light, the room shim-
mers in Roan's ether-eyes. Even the faces of the people
glow. A young woman motions the two tall men forward. "Put
him on the bed."

The man with the beard speaks respectfully to her as they lay
Roan's body down. "I wasn't sure, Miss Alandra, but I was thinking this might be the one you was telling us to look out for."

"You did well. Thank you."

"His finder said he had some gold on him. No telling if it's
true or not, Miss Alandra, but if it is..."

She gives him some coins. "For your trouble. If there's any
more I'll let you know."

Roan hovers close to her, studying her face. Why does her voice sound so familiar?

"We'll go make our report to Governor Brack now."

"Please. No need to keep him waiting."

Roan watches the men leave. The woman called Alandra touches his wrists, feeling the pulse on both sides of his body.

"The toxin's spread through your abdomen and to your brain. Your heart and lungs are weak but still functioning."

Roan can see that his eyes are closed. Why is she speaking to his unconscious body?

"You're not what I expected."

The white cricket crawls out of his pocket and onto the woman's hand.

"Wonderful," she sighs. "Hello." It's obvious she's awestruck by the insect. Setting it delicately aside, she lifts a sharp blade and cuts off Roan's shirt. As she removes his shoes and pants, his knife and coins fall from their hidden pocket. She picks them up, lifts a floor stone, and deposits them inside, along with his pack and hook-sword. She then turns her attention back to Roan, placing her hands over his swollen blue-black arm. She doesn't touch the arm but glides just above, her eyes closed. Then, combining powders and infusions, she gently smoothes them into a wet, gray-green clay, in which she encases Roan's arm.

Alandra slides a tray out from beneath the bed. Hundreds of needles rustle. She selects a very long, thin one, thrusting it an inch into Roan's stomach. The needle instantly begins to vibrate.

Roan, until this moment entirely free of sensation, is startled by a stabbing pain.

With deft precision, Alandra inserts more needles, from the soles of Roan's feet to a spot between his eyes. When she's done, a forest of wildly quivering needles juts out from his skin.

Roan's ether-body quivers in the same frantic rhythm.

Next, Alandra reaches into a jar filled with what look like Nethervine thorns. Plucking one out with tweezers, she drops it into a mortar and methodically crushes it into a powder. Adding various substances and a few drops of a clear liquid, she creates a small tablet that she places under Roan's tongue.

A singular fatigue envelops Roan as he drifts along with Alandra into a room full of jars. This must be her apothecary. Sliding her fingers to the back of a high shelf, she lifts out a small, inconspicuous vessel. Pinching a tiny amount of the substance inside, she nestles it on her tongue and swallows. She settles into a chair and closes her bright green eyes. After a few deep, long breaths, she is still.

Suddenly heavy, Roan is slowly drawn back over his own resting body. He descends, weary, folding back into himself. Now one.

At first, the searing pain is unbearable. But soon the medication radiating out from under his tongue puts him to sleep.

TALL PILLARS AND HIGH CONCRETE WALLS. EMPTY SIDEWALKS STRETCH FOREVER.

A MISSHAPEN MAN MADE OF CLAY CRIES OUT AS HE SINKS UP TO HIS WAIST IN THE CEMENT SIDEWALK.

"I'M DROWNING!" THE CLAY MAN CALLS. HE HEARS A MUF-FLED VOICE BEHIND HIM, BUT HE CANNOT TURN TO SEE THE SPEAKER.

"YOU MUST PULL YOURSELF OUT."

"WHAT DO I DO?"

"QUICKLY. THERE ISN'T MUCH TIME. RAISE YOUR HAND."

HE LIFTS HIS LARGE, AWKWARD HAND. THE UNSEEN FIGURE'S HAND EXTENDS TO HIS.

"PRESS AGAINST MY PALM."

"IT HURTS!" THE MAN GASPS, AND JERKS AWAY.

"GOOD, YOU'RE STILL ALIVE. TRY AGAIN. NOW!"

THE CLAY MAN SHEDS TEARS OF EXERTION AND ANGUISH BUT SLOWLY DRAWS HIMSELF UP AN INCH.

I AM THE CLAY MAN, ROAN THINKS. THE CLAY MAN IS ME.

"KEEP WORKING. YOU HAVE A LONG WAY TO GO."

Awake but very weak, Roan tries to open his eyes.

"Rest," Alandra whispers to him.

"Will he live?" asks a voice.

Prying one eye open a crack, Roan sees a middle-aged man dressed in black through the blur of his lashes.

"I don't know yet, Governor Brack," Alandra answers.

"Did he say who he was?"

"He hasn't regained consciousness."

She's lying to him. She must not trust this man, Roan realizes. Or does she have plans for me she doesn't wish to share?

"Where's the gold?" asks the governor.

Alandra shakes her head. Brack shrugs. "That companion of his likely poisoned and robbed him, then brought him to us in a fit of remorse."

"Perhaps."

"How will he pay for your time?"

"The season is on, and spare hands are hard to find. I'll use his labor once he's well enough."

"If he balks," the governor mutters, "we'll throw him in the lake."

Alandra glares at him. "I'm not saving him just to see him dissolved."

Brack takes her hand. "Forgive me. My concern is for the community. We need you, Alandra. The children are your priority. It disturbs me to think an outsider might distract you from your duties."

"Thank you for your concern."

Roan watches Alandra close the door after Brack and take a long, deep breath. When she returns to Roan, she takes his wrists in her hands.

"Your pulse is growing stronger."

She reaches into his mouth and takes his tongue in her fingers. Roan gags and his eyes fly open.

"Don't move!" Alandra warns, examining his tongue. "Good, there's some color. You've improved already. The needles have done their work."

Within a few minutes, Alandra has extracted all the needles, and she supports Roan as he sits up unsteadily.

"Where I come from," he says hoarsely, "needles are used for sewing cloth, not people."

"Ah, and where is that?"

Cautious, Roan answers vaguely. "The other side of Barren Mountain." He looks around and notices that the room is lit with lamps. Here is something he's only read about. Excited, he asks, "You have electricity? Light bulbs?"

"We have a generator. And solar power," she smiles. "My name's Alandra, what's yours?"

"Korr," Roan replies warily.

"Hmm, interesting name."

The more he hears Alandra's voice, the more certain Roan is that he knows it. Where had he met her? Could it have been in Kira's village? But an even more burning question demands an answer. "Where is my friend?"

"He left you at our gates and fled, some would say like a criminal."

Roan shakes his head. "No, he...he hasn't been around people very much. Shy."

"You're lucky he brought you when he did. Another few hours, and I couldn't have saved you. As it is, you still need a lot of rest, and your arm mold must be changed every two days."

"I can't stay here. I have to meet someone."

"Your appointment will have to wait. The longer Nethervine poison stays in your body, the more powerful it becomes. If even the smallest amount is left unchecked, it will reassert itself and death will follow. My treatment takes time. But it will remove all the toxins from your body."

The woman has saved his life, after all. And Roan feels too weak to do much now. He'll stay a few days, then slip away as soon as he's strong enough.

As if she could hear his thoughts, Alandra smiles. "You'll need a month to fully heal. Any less, and the poison will kill you. There's an extra bedroom here you can stay in."

"I need to find my friend."

"You think he's still out there?"

"I know it."

She considers. "I'll take him some food and water."

"When?"

"Now. If you promise to rest."

"You don't know how to find him."

"There's only one place he can hide. In the forest of stick trees. I'll sing to him and leave the sack hanging from a branch. If he's there, he'll find it."

"You could be followed. He wouldn't like that."

"I'm the healer here. I move freely. There are herbs and roots to gather. No one questions my activities. Do you promise to rest?"

"Yes," agrees Roan, although he is determined to sneak out for a look around as soon as she leaves.

Alandra picks up a small jar and dips a spoon into it. Propping up his head, she holds out a spoonful of gray-brown material for Roan.

"Open up," she orders.

"That looks like dirt."

"Does it?" she says, putting it in his mouth. "Swallow slowly."

It is slightly acrid but leaves no aftertaste.

"Any effect?"

"No, nothing."

"Here, let me help you lie back down."

"I'm not tired," Roan replies, and immediately falls into a deep sleep.

At daybreak, Roan is awakened by pokes and prods.

"He's alive, isn't he?"

"Nope, he's deader than dead!"

Roan's eyes pop open, and his examiners shriek. There are several of them, none more than about six years old.

"Who are you?"

"We're Bub and Jaw and Gip and Runk and Sake," says Bub, the biggest, a round-faced boy.

"I'm Lona," says the smallest, a bright-eyed girl with dark skin.

"I'm Korr," Roan says, noticing that the children are holding thin brushes and cups filled with colors.

"Alandra says we can paint your arm mold," Lona tells him.

"Well, if she says so," Roan replies.

The children immediately descend on Roan's cast with bright pastes.

"Where do you come from?" Bub asks.

"There's a big mountain, a long way from here. I came from the other side."

"What's it like over that side?" asks Jaw, whose pearly little bottom teeth jut out.

"Nice. We have a hollow tree forest."

"Hollow trees! Are they tall?"

Six curious faces wait for the answer.

"Some are a hundred feet high. And so wide you can crawl up inside them."

Bub is skeptical. "You're making up stories," he accuses.

"No, it's true. Even my little sister went climbing inside our favorite. We called it Big Empty. We'd climb up with our friends and there was room for us all to sit on top. When it was clear, we could see miles away."

"How old's your sissy?" asks Lona.

"She'd be turning eight this year."

The children nod their heads knowingly. "They took her?"

Roan, startled, stares at them. "How did you know that?"

"'Cause that's what happens," says Lona. She sticks her finger in her cup and smears green paint on Roan's nose. Roan laughs, gets his thumb in the cup, and daubs her chin. In a moment, all the children are splattering paint on each other.

These children are special, Roan thinks. But no, it's that they're the first children he's seen since Longlight laughing and having fun. Then he notices something one of the children has painted on his cast. A circle sitting on an inverted triangle.

It's the same symbol little Marla drew in Saint's village. Before he can ask any questions, though, Alandra steps into the room, scattering the boys and girls and shooing them out the door. She hands Roan a towel, thick and soft, woven from a completely unfamiliar material.

"What's this made of?"

"Cotton. We trade for it."

"Cotton. I've read it about it. It must be expensive."

"Must be. Would you like a look at Fairview, our village?"

"Yes," says Roan eagerly.

From a closet, Alandra brings out a metal chair with wheels. Roan stares.

"Where did you get this?"

"As I said, we trade for things."

"With who?"

"Sit down. I don't want you on your feet yet."

Roan settles in the chair, and Alandra pushes him outside. The houses on her block are beautifully covered in ceramic tiles with glazes of dazzling hues. Each house has a small, immaculate garden festooned with flowers. Roan even admires the road itself, which is made of sparkling slate. Leaning back as Alandra rolls him along, he sees shiny solar collectors dotting all the rooftops and wires, connected by poles, hanging overhead. They carry electricity, he surmises. The whole community seems to glow.

As far as Roan knows, goods and technologies like these are only available from the City. Fairview must have strong connections there, maybe even connections to Saint. Those links don't bode well for Roan. He won't be safe here for long. He may already be in danger. The moment he's able, he'll flee.

Instead of an outdoor market, there are shops with big glass windows along the main street. Behind each window lie wonders beyond Roan's imagining. Electric bread toasters, eggbeaters, and other shining appliances that he's never even seen in books; all kinds of meats; clothes in the most amazing variety of fabrics and styles. There is an outdoor place where people sit drinking sparkling liquids from glasses or sipping from steaming, finely crafted cups. Roan's intrigued by their frilly clothing, which he can't imagine would be useful for anything but sitting at tables in order to drink, eat, and talk.

"You seem shocked," says Alandra.

"I've never seen anything like this. It's a different world."

"Same world, more extreme."

Two finely dressed young woman, each appearing about five months pregnant, saunter over to them. "Who's this, Alandra?"

"He's the one they found at the gates," says the other, lighting a thin cigar.

"His name is Korr," Alandra tells them, then singles out the one with the cigar. "How are you feeling, Isobel?"

"Fine," Isobel says, dragging deeply. "That remedy you gave me worked like a charm."

"It would work better if you put that out."

"Don't be a nag," Isobel says, blowing out a stream of smoke. She catches Roan staring at her.

"Don't tell me you don't approve either."

"Where did you get it?"

"From the store," Isobel replies, puzzled. She gives Alandra a look. "Cute. But odd."

"Would you like one, Korr?" asks her companion.

"He's too weak." Alandra looks pointedly at Isobel. "And remember, when you start your sixth month, you have to stop. That's in three days."

"I know the rules. That's why I'm chain-smoking now."

Continuing the tour, Alandra points out the building where water is purified. Smoke spews out of the plant's chimneys, and there's a steady hum from the generators inside. "Our water table's infected by the lake. Before we had clean water, our people were ill all the time."

In Longlight, the community used the stuff of nature to purify soil and water: porous stone, healing herbs, mineral compounds. Fairview's method of decontamination uses machines, apparently, adding more pollution to the land. Like much of what Roan sees here, it's strangely contradictory. Alandra points out a thick plume of smoke rising from a single tall chimney up ahead. "Another generator," she announces. "It's powered by the red stick trees near the lake. They grow fast and are rich in resin."

Roan faintly remembers Lumpy pulling him through those

trees, by the steaming lake. He hopes Lumpy is still out there, still safe. He needs to thank him for saving his life.

Roan wakes from his nap later that afternoon to find Alandra returning home with an empty satchel.

"Your friend ate every bit of food I left for him. The satchel was still hanging on the branch where I left it. Contents missing."

"That doesn't mean it was my friend who took it."

"He's made himself a crawlspace using a mossy pad for cover."

Roan eyes her. "You know where it is?"

She nods. "He knows what he's doing. Herders graze their sheep and cattle in that area, and peddlers often go through there. I even saw some signs that Blood Drinkers had been that way."

"I have to get to him!"

"Don't worry," Alandra says. "There was no sign of any struggle taking place. Another thing," she adds, "this friend of yours likes to eat bugs."

Roan leans in. "How do you know that?"

"There's a small termite hill there. I found legs and feelers scattered around."

Roan smiles. Lumpy's alive and feasting on his favorite cuisine.

# DIRt

taLes have been toLd of a dirt and
those who eat it. Let them waLk in
their dreams, if they wiLL. as Long as
they Leave the worLd to me.
　　——Lore of the storyteLLers

THE LONGER HE'S IN FAIRVIEW, the more Roan finds
himself consumed with questions. Alandra is young, at
most a year or two older than he is. She's a busy healer who
spends every waking moment looking after the residents. She
is gracious besides: readily agreeing to take provisions out to
Lumpy, making the snow cricket a little bed in a trinket box
and providing it with succulent grasses to nibble on.

But Roan can see that Alandra's taken on too much respon-
sibility. A great sadness seems to weigh on her, a dark cloud
that seldom lifts. She never questions Roan's past, though, so
he doesn't feel he can pry into hers, and his feelings for her are
tinged with uneasiness. She seems to be silently judging him,
and Roan is sure he's falling short of her mark. He longs for

the sympathetic ear of someone he trusts. The old goat-woman hasn't appeared to him since the day he arrived in Fairview. Nor have any of the other figures from his dreams. Have they abandoned him?

During the long hours Alandra's away from the house, Roan exercises to maintain his fitness, tensing and relaxing his muscles. He visualizes his martial arts movements, mentally perfecting his technique. His instincts tell him he won't be safe in this town for much longer. When the time comes, he has to be ready. At the end of his workout, he revels in the time he has to play his recorder, delighted to be teaching himself new melodies.

One morning, Roan takes a moment to examine Alandra's bookshelves. Most of the books in her library are concerned with medicine and healing, but there's some poetry and even a few volumes in a language he doesn't recognize. He's laboring over the words in one, trying to guess their derivation, when the sudden appearance of the well-fed man dressed in black thwarts his efforts.

"So, Korr, you're a reading man."

Brack, the governor of Fairview. What is he doing here? Roan has met him a few times before, during his wheel-arounds with Alandra. Although they've done little more than exchange pleasantries, Brack has barely managed to mask his antipathy toward Roan.

"Yes, I know how to read."

"Well, not many of you around, to be sure. Reading is on my list of important things to learn. Right under finding out who you are, where you're from, and why you're here."

Roan chooses his words carefully. "I'm from the other side of Barren Mountain."

"Yes, yes, I've heard that, but I'd prefer a more precise accounting."

Roan meets the man's gaze straight on. "My town is called Rainfall. We're governed by the Lee Clan."

"And why did you leave?"

"Our village has a tradition. When you turn sixteen, you go out on the road, see the world. Then, when you come back, *if* you come back, you are considered a man."

"So you're not a man yet."

"Exactly."

Brack scowls. "Have you settled your bill with Alandra yet?"

Roan's relieved to move on to other matters. "A bill hasn't been mentioned."

"We're a generous people here in Fairview, but we don't have much patience with freeloaders. Everyone pays their way, and if they don't, we have a place to put them."

"Once I'm out of this chair, I'll work until my debt has been paid."

"Thank you, Governor, but I can do my own bill collecting." Without either of them noticing, Alandra has made her way into the room and is eyeing Brack coolly.

"Forgive me, Alandra, I just wanted to be sure..."

Alandra smiles. "I appreciate your concern. Truly," she says. Roan doesn't miss the flush that crawls up the governor's face as she touches his arm.

Brack bows to Alandra, then nods curtly to Roan as he goes.

Once the door closes behind Brack, Roan can't stop himself from making a personal observation. "He likes you."

"Yes."

"He seems...old for you."

"In the early days, when Fairview was sacked, my parents were killed. I was left for dead. Brack found me and carried me to a hospital. They saved my life. When I came back to Fairview five years ago, he remembered me, took me under his wing. He hasn't gotten out of the habit. I'm like a daughter to him."

"That look he gave you wasn't exactly what I'd call fatherly."

"It's more complicated than you imagine," Alandra says with unexpected vehemence.

"It didn't seem that way."

She glares at him. "You have no right to talk to me like that."

Roan looks down at the floor. "I'm sorry. You're right. I just—"

"What?"

"I don't trust that man," Roan says without looking up. But after a moment, Alandra speaks with a softness in her voice.

"I appreciate your concern, Roan of Longlight."

Roan's jolted by surprise and fear. "How do you know my name?"

Alandra walks into her apothecary, indicating that Roan should follow. Wheeling through the doorway, he sees the shelves remain crammed with jars: jars tall and stout; jars in strange shapes, one like a turtle, another like a snail; jars translucent, opaque, and sparkling; jars filled with powders in a vast array of shades. Roan recognizes some of the powders, because Alandra's been feeding them to him for different purposes. One the color of cobalt to defeat the Nethervine poison; an amber one to heal his wound; a turquoise dust to strengthen him. Then, on a high shelf, he spots the small, nondescript jar of violet powder half-hidden behind a large, handsomely glazed container.

"That jar. May I see it?"

Alandra passes the jar to Roan. His hand dips, unprepared for how heavy it is.

"The weight doesn't match its size."

"It's very special."

Roan nods. "I saw you eat some of this."

Alandra can't hide her surprise. "When?"

"When I first came here."

"You were unconscious."

"Part of me was, and part of me wasn't. I can't explain what happened. But I saw you take this."

Alandra stares at him dumbstruck, and he knows. "You met me in the dream. You're a Dirt Eater. The goat-woman."

"My mentor taught me many things about soil and healing. But one of the most"—Alandra stops, searching for the right word—"*compelling* things she gave me is in the jar you're holding. Go ahead. Open it."

Roan removes the lid. He looks closely at the dark purple soil.

"Everything in my apothecary is dirt. This dirt comes from a place far from here, where a meteor fell over a century ago. Your great-grandfather discovered it."

"My great-grandfather had something to do with this?"

"He had everything to do with it. He was the first Dirt Eater."

A flurry of emotions surges through Roan. Did my parents know my great-grandfather was a Dirt Eater? They must have, Roan thinks. Did they believe I'd become one too?

"When we eat this dirt we are able to travel to the Dreamfield. I was lucky to have a mentor who was one of the disciples of your namesake."

Roan considers the information. A woman's face comes into his mind, and he says the name out loud. "Sari. Sari is a Dirt Eater."

Alandra nods.

At once, everything clicks into place for Roan. "Sari found you in the hospital. She trained you and then sent you back to Fairview. Sari is the mountain lion, isn't she?"

"Yes."

"There's still so much I don't understand. Tell me, why can I go to the Dreamfield without eating the dirt?"

Alandra hesitates. Roan finds her expression hard to read, but the hint of resentment in her voice is unmistakable.

"There has never been a Dreamwalker like you. You go without the dirt, without training, without struggle, without knowing anything at all."

Alandra's words hammer at Roan. He's desperate to learn more. "How long have there been Dreamwalkers?"

"As long as there have been dreams, or so the myths say. But the art was lost. The first person to recover it was Roan of the Parting, your great-grandfather. Still, we are all bound to the dirt. Somehow, though, he had faith you would come."

"How?"

"No one knows how. We just know you are the one he foresaw."

"What about my sister?"

"I've told you all I can for now."

Roan bristles. "Why won't anyone tell me what's going on? I need to know!"

Alandra stiffens. "A little knowledge in the hands of the ignorant is a dangerous thing."

"Who are you to judge me?"

She glares at him. "Have no fear, Roan of Longlight. I would not presume. But I agree with the assessment of those who do. Your attitude proves you're not ready."

"If I'm ignorant, it's because I was kept that way. I have shown nothing if not a willingness to learn."

"Yes, and everything depends on it. Sari believes in you; I pray she's right."

Alandra pinches some dirt from her jar and inserts it between her gum and cheek. She wheels Roan into the living area, then sits down beside him on a soft chair.

"In a few minutes, I'll become drowsy, and then I'll be there. In the Dreamfield. You need to close your eyes."

"I've gone there with my eyes open, too. I've seen the lion that way, I've heard the rat speak to me. But it was never under my control. They just appeared."

Alandra nods, a look of grudging awe on her face. "Follow the line of light from the soles of your feet up your legs, through your spine, and out the top of your head." She taps a slight indentation in the center of his skull. "Go with the light out of this spot. And keep your eyes closed. That way, if anyone comes into the room, they'll think we're napping."

Roan closes his eyes and lets his attention drift down to his feet. He breathes softly through his nose, as if drawing some unseen energy up from the floor. Then, like the first flames from a smoldering fire, a column of light slowly rises. Up his legs, merging at his pelvis, shooting through his back and neck and head. A hole opens at the top of his skull and, as the light pillars out, Roan's consciousness flies with it.

# the dreamfield

creatures of wonder and mystery. if
only a few of the tales were true. but
i've never seen a snow cricket and
i'm betting neither have you.
——Lore of the storytellers

SMOKE FILLS HIS LUNGS. EVERYWHERE ROAN LOOKS, HOUSES ARE ON FIRE. WALKING IS AWKWARD. BENDING TO RUB HIS LEGS, HE SEES THEY'RE MADE OF CLAY. SO ARE HIS HANDS. IN FACT, HIS WHOLE BODY IS MADE OF IT.

"ALANDRA!" HE CALLS. NO RESPONSE. ROAN'S VOICE FEELS THICK AND STRANGE IN HIS THROAT.

"ALANDRA!" HE SHOUTS AGAIN, HIS VOICE BOOMING ALONG THE EMPTY ROAD. THE ROOF ON A HOUSE COLLAPSES, SENDING A SHOWER OF SPARKS INTO THE AIR. ROAN IS UNEASY IN HIS BIZARRE, UNWIELDY BODY. HE SITS DOWN TO REST, BARELY GLANCING AT THE HUGE WHITE STONE THAT SERVES AS HIS SEAT. THEN IT MOVES AND HE FALLS TO THE GROUND. THE STONE IS A GIGANTIC SNOW CRICKET THAT IS NOW CLAMBERING DOWN A

ROUGH TRAIL THROUGH A THICKET SO DENSE THAT THE BRANCHES ETCH ROAN'S CLAY SKIN AS HE FOLLOWS IN PURSUIT.

IN THE DISTANCE, SOMEONE IS SIGHING, AND THE CRICKET LEADS HIM TO THE SOURCE. ENTANGLED IN A MORASS OF SHARP SPINES IS THE GOAT-WOMAN: ALANDRA. THE SPINES PIERCE HER, JUTTING THROUGH HER HANDS, HER ARMS, HER FEET. THREE BARBS PUNCTURE HER LIPS, PINNING THEM TOGETHER. ROAN CAN SEE THE PAIN IN HER EYES.

TRYING TO CLEAR THE THISTLES THAT SURROUND HER, HE BREAKS OFF A SMALL PIECE OF BRANCH. ANOTHER GROWS IN ITS PLACE, WITH TWICE AS MANY THORNS. SO INSTEAD ROAN BENDS THE BRANCHES BACK, THEN WEAVES THEM SECURELY TOGETHER.

IT'S SLOW, METICULOUS WORK. FINDING THE RIGHT BRANCHES, FITTING THEM TOGETHER, LETTING THE SPINES LOCK ON EACH OTHER TAKES ALL HIS CONCENTRATION. BUT GRADUALLY HE MANAGES TO FREE ALANDRA FROM A LARGE SECTION OF THE FORBIDDING PLANT.

IN THE INTENSITY OF HIS LABORS, HE HAS FAILED TO NOTICE THE FAINT GREEN AURA THAT HAS NOW GROWN TO SURROUND HIM. HE LOOKS AT IT CURIOUSLY, BUT A SIGH FROM ALANDRA DRAWS HIM BACK TO THE MOST CHALLENGING PART OF HIS TASK. "I'M GOING TO TAKE OUT THE SPINES NOW, ALANDRA. ARE YOU READY?"

THE FIERCE LOOK IN HER EYES INDICATES ASSENT. ROAN PAINSTAKINGLY LIFTS A BRANCH, AND WITH STEADY FORCE EXTRACTS THE THREE SPINES FROM HER LIPS. THE MOMENT THEY'RE REMOVED, HER WOUNDS HEAL.

NEXT ROAN PULLS OUT THE SPINES THAT PENETRATE HER FEET, HER CALVES, HER CHEST, HER HANDS. AND AGAIN, TO HIS GREAT RELIEF, THE WOUNDS HEAL INSTANTLY.

WITH HIS CAUTIOUS HELP, ALANDRA STEPS AWAY FROM THE BRAMBLES, TOUCHES BOTH FEET ON THE GROUND AND TOPPLES. ROAN LOSES HIS BALANCE AS HE TRIES TO CATCH HER, AND THEY ROLL LIGHTLY ONTO THE MOSS.

THE OLD GOAT-WOMAN LAUGHS UPROARIOUSLY, SO BOISTEROUSLY SHE'S SLAPPING HER KNEES, TEARS FORMING IN THE CORNERS OF HER EYES. ROAN CAN'T HELP BUT CHUCKLE TOO. EVEN THE GIANT CRICKET'S AFFECTED, WAVING ITS FEELERS. AFTER A LONG WHILE, THE GOAT-WOMAN'S EYES NARROW.

"YOU HAVE AN AURA."

ROAN LOOKS AT HIMSELF. THE COLOR'S INTENSIFIED.

"YOU RELEASED IT IN YOURSELF WHEN YOU RELEASED ME. IT IS A PROTECTIVE BARRIER." SHE CLOSES HER EYES FOR A MOMENT, AND SUDDENLY SHE IS GLOWING GREEN AS WELL. "NEXT TIME IT WILL BE THAT EASY FOR YOU, TOO."

"WHY WERE YOU CAUGHT IN THE BRAMBLE?"

"PARTLY FOR YOUR INITIATION——TO WALK WITH COMPLETE FREEDOM IN THE DREAMFIELD YOU MUST GAIN AN AURA. BUT IT WAS ALSO A STEP IN MY ONGOING PROCESS."

"AND WHY AM I CLAY?"

"BECAUSE YOU'RE GESTATING. YOU WILL GET YOUR DREAM FORM ONE DAY. WHEN YOU'RE READY."

HER HEAD SNAPS AWAY SUDDENLY. "THE CRICKET'S MOVING!" ROAN FOLLOWS AS FAST AS HIS AWKWARD CLAY LEGS CAN

CARRY HIM, STAYING CLOSE TO ALANDRA, WHO SCAMPERS ON HER DELICATE HOOVES.

PAST THE LONG BROKEN TRAIL, THE LANDSCAPE IS DOTTED WITH SMOOTH RED TERMITE HILLS, EACH AROUND FIVE FEET HIGH. THE TERMITES SCURRY ABOUT THEIR BUSINESS, CRAWLING ALL AROUND A SLEEPING FIGURE.

"LUMPY!" ROAN MOVES AS QUICKLY AS HE CAN TO ROUSE HIS FRIEND.

"YOU COULD TRY WAKING HIM FOREVER AND NOTHING WOULD HAPPEN. IT WAS YOUR LONGING THAT BROUGHT HIM HERE."

"I'M WORRIED ABOUT HIM," ROAN SAYS. "THE FORGOTTEN MADE A SALVE TO EASE HIS PAIN, BUT IT WAS LOST IN THE NETHERVINES."

SUDDENLY THE CRICKET'S SHELL BURSTS OPEN, REVEALING TWO ELEGANT, TRANSLUCENT WINGS. ROAN AND ALANDRA WATCH FASCINATED AS THE WINGS WHIR, MOVING SO FAST THEY BLEND IN INVISIBLE MOTION. THE CRICKET RISES FROM THE GROUND, THEN HOVERS ABOVE THEM. THEY RAISE THEIR ARMS, EACH GRASPING ONE OF THE HUGE INSECT'S HARD LEGS. SOON THEY ARE SOARING.

ROAN LOOKS DOWN. BEHIND ARE FAIRVIEW AND THE RED STICK TREES; BEFORE HIM THE TOXIC LAKE'S MURKY WATERS ARE BEGINNING TO CLEAR. IN MOMENTS THEY'RE AT ITS FAR SHORE. OVER LAND AND JAGGED HILLS, STEEP CLIFFS AND NARROW ROCKY LEDGES, THE ENTIRE LANDSCAPE IS IMPRINTING ITSELF ON HIS MIND, EVERY CREVICE AND PATHWAY OUTLINED, EVERY OBSTACLE OBSERVED.

PASSING OVER A GIANT CHASM, ROAN IS ASTOUNDED ONCE AGAIN TO SEE SOMETHING HE HAS ONLY OBSERVED IN PICTURES: A LUSH GREEN FOREST WITH HEALTHY, TOWERING TREES THAT STAND TALL AND STRAIGHT, SO CLOSE TOGETHER HE CAN SEE SQUIRRELS LEAPING FROM ONE TO THE OTHER. LITTLE RED AND BLACK BIRDS DART THROUGH THE BRANCHES, BRILLIANT AGAINST THE VERDANT FOLIAGE. ROAN AND ALANDRA MARVEL AT THESE WONDERS AS THE CRICKET GRADUALLY DESCENDS UNTIL IT HOVERS SO THAT THEY MAY SET FOOT ON THE SOFT, RICH HUMUS. THE FRAGRANCE OF HEALTHY GREEN FIR IS INTOXICATING. IT'S A SCENT SO NEW, SO FRESH, SO DELICIOUS THAT THEY BOTH FEEL GIDDY.

ALANDRA, THE OLD GOAT-WOMAN, SMILES. "THANK YOU."

"WHY ARE YOU THANKING ME?"

"FOR THE POWER THAT BROUGHT US HERE."

ROAN CAN BARELY GRASP HER LAST WORDS BEFORE SHE FADES.

When Roan's eyes open, he sees Alandra standing by the window, stretching her arms.

"Be careful for the first ten minutes or so," she says. "You'll feel half here, half there. It's easy to lose your balance after you've traveled freely in the Dreamfield. You need time to adjust to being back." She notices the little white cricket sitting on Roan's shoulder. She leans close to it and whispers, "Thank you." The cricket's antennae flutter. "Now we know where we must go."

"Do you think that place was real?" Roan asks.

"Yes, I'm certain of it. But we have another task to complete first. A new group of children have arrived at the Home. I think you should meet them."

"Will Lona and Bub and the others be there?"

"That's where they live."

Roan hasn't seen the children since the day they painted his cast. Their faces and voices resonate in his mind, and he still wonders if there's more to them than meets the eye.

As Alandra wheels Roan toward the school, she explains that it's a residence as well, the place where all the children of Fairview live. From time to time, children from nearby villages are brought there too.

The Children's Home is a tall, ungainly house painted powder blue. Swings, slides, and climbing apparatus cover the huge front yard. Children swarm everywhere on the immense playground. They're strong and active, full of spirit. Roan relishes the sound of so much laughter.

When Bub sees Roan roll up in his chair, he whoops with glee and charges toward him.

"Korr! Korr!"

Other children follow, crowding around Roan, jostling for his attention. Soon Mrs. Fligg, every inch the jolly matron, bustles over to them. "So this is the Korr we've been hearing so much about!" she exclaims, shaking Roan's hand heartily. "It's about time we met. Welcome, Korr. My little darlings have told me all about you. Sweeter than sugar, aren't they!" She laughs merrily, pulling Lona close to her and giving her a big hug and a kiss. Lona holds out her hand. Mrs. Fligg chortles and puts a red candy into her palm. Then she nods to Alandra. "Come meet the new arrivals."

"No, no, stay with us, stay with us!" yells Lona.

"Korr will be with you in a minute," Alandra says. "He just wants to say hello to the new children." Mrs. Fligg leads them over to a jungle gym, where eight solemn children are perched on the bars.

"They're still adjusting to their new environment, coming from all those different towns. It's a wonder I can get the poor darlings to eat a thing." Mrs. Fligg looks up at the new arrivals. "Children, this is Alandra, our healer. And her friend, Korr."

Eight pairs of eyes drift somberly onto Alandra. But once the children see Roan, a startling transformation takes place. One by one, huge smiles appear on their faces. They pour off their roost and surround Roan. "I'm Dani!" a towheaded seven-year-old announces to Roan, grabbing his hand. A little boy, no more than five, hugs Roan's leg. "Play!" he shouts. The children beg for his attention, for his touch, and Roan's more than willing to give it.

The Fairview children join the tumult. Lona leads the stampede, jumping onto Roan's lap.

"Give us a ride! Pretty please!"

"Yes!" roar the kids.

Roan pumps the wheels of his chair more and more vigorously as shouts of "Faster! Faster!" ring in his ears.

Jaw and Bub and a few others decide to help. They get

behind Roan and propel the chair with all their might up the walkways, around the play yard, then up a steep ramp, which they struggle to ascend. Once at the top, as many as can fit jump on, and Roan and his passengers zoom down, shrieking at the top of their voices. At the bottom, the wheels hit a pavement stone and they all go flying, tumbling on the grass in a heap.

"Eeks, are you okay, Korr?" asks an anxious Bub.

Roan lets out an agonized groan that makes the children wince. Tears well up in little Lona's eyes. Then Roan rights the chair with his good arm and hoists himself back in. "What're you standing there for? Let's do it again!"

The kids cheer. Lona jumps back in Roan's lap and they're whisked at top speed over every inch of the playground. Finally, when everybody is utterly spent, they gather around the water fountain taking turns for a drink.

"Will you come back next day?" asks Lona.

"I'll try to," Roan replies.

"And you'll bring the chair?" pleads Bub.

"I'm only in it for a few more days."

"And then you're leaving us?"

"No, I'm here for another two weeks on account of the arm mold."

"Then we'll be leaving you," says Jaw.

"Where are you going?" asks Roan, puzzled.

"To our parents," Grip pitches in.

"I don't understand. Don't your parents live here?"

"No," answer several of the kids at once.

"Do they come for visits?"

The children laugh at his question. "How can they?" says Bub. "We never met 'em yet!" Roan is beginning to understand. This must be an orphanage. But then why do all of the children of Fairview live here?

"On Family Day," says Lona happily, "we all get to meet our moms and dads. Jabberwocky Wagon's coming to take us. All of us are going."

"The Jabberwocky Wagon?"

"It's how we get there," explains Jaw. "To our parents."

"It's the best of the best," says Lona, pointing to the circle-on-triangle symbol painted on Roan's cast. "And you won't believe what it has inside."

Alandra speaks up, her face expressionless. "Korr and I have to go now."

The children grumble with disappointment. Then Mrs. Fligg calls them in for lunch. They shout good-bye and scramble to the house, racing to be first in line.

Alandra turns to Roan. "You have a way with them."

Roan smiles. He'll keep how he feels about the children to himself for now. "Yeh, they master, me slave," he says with a laugh, then, "You didn't tell me this was an orphanage."

Alandra winces a little at the question. "We have a different philosophy about parents and children in Fairview. Brack has convinced people that blood relationships are too painful. Better to cut them off early."

"But to give your children up—"

"We sell them," Alandra says flatly. "Our community's doing well, and the world needs children. That's what the governor says. The City is filled with rich couples who are barren, desperate for children of their own. Brack has guaranteed that these new parents will offer our children a good life."

"And bring wealth to the citizens of Fairview," says Roan, dismayed.

"Before Brack came to Fairview, it was ravaged. The people were starving, the buildings were ruined, the water was poisoned. His economic policies rebuilt this town. People are loyal to him. They do whatever he asks."

Roan can't hide his disfavor. "And when this group of children is sent for adoption, how long till the next crop comes along?"

"Times vary. Some prospective parents want infants, others want older children."

Alandra turns Roan's chair up a paved boulevard leading away from the Children's Home. Once they're a safe distance away, she speaks softly.

"It's a lie," she whispers. "A few children may find homes, but the majority are sent to laboratories for experiments. The lucky ones are killed, their body parts used to replace the aging organs of the Masters of the City. I've been waiting for you to come. We have to save these children, take them away from here."

Roan turns in his chair to see Alandra's face, to be sure she's serious.

"Please look straight ahead. Smile and nod as if I've said something amusing."

Roan faces front and forces a smile. It's easy to forget that for all the welcoming faces, they are not among friends. He wonders if it's the same in Kira's village. The only children he saw there were in some way disabled, perhaps rendering them unfit for sale. What strange fortune.

"I returned here five years ago at Sari's behest, to take on this trusted role in the community. For those five years I've been healer to the mothers and the children, keeping them healthy for the cursed commerce. It was easier to watch my parents die. At least then I was too young to do anything, I was helpless. But now that you're here, my ordeal is over. The time for change has come. If you hadn't fallen into the Nethervines, the operation would already be underway. But in a few days you'll be able to move freely and we can finally set the plan in motion."

"What plan is that?"

"To take the children to the place we saw in the dream."

"Alandra, we flew. How do we get fourteen children there?"

"We'll find a way."

# the attack of the
# blood drinkers

for seven years, the earth burned
and the flame unleashed a black fog
that choked the valleys of the great
nations and their people, starving,
perished. the dreamwalkers awoke
and it came to be that the fate of the
survivors was left in their hands.
—the war chronicles

WHEN ROAN AWAKES the next day, the wheeled chair is gone.

"You're ready to walk," Alandra announces. Though he's little unsteady at first, Roan quickly finds his feet again.

He wastes no time announcing his first objective. "Lumpy," he says to Alandra.

"Yes. The three of us have much to talk about."

Roan is surprisingly nervous as they approach the town gate. He's grown complacent and has come unprepared. He lowers his head, allows his body to look soft, weak, as if not fully recovered from his illness.

"Off again gatherin', Alandra?" calls out the gatekeeper.

"Yes, I have to put my patient to work."

As the gatekeeper gives him a curious look, Roan shadows his eyes as if from the sun and offers an easy smile.

"Good to get some fresh air, eh, fella? You look lots better than when we plucked you from the scrub out there."

"Yes," says Roan, "thanks to Alandra."

"She's something, ain't she? Don't know what we'd do without her."

At the sight of open country, Roan longs to break into a run. But after Alandra gives the gatekeeper a friendly wave, she sets the pace at an unhurried gait. They are two people on an easygoing stroll to pick some herbs.

"He's Brack's man, isn't he?"

"That's right."

"The second he closes those gates, he'll report to the governor where we're going."

Alandra links her arm through Roan's. "He'll report to Brack, and Brack will take no notice. Bringing a patient with me to pick herbs is something I do all the time. Nothing will seem more natural."

They amble until Alandra points to her empty satchel hanging from a tree branch.

She lifts an eyebrow. Roan grins. "Hey, termite eater!" he calls in a low voice.

"Roan!" Lumpy leaps out from his hiding hole. Seeing Alandra, he stops in his tracks, covering his face. Alandra can't help but smile.

"I fed you for almost a month, and that's the thanks I get?"

"Don't worry, Lumpy, she's okay," Roan informs his friend. He wraps his arms around him. "Thanks for bringing me here...and for waiting." Roan lifts Lumpy into the air, both of them startled and pleased by the spontaneous display of affection.

"Guess you've recovered!"

"Not quite," explains Alandra. "Another few days in the arm mold before we set him free. I hope you don't mind."

"Not so long as you keep bringing me those berry cakes."

Alandra holds out a stuffed-full satchel for him. "There are more for you in here, plus some tools you might find useful."

Lumpy digs through the bag and pulls out a jar. Opening it, he sniffs, and his eyes open wide. "Salve."

"I'm working on something to heal your skin, but at the moment, this is the best I can offer. Let's put some on you now," Alandra offers.

"You're one of the healers the Forgotten told me about," Lumpy says, his face filled with respect. Alandra nods and begins to rub the cream on his arms, neck, and face. Lumpy takes off his shirt and pulls up his pant legs, and Roan applies the salve to his friend's back and legs. While they finish, Lumpy hugs Alandra gratefully.

"So is this where you sleep?" asks Roan.

"No, just one of many hiding holes." Lumpy leads them to some rocks set on mossy ground. "Here's home," he says, slipping his fingers under the moss. Lifting it like a blanket, he reveals a hollowed-out area below.

"It may look rough, but believe me, I'm happy to have it. These woods are scary."

"Marauders?" Roan asks. "I don't suppose robber bands could resist a place like Fairview."

"Fairview is under the protection of the Friends," says Alandra.

Roan and Lumpy exchange a nervous look.

"I haven't seen a Friend," reports Lumpy, "but I have seen plenty of Blood Drinkers. Mainly they lurk around at night, scouting. When I hear them coming, I raft out onto the lake."

"You made a raft?" Alexandra asks excitedly.

"That water'll burn most things it touches, but the stick trees are impervious to it. And they float. So I wove some together. When I'm out on the raft, the Blood Drinkers can't sniff me out. That stink'd mask anything. And even if they could, they wouldn't dare step in the water. So it's pretty good cover."

"The smell must be hard to take."

"Breathe it in deep a couple of times and you get used to it quick."

"How long would it take you to make three rafts, each big enough to hold four or five children and one or two of us?" Alandra asks.

"Are you serious? What's this about?"

"An escape. How does a week sound?"

"I might be able do it if those Blood Drinkers weren't lurking around."

"Then you'll need some help." Alandra whistles, and from behind rustle of branches, a smiling figure emerges.

"Lelbit!" yells Lumpy, rushing over to her. She takes his hand and puts it on her heart. Roan looks questioningly at Alandra.

"She was sent by the Forgotten to watch over you."

"It was *you* who pulled us out of the poison forest. You built the harness!" Lumpy exclaims.

Lelbit shrugs humbly.

"Why didn't you let me know you were there?" Lumpy asks.

"Her ability to protect you would have been compromised if her presence was known," says Alandra. "But our plans have changed. Those rafts need to be made before the truck comes for the children."

While Roan collects the herbs that are their cover for having left Fairview, Alandra explains the situation. Time is short, but with Lumpy and Lelbit's help, success now seems possible.

In the burgeoning heat of mid-spring, Roan and Alandra prepare for the escape. If they are discovered, they know the offense will reap a terrible punishment. They fill large water sacks, stitch child-sized rucksacks and pack them with bedding and food. Roan creates a map based on the terrain he saw in the flying dream. Together, he and Alandra estimate the distance they need to cover. Roan's tension builds with every passing day. An innocent knock on the door fills him with apprehension. A simple question from a shopkeeper makes his adrenaline surge. If they're found out, Lona and the rest of the children will die. They cannot fail.

This is not the only burden weighing on Roan. He finally feels he knows Alandra well enough to ask for an answer. "Why, from the time I first started dreaming, have you, Sari, and the others kept my sister from me?"

Alandra sighs. "The Masters of the City have Stowe. Some Dirt Eaters control her. The Turned, we call them. Collaborators with the City during the wars. It was the Turned who discovered Longlight, then revealed the location to their masters. The City sent Saint to capture both you and Stowe. He betrayed them by keeping you. Now they're using Stowe to find you. The power each of you possesses is formidable, but you and Stowe together would be unstoppable."

"Isn't there some way to get her out?"

"Even if you did manage to find her without the City knowing, she'd expose you. Then they'd do the same thing to you as they're doing to her. Roan, your sister has changed. Right now, she's one of them."

"What have they…"

"They've awakened her to her adult power. When that's done to a child, a terrible negative force is unleashed. The person becomes a distortion of who they are, of what they might have become."

"Can she be turned back?"

"That may be possible one day, but for now, no. We would compromise everything we've struggled for. But maybe you're ready to see where she is. It might help you understand. Come," says Alandra.


ROAN IS IN A CREVICE. HIGH WALLS ON EITHER SIDE, ABOVE HIM SKY. THE WIDE ROAD HE STANDS ON IS CONCRETE, MUCH OF IT BROKEN AND TURNED UP IN HUGE SLABS. IN FRONT OF HIM SITS THE BROWN RAT.

"IF YOU REVEAL YOURSELF TO HER, IT WILL BE THE END OF YOU, OF HER, AND OF EVERYTHING THAT LONGLIGHT HOPED FOR," THE RAT SAYS TO ROAN.

"WHO ARE YOU?" ROAN ASKS.

"I AM MANY AND FEW." THE RAT LOOKS AT THE GOAT-WOMAN. "ALANDRA. QUICKLY. BE CIRCUMSPECT."

THE OLD GOAT-WOMAN NODS TO ROAN. ATOP A METAL LADDER, ROAN GAPES AT THE SIGHT BEFORE HIM. A HUGE METROPOLIS, BUILDINGS TOWERING INTO THE SKY, CONSUMES THE HORIZON.

"THE AURA," SHE SAYS. "WE'LL NEED IT TO DISGUISE OURSELVES."

THIS TIME, ROAN ACHIEVES THE LUMINESCENCE EFFORTLESSLY.

"WATCH," SAYS ALANDRA AS SHE DRAWS HER GREEN AURA

BACK INTO HER SKIN, MAKING HER INDISTINGUISHABLE FROM HER SURROUNDINGS. "TAKE MY HAND."

ROAN'S CHARGED WITH SENSATION. "I SMELL DIFFERENT."

"BLEND WITH ME, WE ARE EARTH NOW. CAN YOU SEE THE BRIDGE INTO THE CITY?"

"YES."

"IMAGINE YOURSELF THERE."

THE AIR AROUND ROAN CONSTRICTS HIS CLAY BODY. BETWEEN HIM AND THE ENDLESS SKYSCRAPERS, THE DENSE AIR SWIRLS AND EDDIES INTO PATTERNS THAT APPEAR SO SOLID THAT ROAN REACHES OUT A HAND TO TOUCH THEM.

"WE ARE AT THE EDGE OF THE DREAMFIELD," ALANDRA EXPLAINS. "HERE WE CAN SEE THROUGH IT AND GET GLIMPSES OF THE ACTUAL CITY."

"ROAN! ROAN!"

ALANDRA NUDGES ROAN. "SHH!" SHE HISSES.

HE HEARS HIS NAME AGAIN AND AGAIN, COMING FROM DIFFERENT DIRECTIONS.

ALANDRA POINTS. "SHE DOESN'T KNOW YOU'RE HERE."

ON TOP OF BULGING LAMPPOSTS ARE SHINING SILVER SPEAKERS. AND FROM EACH ONE THE SOUND OF STOWE'S VOICE CALLS ROAN'S NAME. A STRANGE YELLOW LIGHT PROJECTS FROM BEHIND SOME TOWERS A FEW BLOCKS AHEAD. ALANDRA EXTENDS HER HAND AND SHE AND ROAN ARE DRAWN TO ITS SOURCE.

THEY ARE PRESSED AGAINST THE GLASS OF AN ENORMOUS DOME. AT FIRST THE LIGHT IS BLINDING. BUT SOON WHAT'S INSIDE BECOMES VISIBLE. IN A VAST CONCRETE MORGUE LIE

THE BODIES OF DOZENS OF CHILDREN. HOVERING OVER THEM, SURGEONS LACERATE AND EVISCERATE. HERE, A LITTLE GIRL, HER ABDOMEN EXPOSED, HER LIVER EXTRACTED. THERE, A BOY, SKULL OPEN, HIS BRAIN PROBED.

ROAN STRUGGLES TO CONTROL HIS RAGE AND GRIEF. HE QUIETS HIS BREATH WHILE ALANDRA CRIES SILENTLY.

THEN HE SEES HER. HIS SISTER, STOWE, HER HANDS DRIPPING WITH BLOOD, HER GAZE FEROCIOUSLY ENERGIZED. A TALL, THIN-NOSED MAN LOOMS OVER HER, LONG FINGERS STROKING HER HAIR.

ROAN WATCHES, DISTURBED. "WHO'S THAT WITH HER?"

"A TURNED ONE."

AT THAT MOMENT, THE MAN SNAPS HIS HEAD SKYWARD.

"PULL BACK!" ALANDRA CRIES, AND THEY ROLL JUST AS A HIDEOUS VULTURE-LIKE BIRD, RED BULBOUS SKIN HANGING OVER ITS BEAK, CASTS AN OMINOUS SHADOW OVER THEM. ALANDRA AND ROAN REMAIN PERFECTLY STILL.

"THIS WAY," SAYS THE RAT. AS THE DREAMFIELD COMPRESSES, ROAN FEELS HIS BODY COLLAPSE DOWN TO A MICROSCOPIC LEVEL AND DART BETWEEN MOLECULES IN THE EARTH. LOST IN THIS EERIE TIMELESSNESS HE IS UNCERTAIN OF HOW MUCH, IF ANY, TIME HAS PASSED. HE ONLY KNOWS THAT IN ONE MOMENT HE IS OF HUMUS AND WATER-SOAKED EARTH, AND IN THE NEXT HE EMERGES INTO DAYLIGHT.

FAR UP IN THE SKY, NOW JUST A SMALL STAIN AGAINST THE BLUE CLOUDS, HE CAN SEE THE SILHOUETTE OF THE GIANT BIRD.

"WE ARE SAFE NOW," SAYS THE RAT. "BUT IT WOULD BE WISE FOR YOU TO WAKE."

Alandra reaches across to Roan, anticipating his grief.

"Maybe one day, when you've fully come into your powers, it might be possible—"

But the clanging of alarm bells interrupts her, deflecting their concerns outward.

"Blood Drinkers are attacking the gates," Alandra informs Roan.

At the wall, the town guards are in position, loading their crossbows. Governor Brack's on the ground shouting orders. Leaving Alandra behind, Roan runs up the steep steps of the wall, hoping to get a better look at the enemy. He reaches the top and peeks over the rampart. On the ground below is an army of Blood Drinkers. Roan's heart sinks at the sight of the vile creatures. They are moving toward the wall in groups of three, each group carrying a ladder. He knows what they'll do to the people here, to the children, if they get past the walls. And he knows that he'll fight to protect them, even if it means exposing himself.

The guards aim their crossbows and fire, wounding several of the Drinkers. But this only seems to galvanize the predators. Seemingly oblivious to the pain, the Drinkers simply break off the arrows that strike them and continue their charge. The first ladder is placed up against the wall. Three Blood Drinkers begin climbing, one after the other, brandishing menacing knives that glint in the light. Roan leans over the wall, grabs the ladder, and pushes it backward. An angry hiss escapes the Blood Drinkers as they fall to the hard-packed ground below.

"Stand away!" orders Brack, who has climbed up beside Roan and holds a bottle on a stick. He places the stickend into a holder on the deck. "Move back!" he commands his troops, as he lights the end of the bottle. Sparks flare as the bottle rises to a great height, then explodes, releasing a huge cloud of yellow smoke into the sky.

Roan stares at the spectacle. He's heard of fireworks and rockets, and though the effect is exceptional, he wonders at its purpose. The Blood Drinkers certainly seem undeterred.

"Hold the vermin off another half-hour. That's all we'll need," Brack orders.

There is no time for Roan to figure out the meaning of Brack's words as more ladders strike the walls. The first are easily toppled, but in short order a dozen more are shoved against the walls.

Roan feels a clammy hand on his shoulder. A Blood Drinker, its sharpened teeth gaping, raises a knife. Roan dodges, kicking his attacker in the stomach. The Blood Drinker flies at him, but Roan shifts his weight and sends the predator sailing back over the wall, where it crashes into a ladder, smashing three of its comrades to the ground.

Many townspeople are helping with the fight, but they're hopelessly outnumbered by the pale monsters. It won't be long before the walls are breached and the massacre begins.

Then out of the stick-tree forest bursts a band of raiders, some forty strong. Their ears and lips are pierced with shards of rock, their bodies painted and armored. Brandishing battle-axes and spears, the raiders break the ladders, and hack, spear, or trample the Blood Drinkers with terrifying precision. In less than an hour, the slaughter is over.

The warriors scramble like beetles, collecting anything of value from the dead. The bloodied remains are dragged the whole distance to the lake, and the corpses are rolled unceremoniously into its acrid waters.

Roan watches the victors return through the gates. Staying low behind the battlement, he examines their faces closely. He's never seen any of them, but that doesn't guarantee they won't recognize him. If they're allies of the Friends, chances are they know his description; they may start asking questions. Observing Alandra leaving the area, Roan runs to catch up with her.

"Complicates things, doesn't it?" he asks her.

"It depends how long the raiders stay."

Suddenly the governor's upon them. "Alandra! There are wounded. Could you tend to them?"

"I'm on my way," she replies without stopping.

"I see you're a warrior," comments Brack, cutting in front of Roan so there's no escaping him. "Much more to you than meets the eye."

"Another week of assisting Alandra, and my account with her will be settled."

"So soon?" says the Governor. "Well, I'm sorry to hear that, Korr. You were a true asset in the battle."

"I only do what's required. Your town has been good to me, Governor Brack, and I regret that I must move on."

"I'm holding a banquet tonight to honor our champions, and you will be my special guest," says Brack. "No, no, don't protest, you were valiant today. So surprising. The ambassador himself will be attending. You must meet him."

"It's just...I'm not much good at such occasions," says Roan, hoping to beg off.

But it's clear the governor won't take no for an answer. "I insist," says Brack imperiously. "I'll see you at eight."

Roan worries as he watches the governor swagger off. If he doesn't go to the banquet, it will raise suspicion. If he does, he risks being identified. He can only hope Alandra knows how to navigate these dangerous waters.

# the ambassador's gift

on the night the birds disappeared
forever from the city, all the children woke screaming. and they
would not be comforted.
            —the book of Longlight

"I BOUGHT THIS FOR YOU to wear to the banquet," says Alandra.

Roan eyes the proffered package with trepidation. "Are you certain I should go?"

"Brack has reminded me twice to bring you. You revealed too much in that battle."

"Should I have done nothing?"

Alandra shrugs, conceding the point. "I've arranged an inconspicuous seat for you, well out of the raiders' view. Once the meal's over you can slip away." And she leaves him to change.

Roan opens the package. The suit inside is black and of a fabric so light and soft he's amazed it has any substance at all. Both the people of Longlight and the Forgotten fashioned beautiful clothes, but they had to be functional. These are something other, sensuous and unfamiliar. He doesn't trust them.

When Alandra emerges from her room, she is dressed in a flowing gown, her hair in braids and ringlets. Her lips are glazed with red. Roan stares at her dubiously.

"What's wrong?" she asks.

"You don't look like you."

She shrugs. "There's no choice. This is how the women of Fairview dress for these events."

Alandra guides Roan along Fairview's main street to the banquet hall. Roan feels awkward and unsure in his new clothes, but he blends in handily with the throng that meanders among the opulent marble pillars and gilded moldings.

"This building is Governor Brack's pride and joy," Alandra says in a low voice. "It's a monument to his resurrection of Fairview. He loves nothing more than to honor the high and mighty here."

There are about a hundred people in the hall. The most prominent citizens of Fairview, all dressed in their best, have come to express their gratitude to the raiders. The mercenaries themselves are washed and shaven, and Roan notes they've shucked their body armor for the occasion. It's clear they are welcome here.

Alandra escorts Roan to his spot. As promised, she has managed to seat him at a table far off to the side. "I told the governor your condition was still delicate and required it," she murmurs. Once Roan is settled, she goes off to her own place, next to Brack at the head table.

A puffed-up fellow in garish red and yellow silks monopolizes the attention of everyone at Roan's table. He clearly fancies himself a gourmet, predicting, from the appetizing scents that fill the room, what the great chef Yasmin has prepared. "No doubt," he postulates as he sniffs, "rack of lamb, and when it comes, smell it first! The meat will have been steeped in her ten-herb marinade. It's like nothing you've ever tasted. Glazed yams and potatoes, eight-succulent-vegetables-in-savory-sauce, and ah yes, seasoned breads." Though he cannot yet smell the desserts, he assures everyone that the most indescribably luscious pastries are certain to follow.

The man's pregnant wife is silent beside him, making no attempt to disguise that she's decidedly bored with her husband, the menu, and the event. She nods at Roan with feigned interest and he bows low, hoping to minimize his exposure.

Roan is happy to see the raiders are already deep into the wine, making toasts and singing bawdy songs. The more preoccupied they are with their revelry, the less chance there is one of them will cast eyes on him.

The assembly applauds as Governor Brack rises. With a solemn gesture, he calls for silence.

"Citizens, we are here tonight to honor our mighty protectors, who have once again fulfilled their obligations to us." At Brack's right, Alandra joins politely in the applause. "All of us in Fairview, gentlemen, offer thanks to you and to the

Friends you serve, from the bottom of our hearts. And now," continues Brack, "it gives me great pleasure to welcome the man who was my partner in making a miracle, the resurrection of Fairview: the ambassador, Mr. Harrow Wing."

Roan's body grows cold as a man in a feathered cloak and beaked helmet enters the room. It is the Bird Man, the one who visited Longlight, the one who made the demands his father would not meet. Roan hunches over his plate, the pulse in his heart throbbing.

"Dear friends, it does my heart good to see how Fairview has prospered. I look around me and recognize so many faces." Though he can't identify it, the voice makes Roan's hair stand on end. Expecting the worst, his eyes dart to the hall's exits. The ambassador sizes up the room. "Oh, Malaborn White, still cheating on your diet!" A plump man chuckles and wags his finger. Mr. Wing looks at a pregnant woman. "Alicia Keet, I see you're due again. You are prodigious. What's this, your fourth?"

Alicia smiles at him. "Fifth, Your Honor!" The crowd applauds appreciatively at both the ambassador's keen memory and the woman's fertility. The Bird Man ruffles his brilliant plumes and directs his gaze to Roan's table. Roan lingers over a sip of wine, the glass obscuring his face, and wishes the ambassador's voice wasn't so distorted by the mask.

"Can't miss you, Yorgan Max. We're birds of a feather, you and I!" The vain man in red and yellow silk rises to display his outfit. The ambassador hoots. "I mean, how could anyone forget that hideous suit!" The crowd guffaws as Yorgan Max slides back into his chair, stone-faced.

"I don't think I've had the pleasure of meeting you," the Bird Man says, pointing directly at Roan. "My, aren't you an elegant young man!"

Napkin in hand, Roan dabs the sweat from his upper lip as he slips his meat knife onto his lap.

"That's Korr, a visitor to Fairview," Brack interjects. "A bit of a barbarian, I'm afraid."

The Bird Man cocks his head to the right and to the left as all eyes turn toward Roan. "Come, come, dear Korr. Grace us with a glimpse of your handsome visage." As the ambassador lets out a high-pitched cackle, Roan's stomach lurches. Raven!

The Bird Man coos, "So young and so unique."

Lowering his napkin, Roan wraps his hand tightly around his meat knife.

"Korr. Couldn't you have searched your imagination for an alias with more flare, Roan of Longlight?"

Murmurs of "Longlight" sweep through the crowd like brushfire. Raven caws, "Take him!" and the raiders charge for Roan, while others scramble to block the exits. But Roan has his knife at the ambassador's throat before the first person screams.

The Bird Man raises his hand, indicating everyone should hold their position. Brack, however, lurches toward Alandra, taking her in his grip, the point of his dagger aimed at her heart. Alandra locks eyes with Roan, and Roan drops his knife, stepping away from Raven.

In that moment, the Bird Man turns, smashing a bottle over Roan's head. The last thing Roan hears as he topples amidst a shower of broken glass is Raven's mocking laughter.

Roan wakes in a dark chamber, head throbbing. The floor beneath him is cold and hard, gritty-greasy to the touch. The room stinks of human sweat, urine, and blood. He tries to stand, but the ceiling is too low, and as his head hits it, a paroxysm of pain travels the length of his spine. Roan feels the spot where the bottle hit. It's sore and damp with blood. On his hands and knees, he crawls along the walls until he locates a door. Locked.

Footsteps. Then the muffled sound of voices. The door swings open, and a bright light blinds Roan. He covers his eyes for a moment, but he can tell from their voices who it is. Governor Brack and Brother Raven, the Bird Man.

"Ah, safe and sound," chirps the ambassador. "I couldn't resist the temptation, but such sorrows Saint would have inflicted on our beloved governor had my blow killed you." He murmurs in Roan's ear. "The one you betrayed will soon be here to claim you." Brother Raven turns to Brack. "The physic has been procured." Circling, he slides his finger behind Roan's ear. "I shall relish your presence as a docile obedient Friend."

Feeder, Roan thinks. The men from Fandor.

Raven insolently brushes his wings in Roan's face, then, cackling, takes his leave.

Brack leans in for the last word. "I owe you an apology, Roan or Korr, whatever you call yourself. I thought you were a scrounger at first, but I was wrong. You turned out to be a gold mine. You can't imagine how lavish a reward they've offered for you."

"A step up from selling children, Brack?"

Brack spits in Roan's face, then turns to follow the ambassador, locking the door firmly behind him.

Enveloped again by darkness, Roan props his back against the wall. He wipes his face and takes in a long, deep breath.

THE SKY'S DEEP RED, DOTTED WITH DARK BLUE CLOUDS. FLOWING BENEATH ROAN'S CLAY FEET IS COARSE BLACK SAND THAT DRAWS HIM FORWARD, AS INEXORABLY AS A RIVER'S CURRENT. APPROACHING THE EDGE OF A GIGANTIC SANDFALL, HE FORCES HIMSELF NOT TO STRUGGLE AS IT STEADILY PULLS HIM INTO AN ABYSS.

WHEN HE OPENS HIS EYES, ALANDRA THE GOAT-WOMAN IS WAITING THERE FOR HIM.

"TELL ME WHERE THEY'RE KEEPING YOU," SHE INSTRUCTS ROAN.

"IT'S VERY DARK. NO WINDOWS ANYWHERE. A CEILING SO LOW I CAN'T STAND UP."

ALANDRA NODS. "THE WINE CELLARS. IT'S BRACK'S WORST JAIL."

"SAINT'S COMING."

"WE HAVE TO GET THE CHILDREN OUT BEFORE HE ARRIVES."

"DON'T WAIT FOR ME. TAKE THEM YOURSELF."

"NO. UNDERSTAND: IT DOESN'T WORK WITHOUT YOU."

THE FLOOR BENEATH THEM QUAKES AND CRUMBLES, AND ROAN FALLS IN A CASCADE OF SAND.

Roan's once again captive in Brack's cellars. He stretches, spreading his aching body across the floor. The cricket makes its music. Comforted, Roan gives himself over to the sound. And a new thought emerges.

When he was still in delirium from the Nethervine's grip, Roan had left his body. He'd seen himself and others, heard their conversations, all the while floating invisibly above. Could he free himself from his body again, this time consciously?

Roan settles against the wall, trying to picture the light around his body. At first there is only blackness. But he continues, taming his frustration with his breathing, creating a tunnel of breath-wind through his body. After what must be a hundred breaths, a spark flashes. Roan's mind leaps to grasp it, but it disappears.

A wave of despair washes over him. But then, relaxing into the sound of the cricket's song, he begins again, concentrating on the air filling his lungs. This time, a voice comes to him. His own? Someone else's? No matter.

"Do not reach for it. Let it be."

The blackness around Roan remains heavy and still. No movement. No light. But he stays with his breath. Waits.

Another spark.

This time, Roan lets it go.

One spark becomes two, two become four, four, eight, doubling and doubling until he's enfolded in a brilliant luminosity. With it comes a feeling of exceptional well-being, a sense of connectedness, as if his skin is the meeting place of within and without.

Roan focuses on a point at the top of his head and breathes, pulling the glow in. It fills his head, whirling behind his eyes. He breathes again, and the light spirals through his chest, expanding him. The brilliance jets down his spine, through his legs and feet and—he is floating. Outside his body. He can see himself, the flesh part of himself, sitting in that dark, gritty corner. But the rest of him is something else. He is part of the light.

# the chef's dessert

Here comes the Jabberwock truck,
the Jabberwock truck, with any luck
you'll be on it! to the city you'll go,
and soon you'll know, the surprises
it has in store!
—Lore of the storytellers

Dressed in her gathering clothes, a pack on her back, Alandra speaks to the gatekeeper.

"Off gathering already, Alandra? What if some of the Blood Drinkers come sniffing around for their dead? I'll call a guard to go with you."

"Not to worry, the governor himself told me it was safe."

The gatekeeper chuckles. "Those raiders did a job yesterday."

"Still, too many took wounds. My apothecary's dangerously depleted."

"Well, then, you'd best be getting on with it."

Roan hovers overhead. He relishes his newfound invisibility, though he wishes he could find a way to communicate.

Entering the red woods, Alandra stops and sings.

*Time is wasting, are you near?*

*Now I need you to appear.*

The moss in front of her jolts up and Lumpy, covered in dirt, scrambles out.

"That was fast. I didn't think you'd be able to get here so soon after the battle."

"Where's Lelbit?"

Lumpy looks up. Lelbit drops from the thin branches to the ground.

"I'm glad to see both of you safe."

Lumpy shrugs. "I'd have been dead a long time ago if I hadn't learned how to hide and not be found."

Lelbit snorts.

"Okay, okay, one pair of Blood Drinkers uncovered me, but Lelbit corrected their mistake in a blink."

"Are the rafts ready?"

Lelbit pulls up a mound of moss, revealing the two rafts they've constructed.

"The battle put a crimp in our schedule," Lumpy says. "And these aren't easy things to make. They have to be watertight, able to hold a lot of weight, and raised on the sides."

"Can you finish the next one by yourself? I need Lelbit's help."

"Was Roan recognized?" Lumpy asks worriedly.

"Yes."

Lelbit grimaces, but before she can move, Alandra grips her arm.

"I know where he is. You can enter by way of the water-works."

Roan, hovering above them, smiles to himself. No, you don't. Not exactly.

"I have a plan," Alandra continues. But the roar of an engine sends the three running through the trees to a concealed rise. There they have a clear view of the road approaching Fairview. "Too soon," Alandra sighs.

Roan recognizes him first.

"Saint," Alandra shudders.

Lelbit lifts an arrow to her bow.

Alandra stops her. "No. We have too much to accomplish to risk bringing down the wrath of the Friends."

Following Saint are ten Brothers on horseback. And lumbering along behind the Brothers is a truck. Lumpy's eyes widen. "I heard rumors some were still running, but I didn't believe them."

The Jabberwocky Wagon. "It's come for the children," Alandra curses as the rumbling truck comes closer. The vehicle has a picture on its side of an inverted triangle with a circle on top. It's the same symbol little Marla drew, thinks Roan, the same one that was drawn on my cast. Only this one has a giant tongue that reaches down to lick the circle. Frustrated at his lack of speech, Roan is grateful when Lumpy asks the question he longs to have answered.

"What's that picture mean?"

"Ice cream," sighs Alandra. "Ice cream. The children think the Jabberwocky Wagon is filled with it."

As Alandra arrives back in Fairview, Saint and his entourage are being warmly welcomed by Brack and Brother Raven. The Friends that came with Saint stand by him, while the town's residents, out in full force, admire the extraordinary motorcycle.

From above, Roan observes the livid scar that trails from Saint's ear down the length of his neck. But the prophet seems as strong and commanding as ever. Roan's attention is diverted by the shouting of the children, who run toward Alandra.

"It's here!" yells Lona, bursting with excitement.

"When're we getting our ice cream, Alandra?" Bub shouts.

"I don't know."

"I wanna go now!" yowls Lona.

Alandra takes the little girl by the shoulders. "Don't worry. We've got a few things to do first." She gathers them all close to her and whispers. "This is very important. When you go back to your rooms today, I want you all to fill up your packs with warm clothes."

"They told us we didn't need nothing," says Bub.

"Yeah," adds Gip. "Our new parents will have all that for us."

"Everything new and nice," pipes in Lona.

"I know," replies Alandra, putting on a cheerful facade, "but it's a long journey. And as your healer, I have to be certain you don't catch cold. Be sure to tell the others, all the new ones too. If anyone gives you guff, tell them it's healer's orders."

"Healer's orders, " Lona solemnly repeats.

"Alandra! There's someone here I'd like you to meet!" Brack calls.

Roan wryly observes as Alandra covers her imminent betrayal with a reserved veneer. "Alandra, meet the Prophet of the Friend."

Saint beams at the sight of her. "So this is the healer who saved Roan."

Alandra takes his outstretched hand.

"Thank you," Saint says. "Roan means a great deal to me."

Roan can tell Alandra's surprised at this display of fondness. Saint is utterly convincing, his tone open and honest. It's hard to believe he has deadly intentions.

"Forgive me," Saint says, "but I'm anxious to speak with my disciple. You will be joining us for dinner tonight?"

"It would be my pleasure," Alandra replies.

"Excellent." Saint smiles, and with that, he and the governor head for the wine cellars.

Roan directs himself back to his body. Upon contact, he grows unusually heavy, weighted down by the loose chains that dangle from the wall to his manacled wrists and ankles. Saint is approaching through the open door.

While joined to the light, Roan was free of emotion, but now, in Saint's presence, blood pounds in his temples.

"Hello, Little Brother. It's been too long."

Roan remains silent.

"Don't you have anything to say?"

"Sorry about the bike."

"It was much easier to replace than the other thing you took from me."

"What was that?"

"My trust. You shamed me in front of my men. And you shamed the Friend Himself."

"You invented the Friend. You invented it all. I've seen the proof."

For a moment, Saint is taken aback. Then he nods with understanding. "Is that what this is all about?" he asks. "Yes, I found a book. But only after the Friend revealed Himself to me on the mountain. My revelation was real. I heard His Word. I am His Prophet. The book helps me to understand that experience."

Roan searches Saint's eyes in the flickering light, trying to find truth there. It's impossible to tell.

"The City wants you, Roan. They've ordered me on pain of death to return you to them. You and your sister united would give them unlimited power." He lowers his voice. "Roan, the Friend could use that power to contain their madness. Join me. Together we can bring justice to the Outlands."

"Why should I believe your intentions are any different from the City's?"

"The City is evil, Roan. You've seen the evidence of that. It wants to enslave all of us. I've witnessed the hideous things the City does to people."

"To children, you mean, with your assistance."

Saint grimaces. "Roan. The Friend wants the terror to stop. I want the terror to stop. As we speak, Brother Wolf is at our encampment, making preparations. Join us, Roan."

Roan glares at him. "Were the children of Longlight sold too?"

The Prophet's eyes brim with emotion. "You met Kira. You've been in my empty house. We all make sacrifices, my Brother. I've made them too."

"Brother Saint, you chose your pain."

Saint smiles ruefully. "Stand with me. Stand with the Friend, Roan. King Zheng created a nation that lasted over two thousand years. He had his wall to build, and we have ours. Sacrifices will have to be made. But that is the cost of freedom."

"King Zheng was a tyrant. His nation was never liberated from dominance and control."

"But the unity he brought gave his people the strength they needed to survive."

"A strength constantly tested at their cost."

Saint moves closer to Roan, his eyes desperate. "The City sent me once before to claim you. I protected you then. I will not be given a second chance."

"Then why don't you make a cut behind my ear and insert the drug? Raven said you'd bring it. I know it's effective."

Saint spits out the name: "Raven! Nothing would make him happier. I want an ally, not an automaton."

"I will never be your ally."

Vehement, Saint grabs the front of Roan's shirt. But Roan jerks forward. Looping his wrist chain over Saint's head, he yanks it against the Prophet's neck. "This is for my mother, for my father, for my aunts, my uncles, my friends." Saint flails, but Roan tightens the links, engorged with the fever of revenge. "You...killed...them...all."

"If you kill him, you're the same as him." His voice? Whose is it?

The instant of hesitation is enough. Saint detects the weakness, and a blow to Roan's head breaks his hold on the chains.

Saint speaks quietly. "I have no choice, Roan. Neither of us has a choice. You're with me, or we're both dead."

Roan does not answer.

Picking up his lantern, Saint mutters, "We leave in the morning," and slams the door behind him. Flushed with adrenaline, Roan is left to contemplate his fate in the darkness. He is confused by the concept of choosing between evils. It's something Alandra's done, watching child after child be sent to certain death, waiting for the chance to save a few. And although Saint claims a larger purpose, he's killed too many trying to attain it. Whatever that voice was, Roan's happy it stopped him, or he'd be bearing the same burden.

It takes an eternity to calm himself, but Roan finds his

breath again. Once he does, he floats free, honing in on the sound of Alandra's voice.

"The meal was remarkable, Yasmin, so delicious. And I hear you're making my favorite flan for the dinner tonight."

The chef smiles proudly as she stirs a large pot of custard in the steaming kitchen. "I am, my friend. And today it must be perfect, for the Prophet is here. I had the honor of cooking for him once many years ago. He was especially fond of my flan."

"If I know you, many wonders are in the works."

"Ah, yes, yes, it's lovely to treat an appreciative palate. I waste my time trying to please the others. All they really care about is that," Yasmin mutters, pointing at the large keg of wine in the pantry.

Alandra nods sympathetically and moves close to the simmering custard. She sniffs dreamily. "Could I have a little taste?"

Yasmin chuckles. "Even before it has time to set, you can't resist my flan!"

She puts a spoon in the liquid, blows on it, and holds it up to Alandra's lips.

"Mmm...heaven," Alandra murmurs. "Although, forgive me for saying this, Yasmin, but isn't it missing something?"

Yasmin nods sadly in agreement. "I know, but there's nothing I can do."

Alandra pulls a small package out of her pocket. Yasmin's eyes open wide.

"What have you there?"

Alandra smiles and holds the mystery ingredient under Yasmin's nose.

"Vanilla! You found me vanilla! How did you get it?"

"Trade secret. But there should be just enough."

Yasmin unwraps the precious stick and draws it through the warm cream. "You're wonderful! Thank you!"

Ecstatic, the chef immerses herself in her preparations, allowing Alandra to slip unnoticed into the pantry. She pulls the cork from the raiders' cask of wine, spills the contents of a small vial inside, and replaces the stopper. Calling her good-byes to Yasmin, she heads off along the street.

The water purification plant is her next destination. Roan sees Alandra put on her most gracious smile to greet Master Vorn, the plant's tall, somber overseer.

"I'm sorry to disturb you, master, but I've come to get water for the children's journey."

"That order comes from the Children's Home."

"Normally it would, yes, but with the group being so large, you know, fourteen children, I've been drafted to arrange the transport preparations. I'll need enough for seven days."

Water for the rafts, Roan realizes.

"If it was anyone else, Miss Alandra..."

"And how could I forget? I've brought you more of the vervain I prescribed."

A look of embarrassed relief crosses Vorn's face.

"Oh, thank you, Miss Alandra, thank you. Just give me a few minutes to get the water ready."

As soon as he's gone, Alandra slips over to the big output pipe. She locates the opening, a small hatch on the pipe that allows a dropper to be inserted for water quality testing. She pulls a wrench from her satchel and twists the nut.

Roan watches helplessly as the overseer returns. But it seems Alandra's heard Vorn's footsteps, for she's quickly covering her activity.

"Sorry, ma'am. Bottles or containers?"

"Bottles, please."

"I'll need some time to load the wagon."

"I don't mind waiting, Master Vorn. I've always enjoyed contemplating your remarkable waterworks."

His face flushing, Vorn leaves. And with one more twist of the wrench, the hatch is open. Alandra pulls a pouch from her pocket and tips its contents into the water supply. She replaces the lid and secures the nut seconds before Master Vorn returns.

Thanking the overseer for his diligence, Alandra covers the large-wheeled water wagon and heads home. Roan knows the lake road's a slow downhill all the way to her house, so it's no surprise when she doesn't even pause before moving on.

"Alandra, my love, how are you?" Mrs. Fligg extravagantly intones.

"Thank you for your concern, but everything's fine."

"Who would have guessed? Such a nice boy, that Korr. My darlings just loved him. And you had him there the whole time, living under your own roof."

"I know," sighs Alandra. "People can be so deceptive."

"Well, let's think of happier things, shall we?"

"The Jabberwocky Wagon's driver has requested that the children be given no liquids before the trip this time."

The matron nods. "That makes a good deal of sense, the body fluids and all. It's a wonder they haven't thought of it before. I'll follow his directions to the letter."

Behind her courteous veneer, Alandra clearly wants to shriek. If they make it out of this alive, maybe she'll teach him some of her self control.

When Alandra arrives home, Lelbit's bent over the stove, stirring an herbal potion that bubbles in a large pot. Once the liquid cools, Alandra helps Lelbit submerge big white sheets, then hang them on the rafters to dry.

Alandra pulls up the floorboard revealing Roan's pack and other belongings. She draws out the hook-sword, and light cascades along the finely honed blades.

"Make sure he gets this."

As Lelbit nods gravely, Roan feels his fate and the hook-sword's join once again.

Evening is approaching by the time Alandra makes her way to the raiders' barracks. The lights are off in many of Fairview's homes, and people are snoozing on their porches. Hovering above as she opens the door a crack, Roan spies the mercenaries, half-empty mugs of wine still in their hands, sprawled everywhere, snoring. Whatever Alandra put in their drink has worked well. Satisfied, she closes the barracks door and moves toward Brack's house.

"Alandra!" calls Brack, when he sees her. "Dinner's being served!"

"Sorry, an emergency with one of my patients."

"You look ravishing," murmurs the Bird Man. As he bows to Alandra from his seat, his head drops, snoring.

"Forgive Brother Raven," Saint apologizes, taking Alandra's hand. "He nipped into the warriors' wine."

Raven's defection leaves Brack, Saint, and ten Friends at the table. No one's poured any water from the pitcher, though. Yet Alandra remains composed throughout the meal, even managing to seem charmed by the small talk.

When the last plate is cleared, she ventures flatteringly to Saint, "I've heard so much about you. Your accomplishments are legendary."

"They are not my accomplishments, Alandra, they're the Friend's. Everything I do is on His behalf. I am only His messenger."

"And when you are offered the famous flan of the great chef Yasmin, do you eat it on His behalf as well?"

Saint stares at her. Brack turns white. All are silent, wondering what the Prophet's reaction will be to this sacrilege. After a tense moment, he bursts into laughter, and everyone in the room joins in.

"No, my young beauty, I eat for myself, but with thanks to the Friend!"

Alandra smiles and rises. "Then excuse me while I go into the kitchen to see how the dessert is coming."

Yasmin and all four of Brack's kitchen staff are asleep at the kitchen table. A tray filled with small dishes of flan sits on the counter. Alandra takes a small vial out of her pocket and swallows the contents. An antidote to the "vanilla" she put in the flan, Roan guesses as she whisks the tray away.

"I've been given the honor of serving dessert to you fine gentlemen," Alandra announces, placing a dish in front of each man with an affable smile. "The chef made this especially for the Prophet."

But neither Saint nor any of the Brothers touch the dessert.

Saint smiles a little sheepishly. "I mean no insult to your fine chef, but I've found lately that such rich foods don't agree with me. My men abstain out of respect."

Alandra smiles demurely. "I admire their loyalty, but it will break Yasmin's heart to see her attempt to serve you refused. Such a delicacy is an honor to the Friend. At least have a little, so that all may enjoy."

Saint relents, eating a spoonful. Brack and the Brothers each have a spoonful too. Saint sniffs at his bowl. Smacks his lips. And takes another few bites. Now all are free to dive in, and their bowls are emptied in short order. But Saint leans back, patting his belly. "Forgive me, I mustn't continue."

"Please don't apologize. You've well honored Yasmin's efforts," Alandra tells him. Roan wonders if the Prophet has eaten enough. How long will they have?

Brack slumps forward, drugged by the flan. Saint looks at him, then at Alandra. "The Governor must have been sharing that nip with the ambassador," she says with a wink.

Before she can finish speaking, one Brother after the other falls forward in his seat, snoring. Saint, confused, scowls at Alandra. He jolts up from his chair, knocking it down, and lurches for her. But the drug takes him as well, and he falls in a heap at her feet.

Lelbit waits in the shadows. Alandra sees her and nods.

# fLight

this is the riddle of his coming.
though Longlight has perished,
he will be her son. and he will see
clearly what he has never seen.
and those who walk with him will
share his vision.

—the book of Longlight

A DOOR SLAMS. FOOTSTEPS. A jangle of keys, and the cell door bursts open.

Roan smiles. "Lelbit!"

Intent on her purpose, Lelbit unlocks Roan's bonds, hands him his hook-sword, and leads the way.

In the front yard of the Children's Home, they find Alandra at her wit's end.

"We're not goin' to go with you. We're goin' with the Jabberwocky Wagon!" shouts Jaw.

"I thought we were getting ice cream!" wails Lona.

"We're not going nowhere except with the Jabberwocky Wagon that's taking us to our new folks," Bub states with finality, and he sits down on his pack, just to the right of the snoring Mrs. Fligg.

Once they spot Roan, however, all of the children leap up, begging him to play.

"Quiet!" he shouts over the din, and they instantly fall silent. "First of all, you should know my real name is Roan."

"I like that name!" Lona squeaks.

"I'd like to take you somewhere else, and not in the Jabberwocky Wagon."

"Does that mean no ice cream?" Bub wonders.

"That's right. Because what you were told about the Jabberwocky Wagon wasn't true. It was a story made up to capture you. My friends and I want to leave here forever and find a new place to live. It won't be easy. There might be trouble along the way. Some of us might get hurt. But if we stay here, we'll be hurt for sure. Would you be willing to come with us?"

For a moment, no sound. Roan feels the force of their eyes on him, feels their collective power.

Then "Yes!" the children cheer. "We want to come! We want to come!"

"Good. We have to hurry. And remember, be very, very quiet."

The children pick up their packs, and Roan leads the silent procession through the eerily deserted town. They walk with care in the bright moonlight, alert for any movement, any sound. A pair of raiders snore on the sidewalk, and the children stare fascinated at their scarred faces. Lelbit, pushing the supply wagon she's fetched from Alandra's home, wordlessly shoos them along.

Ahead, the gate is barred, the gatekeeper fallen beside it. Roan extracts the iron bar that locks it shut. While the others wait, he and Lelbit cautiously push open the massive doors. With his finger over his lips, he motions the children to follow him through. The group begins to move, but they freeze at the sound of a man's voice.

"Alandra!"

A hand grips her wrist. Alandra goes pale.

"It's late to be going out," the gatekeeper mumbles, his eyes half shut.

She bends low, her face close to his.

"I know," she murmurs, "but I'll be alright. You should rest now. Rest."

The man lets out a deep sigh, and his chin falls to his chest. Alandra nods to Roan, who guides the children out.

Once through the gates, the group walks as quickly as the children can manage.

"We don't have much time," Alandra whispers to Roan as they near the lake.

Roan turns to face the children. "We're almost there," he says. "See my friend down by the water? Who's going to get to him first?"

"Me! Me! Me!" the children shout as they bolt toward Lumpy. At the shore, where Lumpy has set out the rafts, Alandra wraps treated sheets around each of the children, while Roan, Lumpy, and Lelbit load the vessels with food, water, and supplies.

"The sheets will stop the lake gas from burning your skin," Alandra explains. "You need to stay wrapped up, even your faces, until Roan tells you it's safe to take them off." She gives Roan a worried look.

They turn back to Fairview, scanning it for movement. A light flickers in the distance.

"Everybody on board now!" Roan orders.

Lumpy takes the first group of children, Alandra and Lelbit the second. Roan follows with the last group of children. Poling through the shallow, bubbling water with long oars Lumpy's fashioned out of splayed tree trunks, they push furiously, propelling the rafts out onto the lake as fast as they can.

They haven't gone far when they hear an ominous sound. The roar of an engine: Saint's motorcycle. Roan turns to see him, with the Brothers on horseback galloping behind. Within moments, the Friends have reached the shore.

"Come back!" bellows Saint, his voice thundering over the water. "Come back, Roan. You endanger them all!"

Roan hears Lona whimper, and he calls out to the children. "Don't worry. Stay wrapped up tight and everything will be fine."

The children fall quiet, comforted, but Roan wonders if he

can keep his word. A slew of spears hurled by the Brothers are sailing over the water at them. The weapons fall short, sizzling in the acid waters.

Before the Brothers can launch another wave of spears, Lelbit raises her bow and lets a few arrows fly. One Brother falls. Another clutches his chest. Two more go down before the rafts float out of range.

Roan observes the Brothers' movements. Saint and his men are hacking down branches. In half a day they'll have constructed their own crafts and be in hot pursuit.

"We've got to put as much distance between us and them as we can," he tells the others. "They won't be far behind."

Rounding the point, they get a full view of the lake. It's a sea of toxic, stinking water. No shore in sight. Roan feels the snow cricket wriggling in his pocket. He sits it on his flat palm and waits patiently. Within moments, the cricket positions its head north.

"According to the cricket, that's the way we go," Roan announces, pointing to the watery horizon.

The rafts are sturdy and hold their loads well. The paddlers keep their strokes even and steady, and labor without pause. But the vessels are far from streamlined and the paddlers must take care not to splash, so the going is slow.

By the time the moon sets, the wind is quiet and the lake still. The three rafts pull closer, and Lelbit lashes them together. Bread, cheese, and water are passed around, the children eating and drinking under their protective sheets. The four leaders decide on alternate shifts, two of them sleeping while the other two keep the craft moving on course.

The children, however, do not rest easily. Excitement wakes them, and one by one they peek out of their protective covers.

"You should be sleeping," Roan advises, but his attempt at sounding stern fails miserably. In a moment, all of the children's heads have bobbed out of their sheets.

"I can't sleep."

"Me neither," says Bub.

Roan sings a lullaby to soothe them, something he's almost forgotten how to do. It's one his mother sang to him many years ago.

*Far beyond sea, the waters run deep.*
*Far beyond hill, the mountains are steep.*
*There you will find*
*in Earth and in mind*
*Your dreams never sleep*
*where your heart can keep them.*

As he sings, Roan looks up into a night sky thrilled with stars. He ponders the galaxies within galaxies that brought back his mother's song. And he wonders if his mother ever imagined where he'd find himself this night.

"Breakfast!" calls Lumpy, who's been paddling with Lelbit since taking over the shift.

While the children eat, Lumpy teaches them finger games. They're fascinated by his scars, asking endless questions of him and Lelbit. Jaw, in particular, adopts Lumpy as his special friend. During her rest time, Lelbit takes bundles of cloth from her pack and ties small pieces of the material around some of her arrows. Roan catches her eye. They share a foreboding, and he's glad she's found some way to prepare.

Their short respite over, the travelers separate the rafts and the paddling begins again in full force.

The most startling revelation on the journey is the children. Huddled together on the tiny rafts, forbidden to take off their protective sheets, unable to run or jump, they could easily explode in frustration. But whenever they grow restless, a calming word from Roan is all it takes. He draws their attention to the dappling of moon and sun on the water, the faces of ferocious beasts in clouds, the drift of a seabird soaring in the wind, and they're instantly content.

For three days they paddle, the rafts separate by day, lashed together by night. On the afternoon of the fourth day, Lona's the first to notice the change in the water.

"Can you sniff it? It's smelling kind of nice."

Lumpy leans close to the surface, then looks at his friends. "I wouldn't risk drinking it, but I don't think it has the power to burn." He breaks off a piece of bread and throws it in the water. The bread doesn't disintegrate; it simply bobs on the surface.

"Look! A fish!" Jaw shouts with glee.

The children crane for a look. Sure enough, a carp is nibbling on the bread. There's life in the water here. Roan and

Alandra share a look of relief and anticipation. It confirms what they saw in the dream. In the distance, they make out a shoreline backed by a cascade of hills.

Alandra's call of "Sheets off!" is met by cheers as the kids take in the sun and stretch out their limbs. But their celebration is short-lived.

Behind the group, a craft's approaching fast. As it draws closer, Roan makes out eight men, paddling in unison and achieving great speed. One of the men stands, raising a heavy crossbow horizontally across his chest. A sharp whine accompanies his arrow as it blasts through the air, straight at Roan. Roan's eyes focus on the missile. He pivots, but too late: he is hit. Lelbit replies with an arrow of her own. It's a long way to the Friends' raft, but the shot hits its mark. The crossbowman and his weapon fall overboard.

The children gawk at Roan, the arrow stuck straight through his bloody arm.

He smiles faintly at them. "I'm alright, don't worry. Just think good thoughts, okay?"

Lelbit dips one of her cloth-wrapped arrows into a jar containing a tar-like substance, then lights it with a spark from her fire stone. Drawing back her bow, she sends the flaming arrow hurtling at the approaching raft. It hits the sap-laden sticks, which ignite instantly. As the Brothers frantically attempt to douse the fire, she shoots one arrow after another, until the raft explodes in flames. Their clothes on fire, the Friends have no choice but to leap into the water.

Lumpy lashes the rafts together so that Alandra can attend to Roan while he and Lelbit paddle toward the shore, which is now clearly in sight.

Alandra's fingers hover over the wounded area. "It's missed the bone." Tearing a strip from the bottom of her shirt, she ties off Roan's arm at the shoulder. With a warning look, she commands, "Hold steady." Roan controls his breath as she cuts off the feathered end of the arrow, each small movement a jab of pain. There is a searing tug as she extracts the shaft.

"It pierced cleanly," Alandra says. Giving Roan a quizzical look, she shifts his attention to the children. He sees that each one of the boys and girls is focusing on his wound. He'd asked them to think good thoughts, but they seem to have taken him at more than his word. "Roan," Alandra says, awestruck, "the wound's already begun to heal."

The children are the first to step out onto the warm, white sand. They scramble over each other to cast off their four days of captivity in an eruption of running, jumping, wrestling, tumbling, and mad digging in the sand. While the other three leaders unload the rafts, Roan keeps vigil over the lake. He knows the water alone would not have killed the remaining Brothers, and those who survived are certain to follow.

Once they've unloaded, Roan calls out to the playing children. "I need you!"

Every child instantly rushes over. Lona's a step behind, having buried herself in the white sand.

"What do you want us to do?" Bub and Jaw ask together.

"First we have to put our packs on and fill up our water sacks from the big bottles."

The children bolt into action, and within minutes they are ready for Roan's next instruction. "See those hills? We have to get over them. Whoever finds the trail first gets to ride on my shoulders."

The youngest ones screech with delight as they charge to the hillside. Clambering through the brush, the little horde runs back and forth until, gathering together, they sit, all eyes on the puzzle.

Little Lona is the one who finally stands up and walks along the edge of the stone. When she stops, she begins to bounce up and down. Bub and Jaw join her, taking her hands, and they jump together, over and over, until the three of them disappear.

Lumpy anxiously runs to the spot, followed by the others.

"We're down here!" Bub yells up from the bottom of a gaping cranny in the rock. "You can get to the other side from here!"

Lumpy eyes Roan. "Did you know they'd find that?"

"Had a hunch."

Lumpy shakes his head. "Good. We'll need a few more of those before the day's through."

While Alandra leads the children through the tunnel-like fissure under the rock, the others work to remove any sign of their landing. They break up the rafts and brush the sand to eliminate footprints. Using thin sticks as a base, they weave in grassy material, hoping to disguise the newly exposed opening, though nothing can replace years of natural camouflage. The end result is merely adequate, but with luck, it will buy the group some time.

Arriving at the other end of the tunnel, Roan scans the range of forbidding, rough-hewn hills.

"For me the Dreamfield is poetry," says Alandra, joining him. "It resonates truth, but I can't hold on to it. Not like you can."

"I may remember the way, but it looks like pretty rough going."

"I'd call it treacherous," Lumpy pipes in. "How do we get all these cubs through it?"

At the ready, Jaw reaches up and takes Lumpy's hand. "You don't have to be scared, Lumpy. I'll take care of you."

"Thanks, Jaw," Lumpy says, with obvious pleasure.

Lona, not one to forget her prize, skips up to Roan.

"Bend yourself over, I get my ride!"

Alandra does her best to intervene. "Lona, Roan has a wound on his arm, and there's rough climbing ahead."

"I'm not sitting on his arm, I'm sitting on his shoulders, and there's nothing wrong with them. Besides, I already looked at the trail and it's smooth as a pickle."

Ignoring their chuckles, she drags them around a bend to a decrepit, overgrown road that winds through the landscape.

"See?"

Roan smiles at the bemused Alandra. He bends down and the tiny waif clambers onto his shoulders, queen of the world.

# the precipice

those who turn from the friend shall
be abandoned forever.
—orin's history of the friend

The rigors of the trail and the caretaking of the
children demand all of Roan's concentration. Though
his every step is weighted with a sense of impending danger, he
cannot enter the deep meditative state required to leave his
body and scout the path behind them. For the moment, he's
content to leave that to Lelbit, who's on constant watch at the
tail of the company. His greatest concern is the huge chasm he
saw in the Dreamfield, a chasm they'll soon be approaching.

The night is warm, a blessing since they can't risk announcing their whereabouts with a fire. After dark, the young ones
wrap themselves in their sheets and stare up at the sky while
Alandra shows them the seven stars of the Pleiades, seven sisters placed in the heavens by the god Zeus to protect them
from Orion the Hunter.

"Is that where we're going?" Lona wonders aloud.

"No," Alandra replies. "We will find a safe place here on the earth."

"What if the hunters come again?"

"They'll be sent to their master in the sky."

Roan notices that Lumpy has walked over to Lelbit, who's standing apart. He touches her shoulder and they stand solemnly, arms round each other's waists. There is no mistaking the troubled looks on their faces.

After two days, the narrow, broken road begins to ascend, and the steep slope slows the children down. Lumpy and Alandra take the lead, with Roan and an edgy Lelbit in the rear. Lelbit's vigilance is not made any easier by Bub and Jam, who've fashioned slings out of their belts and appointed themselves her rearguard deputies.

"Looks like a dead end!" Lumpy calls out from high over a dark, bottomless ravine.

Roan points out a dangerously narrow ledge, all that's left of the crumbled road.

"There's got to be another way."

"That's the only way. And it takes us where we have to go."

Lelbit nudges Roan to look behind them. Below, at the start of the rise, are four small shapes, one slightly larger than the others.

The big one is Saint, Roan guesses. "We've got to put more distance between them and us. Let's tie some sheets together for a handhold!"

He and Lelbit get swiftly to work. Twisting, then securing the sheets together, they fashion a kind of rope.

"Everybody! Put your left hand up in the air," Roan instructs, an order some of the younger ones struggle with. "Hold the rope with that hand and follow Alandra. Keep looking forward. Don't look down. If you slip, hold tight to the rope and you'll get your footing back. If you hear noises or shouts behind you, ignore them. Keep moving. I promise to tell you everything that happens back here once we get to the other side."

As the sun begins its downward arc, the treacherous ascent begins. The children cling to the rope and cautiously move forward in single file. Roan shouts encouragement to them, reminding them to keep their eyes on the person in front of them, not on their feet. He has glanced down at the chasm of jagged stone beneath, and he fervently hopes they'll clear this gorge before their pursuers reach them. But looking back, he can see the men have gained ground.

He turns to see Lona, just in front of him, stumble. She shrieks as some rocks tumble off the ledge, plummeting into nothingness. Roan steadies her with his free hand, and she starts to cry.

"Look in my eyes, Lona."

She turns her head so her tear-filled gaze meets his.

"Don't be afraid. We're going to be alright."

"Okay," she murmurs.

"We'll be alright."

She turns back and follows the line. That's when Roan hears Lelbit stir behind him. He looks to see her drawing an arrow. Saint and the three Brothers are almost upon them, holding shields fashioned from pieces of their abandoned raft.

"You two will have to anchor this end. Can you handle it?" Roan says quietly to Bub and Jam, in line just behind him.

"We're the deputies. We can handle everything," Bub replies, firmly gripping the rope. The two bigger boys take their positions ahead, leaving Roan and Lelbit to face the assailants.

"I don't wish to hurt anyone," Saint announces from behind his shield. "It's you I want, Roan. There's much work ahead of us."

"I will not come."

"Bring the children. The others, too. There are so many who need to be saved from the City. Roan, you cannot escape it. You must fight it. We must fight it together."

"I gave you my answer."

"You don't understand. You are needed. If you leave to save these children, you abandon all the others. There are many who need your help. I can't do this alone. Without you, there's no hope for any of them."

Roan feels himself wavering. What *about* the others? How many more will suffer? If it's true that Saint intends to go up against the City, maybe they could join forces to find Stowe.

But a vivid memory of Longlight erupts in Roan's mind. The broken walls, the smoldering houses. The bones of his people floating in the Fire Hole. Those are Saint's methods. The work of a man who would use any means necessary to achieve his ends. Roan must find his own way. A path that does not seek violence. A path that respects peace. He will look in front of him, not behind. It's the only way to honor the death of Longlight.

He locks eyes with the Prophet. "Let us go."

Saint holds his position.

Roan turns his back on the Prophet, takes five steps forward. For a brief moment, the possibility of truce hangs in the air.

Saint bellows, and his men charge. Lelbit whirls, firing an arrow at the lead man, aiming below his shield. As the arrow hits his leg, he crumbles, tumbling into the dark chasm. She lets loose another arrow, and this time the Brother's shield is so close her arrow pierces it. That man also staggers to his death. The Brother shielding Saint lifts his spear. With a frightening growl, he charges, the tip leveled at Roan's heart. Roan dodges his thrust and chops the Friend on the back, then kicks him over the edge.

Regaining his footing, Roan rushes back to join Lelbit, only to see Saint's battle-axe blistering through air. With a horrible crack, it buries itself deep in Lelbit's left side.

"Lelbit!"

Saint rips out the blade, and Roan cries out in despair as his comrade collapses onto the ledge.

Roan draws his hook-sword, meeting Saint's battle-axe with

a crash. The opponents strike their weapons again and again, teetering on the narrow ledge. Seeing Roan's arrow wound oozing blood, Saint aims his fist. Pain jolts through Roan and he staggers, striking desperately with his sword. A point catches Saint in the thigh. Growling with rage, Saint smashes at Roan's wound again. Roan buckles, his head dangling over the chasm. Instantly, Saint's blade is at his throat.

"You never understood, you never—" Saint gasps in astonishment. Lelbit, kneeling behind him, has thrust an arrow through his neck.

The Prophet meets Roan's eyes in desperation. "Help Kira," he rasps, then lurches forward. Roan reaches, but too late. Saint plunges over the edge, toppling into the abyss.

Roan, heart pounding, looks up to see Lelbit still kneeling in the same spot. Her mission complete, she smiles weakly at Roan and crumples into his arms. In the distance, Lumpy waits with the children, safely on the other side of the abyss. Roan stares helplessly at his friend. They both know that what Lumpy has lost he will never have again.

# the way home

the first ones had a vision and the
vision was Longlight. and her father
and her son, it was said, would build
the new world.
           —the book of Longlight

In the shade of the fir trees the Dreamfield had
promised, Lumpy places the final stone on the mound
where Lelbit lies. Jaw solemnly takes his hand and Lumpy cir-
cles his other arm around Bub and Jam. Everyone assembled,
Roan offers the prayer of Longlight.

*That the love you bestowed might bear fruit*
*We stay behind.*
*That the spirit you shared be borne witness*
*We stay behind.*
*That your light burn bright in our hearts*
*We stay behind.*
*We stay behind and imagine your flight.*

Lumpy's reflection appears over Roan as he drinks from a clear, fresh stream. His heart sinks at the sight of the pack on Lumpy's back. But he prepares himself to accept whatever decision his friend has come to.

"Well, I'm off. It won't be easy to camouflage the tunnel. But Lelbit and I had some ideas. It was something she thought we should do."

"It'll mean crossing the chasm."

Lumpy shrugs. "Lelbit would expect me to do it, and she's not the kind of person you cross." Eyes brimming with pain, he sighs. "It'll be like she's there with me, you know?" Looking away, he reaches into his pocket. "This belongs to you," he says, and hands Roan the silver ring.

Roan nods, cupping the ring in his palm. He searches Lumpy's face. "You won't be coming back?"

Lumpy gives him a long look, then winks. "A few of those kids would miss me, I think."

"I would miss you too," Roan says, embracing his friend. "We won't leave till you return."

Lumpy smiles, and with a wave he's gone.

It will be good to camp in this place for a while, Roan thinks. He watches the rippling water, contemplating Saint's final words to him. In those last moments, Roan saw the pain in the Prophet's eyes, the desperation of someone who had run out of options. Lumpy's scars are on the surface, Roan muses. Saint's scars were inside, and they went deep. Roan knows how close his own experiences brought him to the edge of something dangerously similar.

*Help Kira.* The words haunt Roan. Hints of what lies behind them glimmer at the edge of his consciousness. What had Saint said? "If you save these children, you abandon all the others." Kira had spoken of losing a child, and Saint had said there would be others. Who are these others? he wonders. *Help Kira.* Yes, Saint, I will. But I need time. Time to make a safe haven for these children. Time to develop their strength, and to teach them to defend life in the new home we'll create together.

Roan fingers the silver ring Saint gave him, the ring he keeps as a reminder of his shame, when vengeance ruled him. No more.

He watches Lona and Bub toss twigs into the stream. The sticks, teased by the current, dip and spin, then float out of sight. Lona throws in more. An endless flow of water and wood and children's laughter. Alandra, her feet bare, sinks down beside him and dips her toes into the water. She seems so comfortable in this world. But only part of her is here, he knows. The rest of her lies with the Dirt Eaters; he has no doubt they have plans for Roan and these children. Plans he may or may not be willing to join. But that is in the future. For now, Roan decides he wants to trust her.

He digs into his pack and pulls out his gifts. His hook-sword from Brother Wolf and the recorder from Brother Asp, Orin's book and the rag doll his sister Stowe lost in the snow.

He lays Saint's ring beside these objects on the ground around him. He and his sister are the last living members of their village. These gifts are the markers of their journey, and have now become a part of the history of Longlight as well. How he will connect his truth with its legend, he is not sure. But it will be easier, he knows, surrounded by the sound of singing. On the bank, on the stones, on the tree bark, on the children's shoulders, are perched white crickets, creating their ethereal song.

Roan smiles at Alandra and they sit together, feet dangling in the cool water, watching their flock, listening.

# acknowledgments

I WOULD LIKE TO THANK Susan Madsen, Guillermo Verdecchia, Barbara Pulling, and Pamela Robertson for their time and effort and belief. I am deeply indebted to Elizabeth Dancoes for her tireless and crucial contributions. Elizabeth's ideas, advice, encouragement, and artistry have left an indelible mark on this book.

# about the author

DENNIS FOON IS THE AUTHOR of the novels *Double or Nothing* and *Skud*. His many stage plays have received international acclaim, including the British Theatre Award for *Invisible Kids*. His screenplays include the award-winning *Little Criminals, White Lies,* and *Torso*.

Dennis lives in Vancouver, British Columbia, where he's working on *Freewalker*, the sequel to *The Dirt Eaters*.